To Pauline

THE MAGIC OF MOUNT RINJANI

with my very best wishes

Rosalinda

MARY ANN MARTINELL

Published by Rosalinda Beckles
Publishing partner: Paragon Publishing, Rothersthorpe
First published 2010

ISBN 978-1-899820-98-6

Book design, layout and production management by Into Print
www.intoprint.net

Printed and bound in UK and USA by Lightning Source

NOTE TO THE READER

The decision to set the story on the island of Lombok was truly accidental. All I had wanted to do was to find an exotic, tropical island near Bali.

Lombok fascinated me from the start for the variety of fantastic, breathtaking, and romantic settings it had to offer.

I hope that you, too, will enjoy this journey of discovery, and that your senses will be captivated by Lombok's incomparable beauty.

Mary Ann Martinell

A special Thank You to my daughter Deborah, who helped me with the editing and with the choice of cover.

CHAPTER ONE

Selene turned off the alarm clock and groaned. 'Time I got out of bed,' she told herself, yawning. 'Another wonderful day at the office awaits me.' She waited five more minutes then dragged herself out of bed and went through the motions of washing and dressing with the alacrity of a snail.

It was pouring again, she noticed, the raindrops drumming a crazy beat at the window. She turned on the TV, which served her as background noise while she ate a slice of toast and drank her instant coffee.

Once she had finished, she washed the plate and mug used for her breakfast, switched off the TV, and put on her black leather boots. Then she opened her wardrobe, and fetched her long black waterproof coat with matching hood. She picked up her bag and checked that she had closed all the windows. When she was ready, she battled her way out of the door to her red Mini, parked outside one of the garages of the private block of flats where she lived.

The drive to work was like a long, steamy hiccup. Caught in the rush hour traffic, even more intense for the rain, Selene finally arrived outside the shabby, dingy-white building where were located the administrative headquarters of the small Import/Export Company where she worked.

The parking space assigned to her had turned into a shallow pond, so that when she exited the car she was glad she was wearing boots or she would have been ankle-deep in the cold mixture of dirt and engine oil that always greeted her on rainy days.

Selene let herself in, leaving the door to bang shut behind her as she climbed up the steps to the first floor of the building, where the offices were. She hung her coat on a peg behind her desk, trying to stem the rivulet of raindrops falling onto the carpet with a cardboard box, which had contained the paper she used for her printer.

When everything was settled to her satisfaction, Selene switched on the computer, and scanned through her emails.

Little by little, her colleagues arrived. Selene greeted them with a smile, and after the usual remarks on the weather, she resumed her work.

The phone kept ringing non-stop, with clients asking for delivery dates or complaining about faulty goods. Agents called from sunny countries, asking the most updated pricelists and new catalogues. Managers wanted her to book and re-book hotel rooms, where exhibitions were going to take place, and everybody wanted everything done immediately, as if their lives depended on it.

Lunchtime was upon her before long. Selene went into the small room the members of staff used as a kitchen, and retrieved the salad and chicken sandwich she had prepared the night before. She then put on the kettle and made herself a cup of tea.

'Where is Julie?' she asked Laura, the head of the Sales Department.

'She's in Spain with her new boyfriend. She has taken a fortnight off to go there. They are thinking of moving permanently to the Costa del Sol and setting up a business there.'

'What kind of business?'

'They're thinking of selling chocolate fountains for weddings and children's parties.'

'Isn't it a bit risky to up sticks without having a steady source of income?' remarked Sam, a thin, leggy blonde from the Administration Department.

'Well, Julie has already done this kind of work in her hometown, up North. Besides, think, emerald sea, new apartment giving onto a sandy beach at the front and mountains at the back. Sun all year round and all that lovely seafood and wine...' replied Laura, dreamily. She was Julie's best friend and had been on holiday to Spain with her the previous year.

The conversation around Laura became more animated, with

everyone recalling a holiday they had had in Spain or another sun-kissed country.

Selene stood there, sipping her coffee, wondering how Julie could trust a man to the extent of changing her life completely, and even starting anew in a foreign country, away from her family and friends. That was something she could never do.

'Right Girls, back to work!' Laura's words brought Selene out of her musing, and she returned to her desk, to more emails, more calls, more photocopying, more trips to the warehouse, until five o'clock struck and she was able to shut everything down until the following day.

By the time Selene was ready to rejoin her car, the weather seemed to have improved, with a beautiful rainbow beckoning to her all the way back to her flat.

She unlocked the door, picked up her mail, showered and changed. In the kitchen, she popped the rice dish that she had bought at the supermarket into the microwave oven, and settled down to her lonely repast.

While she ate her dinner, she examined her mail. 'Bills and more bills', she muttered to herself. Last of all she puzzled over a white, official-looking envelope, bearing a London stamp.

Excitedly, Selene ripped open the envelope and read the contents of the letter. 'It can't be! It's impossible!' she exclaimed every few lines.

Selene read the letter through more slowly, so that each word sank in. A well-known firm of solicitors based in London informed her that her mother's sister, a Miss Elizabeth Duncan, had slipped on the wet tiles near the steps of her swimming pool. She had hit her head and had fallen backwards into the pool, where she had drowned. This sad affair had happened on the Paradise Island of Lombok.

'Where on Earth is Lombok?' Selene asked herself. She fetched her Atlas and looked at the index page. Lombok, near Bali, was in the Indonesian Archipelago.

'There is certainly some mistake here. No relative of mine could have lived that far...

Moreover, Mother was an only child!'

The solicitors had contacted the wrong Selene Finch. She would call them in the morning and put them right.

Selene slept badly that night. She had nightmares of an evil witch who kept on chasing her around a deep pool of blood-tinged water, her cackle resembling more and more the persistent ringing of a bell, ringing...ringing.

Selene woke up with a start and discovered that continuous ringing noise was only the bell of her alarm clock. In the bathroom, she noticed the bags under her eyes, which looked a deep jade under her ruffled copper-red hair. 'Oh dear, I look like a witch this morning, never mind the one in my dream.'

Selene took a reinvigorating shower, put on a lacy bra and underwear over which she slipped on a pair of black trousers that she wore with a simply cut white blouse over her svelte figure. As a final touch, she clasped a gold chain round her neck. From the chain, there hung the gold Celtic cross her mother had given her when she had graduated. Selene brushed back her long unruly hair into some sort of order, grabbed a cup of coffee and a slice of toast, donned her long black coat, a white woollen hat, gloves, and scarf and drove to the office.

The morning flew by, like any other morning, but during her lunch break, Selene left her colleagues to their usual gossip and stepped into her Mini. She needed to phone the solicitors and did not want an audience to what she had to say.

'Miss Finch? Miss Selene Jade Finch? Your mother's name was Samantha Jane Hill, wasn't it? No, there is no mistake. You need to come up to London, to the address printed in our letterhead and speak to Mr Gabriel Hart, who is in charge of this matter. Ten o'clock Thursday...? Good. See you then. Goodbye.'

Stunned, Selene sat in the Mini, holding her mobile phone, her mind in turmoil.

'This can't be true. I must be dreaming'. Selene pinched herself and the pain that action generated, convinced her that she was wide-awake.

Trying as she might, Selene could not believe what the woman had said. It had to be all a big mistake.

Nonetheless, she spent the hours that elapsed from that moment until the appointment with the solicitor, trying to unravel this mystery. She had no relatives. Her mother had been an only child, and her father ... Well, the only thing Selene knew about him was that he had played in some kind of band and that he had left town without even knowing that her mother was expecting his child.

Her mother had become pregnant when she was sixteen, but despite her young age, she had been wonderful. She and Selene had been very close. They had been more like sisters than mother and daughter. They had never had any secrets from each other, so how could her mother have kept from her that she had an aunt? It was crazy. It was surely a matter of mistaken identity.

Selene journeyed to town by train, not feeling up to the task of negotiating London's traffic in her Mini while her mind was trying to piece together this puzzle. She took a taxi and there she was, outside Hart & Sons, Solicitors.

CHAPTER TWO

Selene pushed the door and the receptionist contacted Mr Hart's secretary. Selene followed her, her heart pounding, into Mr Hart's office and gently dropped into the comfortable black leather chair that seemed to swallow her up.

In a daze, Selene looked up and met the most incredible eyes she had ever seen.

The possessor of such beautiful eyes had jet-black hair, which created a spectacular contrast with his cobalt blue deep-set eyes. His Grecian features were enhanced by a rich brown tan, which, in turn, emphasized the dazzling white smile with which he greeted her.

Mesmerised by the hypnotic gaze he had turned on her, Selene missed his opening words. 'Pull yourself together. What is the matter with you? Can't a man smile and look at you, without you falling into a trance?' Selene scolded herself. 'You seem to have forgotten all about Simon.' That thought sobered her up. She sat up straight and concentrated on the revelations Gabriel Hart was making about her family.

'So, you see, Miss Finch, you are the sole heir of Miss Duncan's estate, amounting to 25 million pounds, give or take a few pence.'

'Wh...What?' Selene felt like a fish trying to breathe after having been taken off the hook and thrown into a basket. Her head was swimming and her knees were knocking together.

'Are you all right?' asked Gabriel Hart with solicitude. 'Miss Knight, can you bring Miss Finch a cup of sweet tea please?'

He was swiftly by her side, feeling her pulse, which had become erratic, not only at the news he had just imparted to her, but also at the proximity of this exquisite specimen of human maleness.

Miss Knight rushed in with a mug of hot sweet tea, which Selene tried unsuccessfully not to gulp down as if her life depended on it, and scalded her mouth in the process.

'That's better, now, Miss Finch, isn't it? I know it must be quite a shock to you to realise that you have become a millionaire, particularly in such unusual circumstances.'

'Are you sure?' Selene let the almost inaudible words fall through her lips. 'You see, there must be a mistake. My mother was an only child. I have never had an aunt.'

'Let me explain. When your grandmother was 16, she fell in love with a boy of the same age, attending the grammar school for boys on the opposite side of the road from her own school. She became pregnant. At that time, unmarried mothers were considered a disgrace to their family and for a baby to be born illegitimate had a stigma attached to it. Because of this, the baby's father was never told, secrecy being deemed the best policy.

Like many other girls in her condition, she was sent away to a mother-and-baby home run by the nuns, which dealt with this type of situation. When the baby was born, it was immediately given up for adoption.

The couple who adopted your aunt was leaving for Indonesia as Sir Charles Duncan, the adoptive father, had been posted there to become the next British Ambassador. In order to avoid rumours about the adoption ever reaching your aunt when she grew up, Lady Duncan had feigned to be pregnant and all the adoption papers were left with my grandfather, who was a judge and one of Sir Charles's closest friends.

My grandfather put these papers in a sealed envelope with the instructions that it was to be opened only after Sir and Lady Duncan's death and that only then should your aunt be acquainted with the name and circumstances of her biological mother.

When your aunt learnt the truth, she asked me to engage a private detective to find out what had happened to her mother and her family. The detective discovered that your grandmother had married a Mr Harry Hill, who worked as a pharmacist in Crawley. They had a daughter, Samantha Jane, who, when she was 16, had a baby whom she called Selene. Your father, as far as we were able to ascertain, played the guitar in a pop group that was on tour there for a fortnight

Mr Hill divorced your grandmother when you were twelve, so you lived with her and your mother. Your grandmother passed away three years ago and last year, your mother died in a car accident.

When all these details were disclosed to Miss Duncan, she was saddened by the news, but at the same time overjoyed at the thought that she might be able to meet you, the only relation that she had left.

However, even before I managed to contact you, she made a new will naming you her sole heir to the estate. As you can appreciate, there is no mistake.'

Selene sat there, bemused. She had learnt more about her family in the last half-hour than in the past twenty-four years of her life. Poor mother! She had always wanted a sister. How had her grandmother felt when her baby had been taken away from her, never to be seen again? And now...all that money. What was she to do with it? These thoughts passed rapidly through her head, but as she saw that Gabriel Hart was waiting for her comments before resuming his narrative, she blurted out, turning her troubled face towards him 'So, what happens now?'

'The bulk of the estate consists of investments and land in this country, a penthouse apartment in New York, bonds and shares, but there is also the property in Lombok, which accounts for ten percent of the amount I've just mentioned to you. The problem with that property is that, according to Indonesian Law, you must reside on the island in order to claim your right as joint owner of it. This means that you'll have to travel to Lombok and reside there until you are issued with the appropriate papers naming you as the owner. After that, you will be able to make up your mind on what to do.' explained Gabriel Hart, patiently.

'But I can't. I have my job. I don't have a passport. I only have an

ID card, which I used to go to France last year, but it's only valid for Europe. Besides, I don't know anything about Lombok. I only know that it is somewhere in the Indonesian Archipelago.' Selene knew that she was babbling, but it was a way of hiding the panic that was taking hold of her.

'Don't worry about your passport and visa. We can sort that out for you. I am rather more concerned about your travelling arrangements. Have you a friend who could accompany you?'

'No, I don't have anyone. My friend Vanessa has just got married to a Canadian and they are trying to start up a new business in Toronto.' Selene passed the tip of her tongue on dry lips. Her mind wandered off, thinking of Vanessa and what a true friend she had always been. It was thanks to her if she had not been bullied at school. She was her rock. The only person in the world she could rely on. She missed her very much. Vanessa would have helped her to cope with the problems created by this unexpected inheritance.

'Well, as it happens, I need to visit some of our clients in the Far East and Australia in eight weeks' time,' Gabriel Hart's voice interrupted her musing, 'so we could arrange to fly to Singapore on Tuesday 26th of February. From there we can fly directly to Lombok. That will give you plenty of time to serve your notice at work, dispose of the few items of furniture you possess, tell your landlord that you shall vacate the flat by the end of January, and buy yourself some suitable clothes. If you need some money, I can let you have enough to cover all your expenses from now until all the legal formalities are over.'

'Please, you're going too fast. Why should I leave my flat? I don't want to live in Lombok, do I?' pleaded Selene, feeling the ground slipping from under her feet and clutching at the little threads of sanity she had left since she had received the letter that had brought her here, in this office.

'Unfortunately you will have to, until you have made your claim on the property as prescribed by Indonesian Law. You see the laws on properties in Indonesia are quite different from ours. The Law on Ownership is based on the Basic Agrarian Law of 1960, and specifically Article 9, which states as follows, 'and here Gabriel looked at one of the papers in his hand and read out loud:

(1) *Only Indonesian citizens can have the most complete relationship with the earth, water, and airspace, within the limits stipulated in the provisions of Articles 1 and 2.*

(2) Every Indonesian citizen, both men and women, has an equal opportunity to acquire a land right and to obtain the benefits and yields thereof for himself/herself or for his/her family.

Your aunt knew Indonesian Laws well and she had taken Indonesian citizenship to avoid bureaucratic problems. She was also aware that it would have been extremely difficult and costly for you to claim the property as your own; therefore, she nominated a person that she trusted, to be name holder of the estate. He is at present putting in a claim for *hak milik* (right of ownership); otherwise, the State will take the land back.

You see, once he has filed the claim and has obtained the abovementioned document, he can make a nominal sale to you. "Nominal" because you will only pay the legal costs and not the property, although it will seem as if he has sold it to you. He, though, will still be acting as name holder, because a foreigner cannot be the owner of land in Indonesia.

Anyway, before your name appears on the deeds, you, as a foreigner, must produce four documents to the notary.

The first document states that the foreigner gives money to the Indonesian name holder to buy land and property and the Indonesian gives this land and property to the foreigner to use, out of his free will. The document also declares that the name holder gives the foreigner permission to sell, let or rebuild the house or property. It must state that the agreement passes automatically to the heirs of the foreigner, provided the heirs reside in the property, as well as of the name holders. All of the property costs (electricity, water, and taxes) have to be paid by the foreigner. The official Sertipikat will be in the foreigner's possession as well as the statement of cession, signed by the name holder. Only with this Sertipikat Hak Milik it is possible to sell the land.

'But didn't the property already belong to my Aunt Elizabeth?' asked Selene, slightly confused.

'Yes Selene. She was the owner because she was an Indonesian citizen, but you are not, that's why you need a name holder.' Gabriel explained. 'Let's proceed. I'll clarify any points you find obscure at the end of this session.' he added.

The second document one must produce must state that the selling of the property is granted to the foreigner or his/her heir and that the name holder gives his explicit permission to do so.

In the third document, the name holder gives permission to let the house or property.

The fourth document commits the name holder to co-operate, if the time ever comes that the foreigner or the heir can own land and property in Indonesia, in making the foreigner the new name holder on the Sertipikat. Should the law change to the disadvantage of the foreigner, the name holder will co-operate in turning the agreement into a lease-contract of 50 years with option for another term.

Do you understand what I'm saying?' asked Gabriel, putting the papers back on his desk.

'You mean to say that the property will remain in this person's name for the time being?' answered Selene, her mind in a whirl after listening to all the legal jargon.

'Yes. It's in the name of a man who is the son of Sir Duncan's best friend, a Mr Vikram Denpasar. He was born and bred in Lombok. He lives in Mataram and my family and I have known him for many years. He is a very trustworthy and honourable man.' answered Gabriel in a calm voice.

'Will I meet him as soon as we arrive in Lombok?'

'Not right away. He is a shrewd businessman, always on the

lookout for more ways to make money. At the moment he is in New York and has no plans to go back to the island till at least mid April.'

Selene felt a migraine coming on. This was too much. Why, oh why couldn't all this be a bad dream? 'But why should I give up my flat? What if I don't like Lombok and want to relinquish my rights to the property? If I came back, I'll have nowhere to go. And what will I do for three weeks alone in London?' she asked, feeling on the edge of a chasm.

'Because it will be far easier to sort matters out if you are already in London. I shall need to see you. You'll have documents to sign, you see. You can book yourself in at any hotel. We shall advance you a certain amount of money to cover your expenses until all the legal formalities have been disposed of. Take a break, do some shopping, live it up a little. You are a millionaire now.' Gabriel told her in what was meant to be a reassuring tone of voice.

'It's all so new to me. Up to the day before yesterday I was a modest office administrator and now, suddenly, I discover that I had an aunt and a wealthy one at that. An aunt that I have never met and never will meet and that I'm to be in possession of a vast fortune. It's enough to make my head spin.' Selene felt compelled to tell him that her world had turned topsy-turvy and that she needed time to adjust to such a great change in her life. But it wasn't just that. He, too, seemed to have woven a magical spell around her, with his kindness and good looks.

It was time for her to go now. She had a lot of hard thinking to do as well as many decisions to make. And no one with whom to share her fears and doubts.

As if sensing her mood, Gabriel Hart took her hand, looked into her eyes and said, reassuringly, 'I know it is a lot to take onboard and that you feel lost and alone, Selene. May I call you Selene?' Selene nodded her consent. 'If you have any worries or need any assistance, please call me and I'll help you the best I can. And please, call me Gabriel.' He squeezed her hand, handed her a business card on the reverse of which he had scribbled his home address and mobile number. He then ushered her out of his office, gave her one of his dazzling smiles and, with a parting, 'See you soon.' left her in the capable hands of his secretary.

'Here you are, Miss Finch,' said Miss Knight, giving her a cheque-book and a credit card bearing her name. 'We have opened a bank account in your name. Here are also a few notes on Lombok, its customs and climate. Please read them carefully, as they may be of use to you when purchasing clothes for your stay there.'

Selene, her head still swimming with everything that she had heard that morning, thanked Miss Knight and left for the station.

CHAPTER THREE

When Selene arrived home, she could not remember anything of her journey back, her brain still coming to grips with the implications of what her future life would be like.

She had a long shower, washing away the grime of the city, then, famished, she made herself an omelette and some salad.

Selene pondered over what had been revealed to her of her grandmother's past. Now some episodes in her childhood and adolescence made sense. Her grandmother's constant warnings about boys, her fretting when she had gone out on some errand and had arrived home a few minutes late. Selene understood now her grandmother's compulsion to be at the school gates to greet her and all those questions about the boys in and around her school. Poor Granny! She must have thought history would repeat itself yet again, if she did not keep a close eye and tight reins on her granddaughter, always preaching to Selene to follow her head, not her heart. However, even her grandmother had not bargained for Simon.

Oh, he had been smooth. He had been so handsome, so polite. His refined good-manners and respectful attitude, his impeccable English had won over her mother and even conquered her grandmother's diffidence against the male of the species. Selene had been bowled over by his good looks, his blue eyes, and his promises of undying love. He had won a scholarship for his Master in Economics at Sussex University and had taken up lodgings in the house next door to theirs. They were both members of the same library, the only place her grandmother allowed her to go unescorted. What had started as a simple friendship soon turned into something deeper. Simon was everything she had always dreamt in a man. Not only was he tall, dark, and handsome, but he had brains, a kind disposition and made her laugh. Every time he invited her out, he made sure she had the time of her life. They had been dating for three months when the bubble of happiness she had constructed around herself burst.

It was near Easter and Simon was due to go home to Oxford to visit his parents. A week before he left, one Saturday morning Selene will never forget, she went to answer the doorbell. There, in front of her, stood a lovely, lithe, good-looking brunette, with wavy long hair and a sweet smile on her lips.

'Hello, I'm sorry to bother you, but I've tried next door and no one seems to be in. Do you know Simon Croft?'

'Yes, as a matter of fact I do. How can I help you?' replied Selene, rather puzzled.

'You see I'm Amanda, Simon's girlfriend.' The girl explained.

Selene became very pale and thought for an awful moment that she was going to faint.

'Are you all right?' enquired Amanda, solicitously.

'Yes,' croaked Selene, who, with an enormous effort of will, had managed to keep her emotions in check. 'It's only a dizzy spell, but I'm all right now. Do come in. The Greens have gone shopping and Simon is at the library.' Selene led her to the sitting room, then, with the excuse of making tea, went into the kitchen, and sat down, trying to stop her body from shaking. Somehow she managed to go through the motions of being a polite hostess, bringing tea and biscuits to her unexpected guest. With an effort of will, Selene sat down facing Amanda.

'I should have told him I was coming, but, you see, I meant to surprise him.'

'Have you been going out long?' asked Selene in an outwardly calm voice.

'We've been together for two years and it's the first time that we've been apart for such a long time. I know he came home for Christmas, but that was three months ago and I needed to see him. I have something very special to tell him. You see, I'm expecting a baby....' Amanda prattled on happily, not realizing what this bombshell was doing to Selene.

Selene was glad she had been sitting when she had heard this piece of news that had rocked her world. She still could not believe how she had managed to survive that terrible day. She had felt like an automaton. She had behaved normally, asking the appropriate questions, and giving the right answers, but it seemed to her as if she were watching someone else doing it, not herself.

Selene had not wished to see Simon again. She had asked her mother to tell her friends and her neighbours that she had come down with a virus and spent the following three weeks in bed, not wanting to see or hear anyone, except her friend Vanessa. She had been unable to eat, only managing to swallow some water or tea and had lost a lot of weight. Distraught by seeing her so ill, her grandmother had suggested she should take her away for a while. She would write to a friend of hers who lived in Brighton, where she had a B & B.

Grandmother's friend had written back saying she would be happy to have both Selene and her grandmother, as she needed a hand with the guests. One of the paid helpers was on holiday. Selene's mother approved of this temporary move and promised that she would let them know when they could safely return home without bumping into Simon again.

As it happened, an opportunity arose for her mother to go and work in Tonbridge, so the three of them moved in a flat in the same building where Selene had later found the one-bedroom flat where she still lived.

It had been a long, painful awakening for Selene who, from that day on, had vouched never to fall in love again.

Once out of her reverie, she took up the notes on Lombok. She was soon intrigued by its history, its caste system and its unique blend of Islam and Animism practiced in the north of the island, where the Wetu Telu people prayed three times a day rather than the five prescribed by the Quran. Islam being the predominant religion on the island, Selene realised the emphasis Gabriel Hart and Miss Knight had put on the type of clothes that she had to buy, as she would have to reside on the island for a long period of time.

Fascinated, Selene read on to learn that Lombok's climate was typically tropical, with temperatures in the 80s and 90s. The rainy season started in October and lasted until May, but, apparently, the word 'monsoon' was mainly applicable to the wind, not the rain, as precipitation lasted just one hour on any one day.

Mataram was the largest city on Lombok and the capital of the West Nusa Tenggara province in Indonesia. Mataram was an agglomeration of a number of villages that had grown together. The main clusters comprised Ampenan, the port on the west coast and the site of the airport; Mataram itself, in the centre; and Cakranegara, the commercial hub to the east.

Apart from the written notes, she found some pictures of the island, of the breathtakingly beautiful Kuta Bay, with its fantastic beach. Other pictures showed the imposing Mount Rinjani, Indonesia's second highest peak. The last pictures were of a fabulous villa lost in a wide stretch of land, all fenced in. The building was her Aunt Elizabeth's villa. It was called *Inggris*, which apparently meant English.

Selene sat there, staring at the incredibly luscious garden with its magnificent swimming pool, the place where her Aunt Elizabeth had drowned.

Suddenly, Selene felt a cold chill run down her spine. It seemed impossible that someone should die in her own swimming pool, in Paradise. 'Because it looks like Paradise. Or very near it.' Selene mused.

Then, without her wishing to, a splendid male face presented itself to her mind's eye. She would see him again soon. They would travel together to the island... and then? Surely someone as gorgeous as he had a girlfriend or a wife. That brought back memories of Simon, which made her feel ill and dejected. Well, she told herself, there were tasks she had to perform before she saw him again.

First, she typed the letter of resignation, which she would hand in at work first thing in the morning. That would be a shock to her employer, but Selene was determined to serve her notice, although she would keep the real reason for leaving the company to herself.

Her grandmother had instilled to her and to her mother the fundamental principle that it was never a good policy to talk to other people about private matters and now Selene, having discovered her grandmother's early pregnancy, understood why.

Putting these thoughts aside, Selene concentrated herself on her next task. She had to sort out her few possessions. That was quickly done, as the bulk of the furniture belonged to her landlord. Anyway, she thought, wherever she would go and live from now on, she had no need for the little tables and nick-knacks that she had bought from second hand shops to adorn her miniscule flat. Her clothes, too, could be dropped at several charity shops in the town centre.

By ten o'clock Selene felt so tired that she went straight to bed, where she slept like a log till the alarm went off at 7 am.

CHAPTER FOUR

Another cold and grey morning greeted Selene, who went through the usual daily routine. Once at the office, she placed her letter on Sue Proctor's desk. Sue was the office manager and the person who had engaged her nine months before. She was a lovely, kind woman, on the verge of anorexia.

Selene was at her desk going through the day's emails, when Sue arrived. Ten minutes later, Sue called her into her office.

'Selene, what's happened? I thought you were happy here, working for us. We are extremely pleased with your attitude to work and the results you have achieved in such a short time'.

'Thank you Sue. Believe me it's nothing to do with the company or with you. I'm very grateful for all your help and kindness, but something has cropped up of a personal nature, which I don't wish to discuss.' 'Let her think I have boyfriend troubles,' thought Selene.

'Well, why don't you take a holiday? Take a fortnight off and....'

'Sorry, Sue. It will take me months to sort things out and I'll have some travelling to do as well, but thanks for the offer', replied Serena firmly.

Sue looked puzzled, but she realised that Selene was determined.

'All right, Selene. You know that you owe us a month's notice, starting from today. But if you change your mind, we'll be happy to have you back.'

'Thank you Sue', Selene responded, relieved. 'By the way, I'd rather you didn't tell the girls. I don't want any fuss.'

'Very well, Selene, as you wish', replied Sue in a resigned tone of voice.

In the end, though, all the girls gave her a good-luck card, with everybody's best wishes, and a silver bracelet. Selene was moved, but glad that she had got over that hurdle.

The next thing Selene had to do was to notify Mr Berry, her landlord.

Mr Berry's reaction was heart-warming. He had been her family's landlord and hers for the past few years and had grown fond of her. He made Selene promise that if she ran into any difficulties, she would contact him and Mrs Berry, who would be happy to put her up at their house, should someone else be renting what, at present, was her flat.

Selene had to make an appointment with the doctor, in order to be inoculated against the usual tropical diseases, as well as obtaining a prescription of tablets against what the Australians call 'Bali belly', a very unpleasant bug caused by the water in Indonesia.

Time flew by, and it was on the eve of her journey to London that Selene received a call from Gabriel.

'Hello Selene? How are you? Have you sorted everything out? Have you already booked a hotel in London?' He enquired solicitously.

'Yes, thank you, Mr Hart. I've booked a room at the Copthorne Tara Hotel in Kensington', Selene informed him, slightly breathless at the sound of his deep virile voice.

'Excellent choice, Selene. Please call me Gabriel. I believe we had agreed on that already. As we are going to be travelling companions, we should dispense with formalities and address each other by our first name. You need to come and sign a few papers Miss Knight has ready for you. Unfortunately, I shall be away on business, so I won't be able to see you. Anyway, I will come and collect you on the 26th of February at 8.30 am. Our flight leaves at 11.00 am. We shall have to sleep over in Singapore, and then take the 3.30 flight to Lombok. Miss Knight has booked a chauffeured driven car, as it is customary on the island, to take us to your aunt's property.' explained Gabriel.

'Fine, I'll be ready', uttered Selene, trying to keep her voice cool and detached. 'By the way, Gabriel, I haven't seen any pictures of my aunt. Is there a reason for it?' Selene asked.

'Yes. Sorry Selene. All her pictures are at *Inggris*. In the confusion that arose at her unexpected death, nobody thought of forwarding any.' he answered, apologetically. Is there anything else that I can do for you?' he added, kindly.

'No. Thank you Gabriel. That's all for now. Goodbye'

'Goodbye Selene. See you soon.'

Selene was still holding the receiver in her hands long after Gabriel had rung off. She had the dazed star-struck look of a teenager with a major crush on her best teacher.

'Snap out of it, girl. Gabriel Hart is not for you. He is too suave and sophisticated, so he is probably a rat like Simon. Will you ever learn?' she berated herself.

Two days later, it dawned on Selene that she had to part with her Mini. It had been her mother's car and Selene had always loved it. She could not do it. She felt as if she had been asked to relinquish a favourite pet. What was she to do?

Selene spent hours agonizing over this problem, when suddenly she had a bright idea. Louisa Berry had always admired her Mini and Selene had lent it to her a few times when Mr Berry had been in hospital. Maybe she could let her keep it for the time she was away in Lombok and ask for it back when she returned.

Mrs Berry was over the moon, hugged, and kissed Selene as if she had been a long lost relative. 'Oh Selene, thank you. You don't know how happy you've made me. I feel as if I've won the lottery. You'll keep in touch, won't you? Look after yourself dear. Goodbye.'

Well, everything had been sorted. All Selene needed to do now was to go to the hotel in London and 'live it up.'

Selene was thrilled at the freedom money was giving her. She was now able to shop at top boutiques, have her hair done at the most chick salons in town. But for all that, the years of penury had taught her moderation and, in the end, she only bought a few items of clothing, though of excellent quality.

She had her hair lightly waved, and styled in a way that the loose ringlets complemented her oval face, giving her an aura of sophistication and simplicity at the same time.

Selene went to see a pantomime and a couple of musicals; visited museums and art galleries, but spent most of her time at the British Museum Library, where she browsed through many interesting articles on Indonesian folklore.

Out of the many myths and legends that characterized Lombok, Selene was particularly captivated by the tale of Rangda.

Rangda, or 'widow', Selene read in one of the articles, *is evil personified. She is a witch that is associated with the spirits of the dead. Several men armed with keris (daggers) accompany Rangda wherever she goes. Under her influence, they go into a trance and stab themselves, but are protected from injury by the presence of Barong, the lion that represents good. Rangda and Barong are engaged in endless battles. Barong is usually, but not always, the final victor. This victory is taken to affirm his protection of the village...*

Though interpreted as good versus evil, the two sides are more equivocal, as Barong does not always win.

Fascinated, Selene decided to read more about this unusual myth and borrowed a book to take back to the hotel.

After a day spent sight-seeing, Selene, her feet aching, regained her room and went to bed early, looking forward to learn more about what she had renamed 'the wicked witch of the East.'

According to the ancient Calonarang manuscript, Rangda was a woman of overwhelming desire or unrepressed fury sparked by revenge. An 11th century manuscript from old Javanese literature tells about a widow who possessed supernatural powers, but unfortunately she used those powers to spread terror over the people. At the end of the story, the widow duelled with Empu Bharadah, a clergyman emissary of the king. During the battle, the widow changed into Rangda, a bloodcurdling figure, whereas the Empu changed into Barong, the supernatural form of a mythical lion.

Rangda is also the queen of the Leyak. The Leyak are humans who practice black magic and have cannibalistic behaviour. Besides the Leyak, demons are said to be the followers of Rangda

As she read those words, Selene felt a cold chill run down her spine. She quickly put the book down on the side table and was unable to sleep. Every time she closed her eyes, a horrible head with popping eyes greeted her.

The following day, Selene took the book back to the library, and from that time, despite the many hours she spent browsing through the folklore of Bali and Lombok, she avoided reading other tales on this perverse and maleficent being.

CHAPTER FIVE

The night before she was due to embark on her journey, Selene was both restless and excited. In a few more hours she would see Gabriel again, and together they would fly off into the unknown.

Room service woke Selene up with scrambled eggs on toast, orange juice and the aroma of freshly percolated coffee. She took her time over breakfast, which she ate with gusto, savouring each mouthful.

After taking a long, hot shower, Selene applied some make up on her face, in the subtle way her mother had taught her. She then carefully selected a jade green suit in cashmere – she would change on the plane, as the weather was still cold in London, but would be hot and humid in Singapore. She decided to put her hair up in a knot, with some loose, springy tendrils caressing her cheeks. Finally, she clipped on the gold chain with the Celtic cross, which was a good-luck charm to her, and sprayed some of the monstrously expensive perfume she had purchased during her shopping spree in the most renowned shops of the capital.

Selene was ready. She took the lift to the ground floor and approached the reception desk. She paid her bill, the clerk pressed the bell, and the porter fetched the two new suitcases that she had packed the previous night. Selene took up a magazine and sat, outwardly composed, but heart pounding, awaiting Gabriel's arrival.

Gabriel came on the dot of 8.30. He looked devastatingly handsome in a grey three-piece suit, well-ironed shirt the colour of his eyes, and Italian hand-made shoes. His aftershave was tantalising her sensitive nose, his warm smile and laughing eyes playing havoc with her senses.

'Hallo Selene. I see you are packed and rearing to go. Have you paid your hotel bill?'

'Yes, Gabriel', she managed to say in a husky voice she hardly recognized as her own, then, regaining control of her emotions, she added, 'I am ready. Let's go.'

When they reached the chauffeur-driven Rolls with its posh leather seats, Selene discovered, to her dismay, that an incredibly attractive, exotic-looking girl, about 24 years of age, was occupying the back seat.

'This is Dewi Rinjani Fairchild.' said Gabriel, introducing the long-legged brunette. 'Her father is English and her mother is Sasak, from one of the old aristocratic families in Lombok. She'll be coming with us, as she's taking some time off from London University in order to go home and visit her family whom she has not seen for four years. She's started her PhD on *The Myths and Legends of Lombok*. If you want to know more about these subjects during our journey, you can ask her. Dewi Rinjani is a real expert. Her father is a friend of my family. Dewi Rinjani and her family will be your closest neighbours on Lombok.' Then, turning towards Dewi Rinjani, he explained, 'This is Selene Finch, Elizabeth's niece and heiress.'

Dewi Rinjani looked at Selene with a mellifluous smile that did not reach her cold blue eyes. It was clear that she considered Selene a rival in her quest for Gabriel's favours.

'So, you're the lucky girl.' she remarked, spitefully. 'To think that Elizabeth didn't even know you and didn't want any dealings with your family, and now you've inherited that splendid property and all that money.' she added venomously.

'Now stop that, Dewi Rinjani.' upbraided Gabriel, a grimace of irritation altering for a moment his handsome features. 'You don't know what the relationship between Elizabeth and her family was and quite frankly, it's none of your business.'

Dewi Rinjani tried to justify herself and, looking contrite murmured, 'Sorry, Gabriel. You know how I feel about that piece of land. After all, it had belonged to my family for generations.'

‘Yes, I know,’ replied Gabriel, taking her hand and patting it. ‘But it was a long time ago, and Elizabeth’s parents paid good money for it.’

Selene’s spirits had hit an unprecedented low. She should have known that Gabriel was another Simon. He even looked a bit like him. As far as rivalry was concerned, Dewi Rinjani could have him, if he was available. Deep down she was sorely disappointed. She had hoped, in her heart of hearts, that he was different from other men, and that the flicker of attraction she had seen reflected in Gabriel’s eyes when they had met, would blossom into a stronger feeling. What a fool she had been! Dewi Rinjani was probably only one in a chain of beauties sat to conquer Gabriel’s affection in a permanent way.

The drive to the airport was agony to Selene. It was impossible not to notice how Dewi Rinjani kept putting her well-manicured hand on Gabriel’s arm, allegedly to call his attention to something she was telling him, nor the way she put her face close to his to whisper in his ear.

On the plane, Gabriel selected the seat in the middle, with Selene on his right and Dewi Rinjani on his left. Selene was glad of the arrangement, because she could look out of the window. The sky was clear for once, so Selene was able to admire the view beneath them.

Now and again Gabriel attempted to speak to her, but immediately Dewi Rinjani would call his attention to something she needed or asked him questions about friends they had in common, excluding Selene from the conversation. Due to the proximity of their seats, Selene couldn’t help but overhear what they were saying and learnt, to her secret delight, that Gabriel was not married and had ended a long-standing relationship a couple of months before she had met him. And why should she be happy about that? She wondered.

After a while, lulled by the droning of the engines, and the monologue Dewi Rinjani had embarked on, Selene fell asleep. When she awoke, she found that Gabriel's head rested on her shoulder. A feeling of tenderness overcame her. He looked so innocent in his sleep. His classical profile, his long dark eyelashes rendered him sexier than ever. His full bottom lip betrayed his sensual nature, the musky scent of his aftershave teased her nostrils. Selene could not help herself. She feasted her eyes on him until she realised that his cobalt blue eyes were looking at her with a sexual hunger that made every nerve in her body come to life. Just then, Dewi Rinjani returned to her seat and addressing Gabriel, exclaimed, 'You are awake finally. Where are we?'

Gabriel sat up straight and, after a quick look at his Rolex, replied that they would be approaching Changi airport, in Singapore, within the next hour.

The other girl's presence galvanized Selene into action. She retrieved a small bag from under her seat and, after excusing herself, she adjourned to the restroom. In the privacy of its small, enclosed space, she changed her warm clothes for a pair of aquamarine, gossamer-light, pure silk, loose-fitting trousers with a matching long-sleeve blouse. She used some cream to remove the make up from her face, and then made it up again, applying a thin layer of blush to her cheeks and caressing her lips with a hint of lip-gloss. She ran her fingers through her hair to bring her soft curls back into shape, and then let her hair loose over her shoulders. A final touch of mascara over her eyelashes, a pair of golden sandals on her feet and she was ready to face the world. The overall effect was of a fragile, delicate, almost ethereal nymph.

When she went back to her seat, she realised that Dewi Rinjani had vacated hers once more.

'You're a very beautiful girl, Selene. I can see that I'll have quite a time chasing off your admirers.' exclaimed Gabriel when he saw her.

Selene's cheeks took on a pinkish hue. To steady her nerves, she sat down and looked out of the window. 'It's a lovely sunny day,' she murmured inanely, to hide her pleasure at his words.

'It will be very hot and sticky when we disembark from the plane, but there should be a chauffeured car with air conditioning waiting for us.' Gabriel informed her.

Gabriel, too, had changed into a white suit with a pale blue short-sleeved shirt, opened at the neck. Selene had to keep a tight control over her senses that were going wild at the sight of his smooth tanned skin and the play of his Adam's apple as he talked.

'Oh, here you are Dewi Rinjani. You look good enough to grace the pages of Vogue.' Gabriel enthused. And, to be fair, thought Selene, Dewi Rinjani did look like a super model in her splendid pink and gold silk sarong. The girl's black hair was swept back, leaving exposed her exquisite shell-like ears adorned by a pair of earrings made from the blue coral found in the sea around Lombok. She had adorned her long graceful neck with a necklace of the same blue coral, which matched the colour of her eyes. The fairness of her skin, which she had undoubtedly inherited from her father, was slightly flushed, as Dewi Rinjani seemed to blossom at Gabriel's praise. His words spurred her on and for what remained of the flight, she kept him engrossed in a never-ending conversation.

The formalities at the airport were soon over and Selene relaxed in the back seat of the hired car. Gabriel had joined the driver at the front, so that Dewi Rinjani had to be content with sitting next to Selene. The two girls sat in silence, Selene looking at the city, as the car sped by, heading for their hotel.

It was six o'clock, local time, but Selene felt very tired. She decided to have a light dinner in her room, therefore she excused herself with the others. Gabriel's look was unfathomable, whilst Dewi Rinjani was clearly pleased to have him all to herself.

CHAPTER SIX

Selene had a long soak in the scented bath of sandalwood and jasmine. She picked at her food, then went to the window, opened the blinds and looked at the splendid display of stars the southern sky was putting on. There were thousands of millions of stars, she mused, so different from the ones visible in England. She stepped onto the small balcony and looked down where the swimming pool was, then to the open doors of the dining room, music issuing from it, mainly Western music, as this was an international hotel. The heat and humidity hit her and she retreated to the welcome coolness of her air-conditioned room. She felt excited, but dejected at the same time. Excited because she was in a different continent, in such an exotic place, but dejected because she thought of Gabriel and Dewi Rinjani together. What were they doing? She pictured the two of them dancing, the closeness of their bodies.... and she was assailed by a sick feeling in the pit of her stomach. She couldn't be jealous, could she? Jealous of a man she had only just met, a man she knew nothing about? It was ridiculous. Ok, he was a very attractive man, but there was more to a man than being handsome. 'But there is,' her heart said, 'he's kind and considerate.

Selene felt a headache coming on, so she took some mild sedative and went to bed. She woke up the following morning at 8.30 feeling refreshed and so full of energy that she decided to go for a swim in the opulent swimming pool she had glimpsed at the night before. She wore a demure light blue one-piece swimming suit with matching cap, and fastened the soft ankle-length bathrobe of the hotel.

Even at that hour in the morning the percentage of humidity in the air was quite high, so it was pure bliss to plunge into the cool water of the pool. Selene enjoyed swimming and she had already completed the full length of the pool three times, when she felt the warmth of cobalt blue eyes enveloping her. She reached the steps of the pool and walked up to him. He was holding an enormous towel, which engulfed her in its softness. 'Thank you', she murmured throatily.

'You are very welcome, Selene,' replied Gabriel, languidly lifting a strand of hair that had escaped from under her cap.

'I would be more careful around swimming pools,' Dewi Rinjani's spiteful words reached her, 'seeing what happened to your aunt'.

'Behave Dewi Rinjani.' warned Gabriel, a hint of frustration and annoyance in his voice.

'Selene, go and change, then come down to breakfast.' he ordered.

'Yes, Sir!' replied Selene, slightly amused at his commanding tone. She raised her hand to her forehead, saluting him as a private would an officer and he laughed heartily at her retreating figure.

She decided to leave sophistication to Dewi Rinjani and went for a plain white linen dress with a jasmine motif at the front and back. She slipped on low-heel sandals, an ethnic copper bracelet, and necklace completing her outfit. She combed her hair in an ancient Greece's sort of style and left her face bare of makeup. Pleased with the young slender image the mirror reflected, Selene sprayed the expensive jasmine perfume she had bought in London and headed for the lift.

When she reached the breakfast room, she saw Gabriel sitting there alone and her heart gave a flip. Without her volition, her face betrayed the happiness she felt inside at meeting him there without Dewi Rinjani.

'Where's Dewi Rinjani?' she enquired.

'On the phone to her brother Michael Taun', replied Gabriel. He got up and helped her sit down, like an old-fashioned gentleman, but he took advantage of the situation by brushing her delicate neck with his warm fingertips. The sensation that ensued took Selene's breath away. He sat down opposite her and gave her a comprehensive stare, 'You look about sixteen. Sweet sixteen and....' He never completed the rest of his sentence as Dewi Rinjani joined them at the table, extremely elegant in a Versace's outfit that would not have disgraced the most demanding jet-set party.

Her presence dampened the seductively tense atmosphere of the few seconds Selene and Gabriel had shared, and breakfast took on a form of mild torture for Selene, under Dewi Rinjani's probing eyes and malicious attitude towards her.

When breakfast was over, Selene declared her intention to go shopping, as there was plenty of time, as their flight from Changi was scheduled for 3.30 pm.

Selene felt confident going shopping on her own. Le Meridien Orchard Hotel, where they were staying, was right in the heart of Orchard Road, Singapore's undisputed hub of shopping. There - as the receptionist at the desk had told her that morning - she would find mall after mall of glitzy clothes, shoes, and anything else she could desire.

Out of politeness, she asked Dewi Rinjani if she wanted to accompany her, but was relieved when the other girl declined, stating that she wanted to rest. Gabriel had some work to do, therefore Selene was left to discover the Aladdin's cave that the city and her newfound money were offering her.

In the end, Selene devoted her time window-shopping, although she stopped at several jewellers' shops, attracted by the variety of jade necklaces, earrings, and bracelets she found. She discovered that there were two types of jade: jadeite and nephrite. The former came in more vivid colours of green, black, pink, russet, white, and lilac. The nephrite variety instead, was a tougher type of jade that lasted longer.

Selene chose green and russet jadeite necklaces with matching earrings, which reflected the colour of her eyes and hair. She also went for a very expensive emerald and platinum necklace also with matching earrings that had taken her fancy.

Exhausted, she stopped for a relaxing cup of coffee at the Starbucks Coffee Bar, where, totally unaware, she attracted the eyes of several male customers, before heading back to the hotel.

It was a few minutes past twelve, so Selene went back to her room for a shower and a lie down. She was awakened by the alarm service an hour later. She packed the small bag she had brought with her, her other suitcases having been left at the airport's luggage depot the previous day. For her outfit to the island, Selene chose a silk, sky-blue sarong, with a bird of paradise as motif on the front, clipped on the russet jadeite necklace with matching earrings she had bought at the jeweller in the Tampines Mall, and then combed her hair up into a knot. When she was ready, she buzzed reception and asked to be put through to Gabriel's room.

'Gabriel? It's Selene. What time would you like me to meet you?' she asked in what she hoped sounded a detached tone of voice.

'In a quarter of an hour at reception,' he responded in his deep baritone, which always made her feel as if she had butterflies in her tummy. 'We'll be leaving at two o'clock.'

Selene decided to go downstairs and buy herself something to read, leaving the art of conversation to her two travelling companions.

However, this time, after takeoff, Gabriel devoted himself entirely to her, describing to her Malaysia and Indonesia, their cultures and peoples. He curtly replied to any questions Dewi Rinjani asked him and curbed any other attempt at conversation the girl initiated.

Tired of being ignored, Dewi Rinjani eventually got out of her seat and went to the bar section of the plane, animated by the presence of some patently wealthy males.

Captivated by Gabriel's knowledge of that part of Asia, but more so by his proximity and electrified by the touch of his hand on her arm, Selene felt in seventh heaven.

CHAPTER SEVEN

As they approached Bali, the magnificent view that unfolded in front of her eyes astounded Selene. Then, as the plane proceeded eastwards, the circular island of Lombok came into view. Mount Rinjani dominated the centre-north side of the island from its height of 3,726 meters. Its horseshoe shaped crater, Amos, filled by the shimmering waters of Lake Segara Anak captured her interest. Selene feasted her eyes on the Tiu Kelep Waterfall, before the plane started its descent towards the west side of the island, to Mataram Selaparang Airport.

'Where is my aunt's villa and where is she buried?' enquired Selene.

'It's in the southern part of the island, at Kunta Bay, in one of the most scenic and sought out spots on Lombok and your aunt is buried in a little wood, next to a temple her parents had had built on the property.' was Gabriel's polite reply.

Kunta Bay, that's probably where the name Dewi Kunta originated. Dewi Kunta was the name of the property where Dewi Rinjani lived with her family. Selene was reminded once again that the two properties had been one in the past, and only a sudden need of money had prompted the sale of the piece of land that, by a strange train of events, was to become her own.

She felt rather depressed at the thought that she would be living so close to Dewi Rinjani. Yet her spirits lifted again as if by magic, once they left the airport. She breathed in the clean air left by the rain and the wind, which had swept over the town an hour earlier, or so their Chinese looking chauffeur informed them, while respectfully opening the car door for them.

It was now 5.30 pm, and they still had a sixty-minute drive to Kunta Bay. This prompted Gabriel to ask them if they wanted to stop for dinner along the way, but, as they had been served boiled rice and spicy shrimps during the flight, both girls declined. All they wanted now was to reach their destination by sunset.

'Well, then,' continued Gabriel, 'the driver will drop Selene and myself at the villa, then he will take you home, Dewi Rinjani. Once everything has been settled at *Inggris*, Wayan, Elizabeth's chauffeur, will drop me off at the Kunta Indah Hotel here in Kuta Beach, where I've booked a suite.

'But, Gabriel, I thought you were going to stay with us.' Dewi Rinjani objected with a pout.

Gabriel touched Dewi Rinjani's cheek gently with his lips, as he would have done with a child.

'You know it's impossible. I have business to sort out in Bali and in Mataram, as well as people to see on this part of the island, therefore a hotel's suite is definitely more appropriate than a family home. Anyway, I'll come and see your family soon.'

Dewi Rinjani brightened up considerably after that, whilst Selene felt as if she had been doused with a bucket of icy water. The tenderness shown by Gabriel's action, together with the hidden promise to Dewi Rinjani, disguised as a visit to her parents, brought a lump to her throat. Furthermore, it sounded as if she would see very little of him. Now she realised that what she had thought of as kindness in accompanying her to Lombok, had not stemmed from any special feeling he had for her, but for Dewi Rinjani. Selene was only part of the business he had to attend to in that part of the world.

Close to tears, Selene turned her head and looked out of the window, whilst Dewi Rinjani listened to the tunes from her I-pod and Gabriel, sitting at the front with the driver, started up a conversation with him.

They left Mataram, skirted the town of Cakranegara. From there onwards the road went southwards, abandoning the acacia trees, the fragrant eucalyptus and the thick forest of palm trees. It curved round the west side of the Praya Reservoir, and finally headed towards the sparsely populated scrubby, barren hills of the south.

By the time they reached Kunta Bay, the sun was setting and Selene thought it had been worth coming all that way just to witness this spectacle of nature. The sun grew enormous on the horizon, spreading flames of light, bathing the water and everything around it with a fiery display of red and gold, and then, quickly, it was engulfed by the sea and the stars appeared, like millions of fairy lights against the velvet darkness of the night. Selene held her breath for what seemed hours. This was magnificent. Not even in her wildest dreams had she believed she would experience something so exceptional, so magical that no words nor canvas or music could do it justice.

Gabriel opened the door for her, but before Selene was out, Dewi Rinjani had managed to come round the car and was now kissing Gabriel lingeringly and passionately on the lips and he appeared to be responding, not in the least embarrassed at this public display of affection.

Selene leapt out of the car and, as if by magic, the gate opened and the light of countless Chinese lanterns turned the already magnificent night into a fairyland. It was a shame that Selene's prince had just turned into a toad.

'Wait, Selene,' Gabriel cried after her, 'aren't you going to say goodbye to Dewi Rinjani?'

Recalled to the social conventions of polite society, Selene found the strength to rise to the occasion, managing to ask the girl to convey her greetings to her parents. As Dewi Rinjani left, a strange horse and cart, all bells and pom-poms, made its way up the driveway.

'What's this?' croaked Selene.

'It's a *cimodo*, pronounced *chi-moe-doe*. As you can see, it's a two-wheeled horse-drawn cart. It's one the most common means of transport on the island.' explained Gabriel 'the entrance to the villa is nearly two miles away. Mei-Lin, your housekeeper, has sent Wayan, her son and your driver, to convey us there in comfort'.

Selene was speechless. She had not realised that the villa had so much land. She was about to ask him how much, when she thought it was probably part of the information he would impart to her at the house.

Gabriel took her hand to help her up onto the vehicle. At the touch of his fingers, her whole being was pervaded by a sensation of warmth that spread from her hand to the rest of her body, colouring her cheeks and her neck. Fortunately, the light of the lamps was not bright enough to expose her reaction to him. If his touch alone provoked such a response, how could she bear to sit close to him in the confines of the *cidomo*, without betraying her feelings at his proximity?

When Gabriel mounted on his seat, Selene moved as far away from him as it was possible. Gabriel, though, perversely closed the gap and turned to her with a smile. 'You rat,' thought Selene, 'you've just kissed a girl and are now ready to seduce another.' The anger she felt at his unspeakable behaviour helped Selene exude a coolness she was far from feeling.

Determined to show Gabriel that she was not impressed by his pathetic attempt to capture her attention, she asked Wayan about the weather. His comprehensive replies together with his own enquiries about their journey accompanied by the pleasant *jing, jing, jingeling- clippity-clop* sound of the vehicle and horse occupied most of the journey so that, before she knew it, they were standing at the front door of the villa.

Selene could only make out the outline of what appeared to be a substantial building and reserved any thoughts on it, after she had had a proper look at it the following morning. All she could see at the light that flooded through the open entrance door was a short middle-aged woman waiting for them. She looked slim yet strong, her dark almond-shaped eyes smiling. Oddly, she was not wearing any shoes or sandals on her feet.

'I Mei-Lin, welcome', she chirped sweetly.

Selene smiled back her "thank you." She liked this lithe little woman in her red and gold sarong on sight and sensed that she would find a friend and ally in her.

Gabriel took his shoes off and signalled to Selene to do the same, explaining that it was yet another of the island's traditional customs to be observed, like the one of not carrying food with the left hand, considered unclean or the one about not drinking anything alcoholic in public.

CHAPTER EIGHT

Mei-Lin crossed the generously proportioned hall, opened a richly carved wooden door, and ushered them into a vast room, filled with the scent of sandalwood.

Selene looked around her and realised that the whole flooring was entirely made of this precious wood, as it is in some temples. Three expensive leather sofas and four armchairs were elegantly placed in one section of the room. Against one of the walls stood the biggest aquarium Selene had ever seen, with colourful tropical fish, sea anemones, and aquatic plants native of the island.

A pot of fragrant jasmine tea had been placed on one of the low carved wooden tables, positioned all around the room. Two cups of fine porcelain and a plate of freshly made rice cakes stood on a silver tray.

While she poured the tea, Gabriel pushed a button, from what Selene had thought was a TV remote. The panel blinds moved back and let in the enormous full tropical moon, the starry sky, and the ocean waves through the panoramic windows, which replaced an entire wall and overlooked the distant bay.

'It's so beautiful', Selene exclaimed, enchanted by the view.

'You are beautiful, Selene', murmured Gabriel advancing towards her.

Selene regained her composure and asked, in a brisk manner, 'Look, Gabriel, I'm incredibly tired. Could we leave the business we have to discuss till tomorrow?'

Gabriel seemed to be taken aback, but he could see that the excitement of the last few weeks and the long journey there had taken their toll. He saw the blanched face and the dark shadows under her eyes. 'All right, Selene. Have a good night's rest. I'll call round tomorrow at eleven.' She gratified him with a thankful smile and was surprised when he took her hand and kissed it. She moved it away as if scalded, then asked Mei-Lin, who had been waiting patiently in the hall, to let him out.

Mei-Lin came back and Selene followed her up one flight of stairs leading to the west wing. They sailed through a picture gallery, and then Mei-Lin stopped outside an open door and let her through.

It was a very pretty room, with a double bed in teak. It contained a walk-in wardrobe with a full-length mirror, a small desk with a bookcase next to it and a plasma TV set on the wall facing the bed. Mei-Lin opened a door and Selene found herself in the ensuite, with tiles made of marble, with embedded fragments of shells. An opulent bath stood next to the shower, with the washbasin, bidet and toilet bowl, facing it. The far wall was taken up by a double set of shelves. The most refined toiletry money could buy had been placed on some of the shelves, with plenty of towels and a bathrobe ready for her use.

'Everything right, Miss?' Mei-Lin called out.

'Yes, Mei-Lin. Thank you. Everything is perfect. I'll see you in the morning.'

'What time you eat breakfast?'

'8 o'clock, please. Some fruit, coffee and pineapple juice.'

'Good, Miss. Goodnight.'

'Goodnight, Mei-Lin. Thank you for your warm welcome.'

Once alone, Selene had a long shower, slipped into a cool cotton nightgown and climbed into the comfortable double bed. Within minutes, she was fast asleep.

Selene had a dreadful night. She dreamt that she was at the bottom of the swimming pool at *Inggris* and that a demoniacal force was preventing her from reaching up to the surface. She struggled with all her might, but she was on the verge of losing her battle when, thankfully, the thrill of the first bird, announcing dawn awoke her. Quickly, Selene got up and pulled back the blinds.

The French windows opened onto a wooden balcony. Selene wrapped herself in the soft bathrobe and stepped outside. There she found a wicker chair with some cushions. Selene snuggled into it, awaiting the sunrise.

It was by far the most fantastic sunrise she had ever seen. The sky seemed to glow with pinks, reds, yellows, and blues. As the sun crept over the horizon, it was greeted by a musical crescendo from the birdsong chorus of hundreds of feathery creatures that welcomed the new day. 'Whatever happens in the future,' thought Selene, 'I'll never forget this incredible journey to the other side of the world.'

CHAPTER NINE

Selene looked around her. Straight ahead, to the south, she could see a series of bays with white sandy beaches, created by an area of high land jutting out into a turquoise sea. To the east, she admired a high rock, an integral part of a mountainous chain of rugged hills.

Just below the balcony, which girdled the house, there was the Olympic-size swimming pool where she had nearly drowned in her dream and where her aunt had lost her life. It looked peaceful in the morning sun, with its tables and loungers positioned to have a full view of the bay. Next to the swimming pool there were some round cabins made of bamboo, where visitors could change for a swim.

Selene got up and walked along the balcony. She now had a better view of the grounds. She glimpsed an enchanting Japanese garden. Little bridges had been constructed over a man-made brook, which turned into a miniature waterfall, tumbling into a pond, completely covered with water lilies. Bar-winged prinias and ashy tailorbirds crept and darted through the bushes in search of grubs. The vivid scarlet-headed flower peckers and metallic blue-throated olive backed simbirds, busily rifled through the hibiscus blossoms to sate their appetite for minute insects and nectar. Farther along, the cheerful green yellow common lora hopped about in the thick crown of a *rambutan* (banyan) tree, now and again betraying its presence with a long drawn-out mellow whistle, slowly increasing in pitch and ending abruptly on a lower note.

She turned round the corner and, in the distance, she glimpsed the paddocks where a white mare and a black stallion were nuzzling each other, whilst a brown colt gambolled and neighed near a grazing pony. Next to the paddocks, there stood a row of outbuildings, probably the stables.

An extended patio area, a tennis court, and a mini-golf course completed the amenities. She had now arrived at the front of the house, with a well-manicured lawn, surrounded by beds of roses and climbing bougainvillea. A maze and a monkey tree completed the effect. Then the long driveway, with palm trees and hibiscus scattered on both sides as far as the eye could see, with outbuildings and greenhouses, the entire property contained by sturdy fences made of eucalyptus. 'And of this realm I am to be the mistress,' thought Selene, in awe.

Impatient to explore inside the house, as well as its grounds, Selene showered and changed into loose white linen trousers and an emerald green, long sleeve blouse. She tied her hair into a pony-tail, with a green ribbon, and barefooted, carrying a pair of moccasins in one hand and a sun hat in the other, left her room.

Along the landing from her room, there was another door. Selene opened it and entered a room similar to hers for size and furnishing, but in pale yellow. The ensuite had white and yellow tiles with a sea horse motif.

Selene directed her steps towards the middle of the building and found the master bedroom. It was wider and more sumptuously furnished than the other rooms. There was a king size four-poster bed, a walk-in wardrobe full of dresses for all occasions and a number of shoes that would not have disgraced the shoe-shop in Tonbridge High Street. The ensuite was in white marble with pink streaks running through it.

On the bedroom wall, there hung the picture of a woman that Selene recognized as her aunt. She could see the likeness with her mother: the long wavy copper hair, the green laughing eyes, the sensuous mouth, the thin nose, the high cheekbones, and determined chin. She was wearing an ankle-length gold and silver sarong, with a long three-quarter-length sleeved jacket of the same pattern. On the exposed section of her arms, she wore gold bracelets and rings on every finger. She looked very beautiful.

Selene continued her exploration on the east wing, where there were two further rooms, which, apart from the colour of the walls and the tiles of the ensuite, were identical to the ones in the west wing. All the rooms, except her aunt's had pictures of birds or landscapes of the island.

She walked down another set of stairs and found herself in the hall. It was wide, with a high ceiling. The niches on both sides of it contained the life-size statues of two Balinese dancers, a man in the left niche and a woman in the right.

In the middle of the hall, opposite the front door, there was an exquisitely carved mahogany table. On the table, there stood a skilfully designed Venetian cut glass vase, where a talented hand had arranged freshly cut roses. The perfume of the roses mixed with the scent of the sandalwood floor, created a pleasing, exotic atmosphere.

Above the table, on the whitewashed wall, there hung a huge mirror in a light teak frame, which made the hall look even more spacious. Selene turned left and saw a corridor with two doors. The first door led to the study cum library. Three of the walls were lined with books from top to bottom. They were books on all subjects under the sun, though she noticed that there were more books on anthropology than on any other subject.

Colourful rugs, woven on the island, were strewn on the wooden floor. There were comfortable leather armchairs and an Edwardian desk with the latest laptop and teak filing cabinets.

On the desk, there was a picture of what Selene presumed were Sir and Lady Duncan, whom her aunt had thought to be her parents. He was a tall, red-haired man, with a military bearing and she a petite blonde, with green eyes and an English rose complexion.

On one side of the desk, turned towards the window, was an old-fashioned telescope.

Selene exited the study and opened the second door. She found herself in a breakfast room, simply furnished with an oval wooden table and some chairs. Several pictures of a splendid English country house, viewed from different angles, broke the monotony of the whitewashed walls, while a panoramic window showed the paddocks in the distance. At the far end of the room, a door led to the spacious kitchen, where Mei-Lin was busy preparing tea for herself and her husband Komang.

'Good morning Mei-Lin. Please don't mind me and continue with what you are doing. I'll make myself a cup of coffee and have breakfast as agreed.'

Mei-Lin smiled her sweet smile and showed Selene where everything was.

Selene took out a mug, poured herself the freshly ground aromatic coffee and left the kitchen. At the far end of the corridor, there were some French windows, opening onto the patio and the swimming pool. Selene did not want to go there just yet, so she retraced her steps to the hall.

On the right of the corridor, there were two doors, but they were further apart than on the east wing. The first door led to the sitting room, which, to her surprise, looked even bigger than it had appeared the previous night. Tired by the long journey, captivated by the views and troubled by Gabriel's presence, she had failed to notice that, behind a pale gold screen decorated with birds of paradise, the room continued into a formal dining room, with a modern crystal dining table, sitting up to 24 people. Of course, Aunt Elizabeth's adopted father had been in the diplomatic service, therefore he and his wife must have been used to entertaining. Her aunt, who had probably lots of friends on the island and in the rest of the Far East, must have done her fair share of entertaining, too.

It was amazing how simplicity, elegance, and modern technology blended perfectly. From the delicate and exquisite figurines in the display cabinet, to the ethnic vases and mats, the masks, the plasma TV that covered almost the entire wall, to the cordless telephones placed in every room, except the study. But best of all, thought Selene, picking up the remote to draw back the panel curtains, was the breathtaking views from the panoramic windows.

Time was ticking on and Selene left the sitting room to walk along the corridor and open the last door. It was a cloakroom with a blue and white mosaic floor depicting a dolphin. White tiles with blue Roman borders reached the ceiling. The suite matched the walls and blue and white towels with a dolphin design completed the overall effect.

Selene checked her watch and hastened to the breakfast room. Mei-Lin, though, ushered her outside to the patio where she had laid a pretty arrangement of tropical fruit, a pot of freshly brewed coffee, and a jug of pineapple juice.

Although the temperature was already in the 80s, it was less humid than in Singapore and Selene enjoyed looking at the surfers riding the waves under the watchful eyes of the locals, through the binoculars Mei-Lin had placed on the table.

Breakfast over, Selene ran to her room where she covered her body in suntan lotion, wrapped the long silk *tudung* (headscarf worn by Muslim women) she had bought in a boutique in Singapore and sped outside.

She passed a pretty cottage-style building on her way to the stables and realised that it was where Mei-Lin and Komang lived.

It was nicely positioned, to ensure total privacy to them and to the inmates of the big house. The garden was a miniature reproduction of the Japanese garden, with the addition of a tall and wide bamboo cage, the home of a family of myna birds.

As Selene walked past it, one of them addressed her with, 'Hallo, pretty baby. How are you?' 'Very well, handsome,' replied Selene, laughing, to which the myna bird added some words in *Sasak.* This put Selene in a light happy mood, which persisted during her visit to the stables. There she met Wayan, Mei-Lin's son, the young man who had driven the *cimodo* the night before. In his heavily accented English, he explained to her that he was in charge of the cars but also of the stables and horses, and helped his father Komang look after the garden.

'Do you live here?' Selene asked him kindly.

'No, Miss. I married. I live in home in village.' He answered readily.

'I saw some horses in the fields this morning' went on Serena, 'Are there more?'

'Yes, Miss. Two more, but older. Titus pulls *cimodo*'.

Selene thanked him with a smile and resumed her rambles around the property.

She had barely reached the Japanese garden, when she spotted a tall, handsome figure walking towards the house, and realised that it must be eleven o'clock, and that Gabriel had arrived.

Selene walked back for what seemed ages, her heart pounding, her breath uneven, but eventually reached the patio, where Mei-Lin had placed a can of Bintang beer, a jug of coconut milk, and two glasses. Gabriel sat there looking at her and this increased her confusion.

He got up, when she came near and greeted her in his deep baritone.

'Good morning, Selene. Had a good night's sleep?'

It was difficult to keep her cool after having walked for hours in the heat and the wind that had sprung up in mid-morning. Moreover, the sight of him in his light cream suit and tobacco short-sleeve shirt was enough to make her pulse race.

He had removed his Panama hat for they were sitting in the shade of a large umbrella made of reeds, and looked superbly relaxed.

'Shall we discuss business inside? Mei-Lin has turned on the air conditioning, and this monsoon wind will increase as the day goes on.' suggested Gabriel.

Selene got up and followed him to the study, bringing her glass of coconut milk with her. 'You know your way well around the house,' she remarked, filled with curiosity.

'Yes. I've been here many times. You see, the role I have in my father's firm is to look after the legal interests of British clients who live in the Far East, Australia, and New Zealand. My grandfather had a vast number of acquaintances, with the result that I've acquired a large portfolio of clients. As I've already explained to you, he and Sir Charles were friends. When Sir Charles died, your Aunt Elizabeth was happy to continue with our services. But now let's get down to the matter in hand,' concluded Gabriel.

For the next hour, Gabriel gave her detailed briefing on her aunt's possessions, which comprised the house, with its 140 acres of land, shares in various multi-national companies, bank deposits and even her favourite charities and other charitable and scientific enterprises.

After half an hour, Serena's head was spinning and she was barely able to make out the words that were pouring forth from Gabriel's lips. She raised a hand and called a halt.

'I'm sorry Gabriel, but you are giving me too much information in too short a time. Let's take a break, eat lunch and then I may be able to absorb more of what I need to know.'

'All right, Selene. You may be still suffering from jetlag. I'm more used to it than you and, sometimes, I forget myself when I start on my legal monologues.'

Mei-Lin had prepared a native dish of *nasi kuming* (yellow rice) and *sate lilit* (mince seafood served in a delicious peanut sauce).

They sat at the polished oval table in the breakfast room, while outside the wind and the rain chased each other like angry gulls, and ate the mouth-watering food, washing it down with *Tuak*, a sweet palm wine of light alcoholic content.

They ate in silence, sampling each mouthful with gusto, sharing this companionable moment, both happy to be together in such a simple, undemanding way.

When the meal was over, they had coffee in the sitting room, where Gabriel showed her the hi-fi equipment her aunt had recently purchased, hidden inside a cabinet with an orchid motif on the panels. Stacks of CDs of Western and Oriental music were stored in another similar cabinet.

It was a magic moment of contentment and Selene selected a piece of her favourite classical author to match her feelings.

Gabriel was the first to break the spell. 'I was wondering, Selene, whether it would be best for me to leave you all the papers for you to read at leisure and come back in a week's time. As you know, I have to see various clients in Bali and in Sidney. I'm leaving this afternoon and will come back next Friday.

Don't forget that Friday is a holy day on the island and that most businesses close half day. Meantime, relax and enjoy this new life and the freedom that goes with it.'

Gabriel's words had the effect of a cold shower on Selene, who came out of her reverie. He was going. He was leaving her for a whole week. Nothing had been said or done to promote any closeness between them, but she knew that she would miss him terribly. She had so many questions for him, which had nothing to do with her inheritance. Was he attracted to her? Sometimes, she thought she saw a spark in his eyes when he looked at her, but, after Simon, she no longer trusted her instincts.

Deep down, she remembered her grandmother's warnings about boys and men and the way they wormed their way into a girl's heart, to discard her once they had obtained what they wanted. Was Gabriel like that? The sight of Gabriel and Dewi Rinjani kissing surfaced to her consciousness and seemed to confirm her worst suspicions.

'Yes, Gabriel. Perhaps it would be best if I had a little time to become acquainted with these papers. I'll see you in a week's time, then. Have a good trip. Goodbye,' her voice trailed off, whilst he kissed her hand, his lips lingering longer than the gesture warranted, and left.

His departure left Selene bereft. She couldn't understand how someone she had only known for such a short space of time was able to make her feel incredibly high one moment, yet so depressed the next. She lay her head back, exhausted, and closed her eyes.

CHAPTER TEN

The next thing she knew, Mei-Lin was calling her name, 'Miss, Miss, wake up. Miss Dewi Rinjani on phone for you.' Still half asleep, Selene took the call.

'Selene?' enquired Dewi Rinjani.

'Speaking.'

'My mother is giving a garden party on Sunday and has asked me to invite you.'

'Yes, well, thank you. What time?' mumbled Selene, her head still fuzzy.

'At 3.30. My brother Michael Taun will come and collect you at three.' and before Selene could add anything more, Dewi Rinjani had rung off.

Slowly, the fog that seemed to be still lingering in her head lifted, and she considered what had just happened. Dewi Rinjani had invited her to a garden party, and, even more curious, she had accepted!

There was no way she could refuse now. Dewi Rinjani's mother belonged to the oldest and most aristocratic family on the island. She was a *Denek Bin*, that is, a woman who belonged to the highest of the four castes of the island. She and her family were her closest neighbours. On this small island of two and a half million inhabitants with very few Westerners residing there – most Westerners having left the island after some anti-Christian riots a few years before – it would have been a great offence not to accept an invitation. Moreover, Selene felt she needed to be part of this restricted circle.

Dewi Rinjani had said that her brother Michael Taun would come for her. Selene only hoped he was friendlier and less abrasive than his sister.

To her surprise, Selene discovered that she had slept for two hours, but, as it looked as if the rain and the wind had ceased for the day, she decided to resume the tour of the grounds. First, though, she felt like taking a shower followed by a cup of the scented jasmine tea she had sampled the previous night.

The kitchen was empty, and Selene rejoiced at being able to do something for herself. She sat in the breakfast room, sipping her tea and thinking of a less tiring way to view the grounds than covering it on foot.

Refreshed, she walked out of the front door and turned left. There were three low buildings next to one another and when she went to investigate, she found that two were garages, housing a Bentley, a jeep, a Japanese motorbike and a golf cart. 'Just the thing I need,' thought Selene, admiring the latter.

Before going off in the golf cart, she had a peep inside the other building and there she saw Mei-Lin ironing sheets. The room was air-conditioned. Mei-Lin told her that it was always kept at a constant temperature so that ironing was not such a heavy chore as it might have been in the heat that had risen to the mid 80s, since the rain had ceased.

Selene told Mei-Lin where she was going, and then headed for the Japanese garden.

She parked the golf cart and spent the rest of the afternoon exploring every tree, every bush, and every flower of that magnificent creation. The sweet music of birds accompanied her peregrinations and, once, she glimpsed a bird of paradise.

Towards sunset, she returned to the house, and watched from the sitting room windows the enormous orb of the tropical sun plunge into the sea. A light meal, consumed on a tray in front of a 'soap opera' from home, courtesy of the satellite dish on the roof, completed her day.

Friday morning saw her up and about at an early hour. Once more, Selene had had a troubled night. This time, in her nightmare, she had been thrown headlong into the swimming pool. She had turned round to see the face of her aggressor, but the sun was in her eyes and Selene had only a glimpse of a long bulky shadow. As she watched, a huge hand was reaching down towards her, it was coming closer and closer, and she knew that soon it would seize her and extinguish the life in her. Selene woke up with a start, perspiring copiously, fighting with the sheets that had twisted around her body during her restless sleep.

After she had calmed herself down with a long, tepid shower, Selene put on the demur bathing costume she had worn in Singapore, with a pale yellow caftan over it. She took a beach bag where she stuffed two big towels, an emerald-coloured swimming cap, a high factor suntan lotion, a pair of expensive sunglasses and a wide-brimmed straw hat she had found on a peg outside one of the cabins near the swimming pool. She walked into the kitchen and picked up a dragon fruit and a bottle of water. Then she went over to the pool, as she had left the golf cart nearby, ready for today's outing to the beach. Almost skipping, she reached it, hopped into it and, going as fast as the vehicle would go, made her way towards the bay. Once she arrived by the fence, she spied a gate and some steps, leading to the beach.

The sand in that part of the beach was a real surprise. It was coarser in places with grains that varied in colour from light to dark like peppercorn. Selene deposited her belongings by a rock and walked into the sea. The crystal-clear water was warm and welcoming. Selene dived into it and swam parallel to the shore. She was alone. She was only aware of a few fishing boats out in the distance and of a couple of surfers farther down the bay.

'I'd like to learn to dive,' she thought. 'It would be a dream come true, to watch the blue corals, the sea anemones, the sponges and angel fish first hand.'

After she had swum to her heart's content, she spread one of the towels on the beach, dried herself, applied to her body some sunscreen lotion and lay down to soak up the sun.

Selene had nearly drifted into sleep, when she felt a presence. She opened her eyes and saw a very handsome, tall, dark-haired man with cold blue eyes looming over her. He was wearing Bermuda bathing trunks. His bare legs and his torso were deeply tanned.

'Sorry,' he grinned, 'did I wake you?' Then he added, in an apologetic tone. 'My name's Michael Taun. I'm Dewi Rinjani's brother. You must be Selene. I've heard a lot about you.'

'If you've heard about me from your sister, I'm afraid it probably wasn't all good.' laughed Selene,' She and I haven't exactly hit it off.' she concluded with a shrug.

'Well, you can thank Gabriel for that. My sister's been after him for years, and she considers every woman a threat to her matrimonial plans.' Michael Taun informed her, still grinning.

'I'd guessed as much. As far as I'm concerned she can have him any time.' declared Selene with feelings.

'When we're better acquainted you must tell me what he's done.' said Michael Taun, sitting down cross-legged on the sand next to her.

He seemed a friendly, uncomplicated man and he entertained her with anecdotes of his childhood on Lombok, a Sasak word that meant, as he explained, 'Chilli Pepper' because of the type of small, dark, round pebbles on some parts of the beach, the ones Selene had puzzled over earlier.

Selene enjoyed herself and when Michael Taun asked if she would go with him on an excursion to Senggigi on the following day, she readily accepted. Michael Taun escorted her as far as the steps at the bottom of her property, then left.

Selene got into the golf cart and drove speedily home, showered, had breakfast, and then decided on a plan for the day.

She would go to see the horses and go for a ride to the woods, where she would visit her aunt's grave. She put on some jeans, a knee-length cotton shirt with long sleeves, and her moccasins. She walked to the stables and went to look for Wayan. He was in the tack room, taking care of the saddles. Selene explained to him what she wanted to do and he opened a cupboard that contained riding hats of various sizes. He then asked her to try on what had been her aunt's riding boots and Selene discovered that they fitted her perfectly.

She and Wayan rode to the little wood. There she discovered the small wooden Hindu temple and some seats. Wayan went in to pray, whilst she looked around for her aunt's grave. She spotted it almost immediately. It had been placed in a secluded corner, with *leis* (garlands) made from a myriad of gorgeous flowers placed on it. It was a simple grave, with a headstone made from some kind of volcanic rock. The inscription read, "Here rests Elizabeth, wonderful daughter and best friend. May she lay in peace on this island amongst the people of this land whom she loved." They were simple words that spoke of a warm, loveable, and caring human being. Selene silently prayed for this aunt she had never known. After a few minutes, though, she had to take shelter inside the shrine, because the wind and the rain had started to play their usual seasonal game. After the brief deluge, she and Wayan galloped back to the stables and Selene returned to the house. It had been years since she had ridden a horse, therefore she felt stiff, and her body was aching all over. Once she was soaking in a hot scented bath, she asked herself whether she had been wise to have spent the day on horseback, considering that she was going on the planned excursion with Michael Taun the following day.

That evening, she attempted some mild yoga exercises, drank a tisane, and retired early to bed, hoping she would finally have a good night's sleep.

Dark. It was very dark. It was a dark, cloudy night with no stars or moon. She felt an evil presence behind her. Something or someone was after her. She tried to run, but she slipped and fell into the swimming pool. Her pursuer was still there. She could feel its malevolent presence. Then she felt a huge hand pushing her down. Selene started to struggle, but to no avail. The hand kept on pushing and pushing until, she abruptly woke up.

What was happening to her? Why was she having recurring nightmares about the swimming pool? Had her aunt's death made such an impression on her that her subconscious could give Selene no peace? Thank goodness she was going to spend a day away from all her worries and cares.

Michael Taun arrived a few minutes late in his Suzuki jeep. He opened the passenger's door for her, and Selene jumped in, impatient to leave *Inggris* for the day. She wore a pair of light cotton trousers and a linen tunic, which reached down to her knees. She wore a tudung and her sunglasses. 'You look perfect.' Michael Taun reassured her.

'Thank you, kind sir,' replied Selene smiling. 'I'm ready to be amused.'

And amused she was. Michael Taun was the perfect companion. He made her laugh with his witty remarks. He told her about the history of Lombok, and he took her to visit the touristy part of Senggigi. They went snorkelling off the point and in the sheltered bay around the headland. Afterwards, they stopped for lunch at the Gara Gara restaurant, which - as Michael Taun explained - catered for all tastes. On their way back to the car, they stumbled upon a typical Indonesian puppet show, a *Wayang Kulit*, which Selene enjoyed immensely.

Selene had had a wonderful day. She had never had so much fun and said as much to Michael Taun. He dropped her off, reminding her of the following day's engagement.

Tired out, but extremely happy, Selene walked to the kitchen for a cup of tea, as well as to give Mei-Lin a little present she had bought her. Mei-Lin was peeling vegetables for the evening meal and looked up when Selene walked in. 'Thank you, Miss. You are very kind.' said Mei-Lin, with a broad smile. 'Oh, Miss, Mr Hart phoned for you, but left no message.' she informed her politely.

Selene's light heartedness disappeared, leaving her with a feeling of disappointment, as if missing Gabriel's call had been a great misfortune. But, she berated herself, 'I can't very well hang around waiting for him to phone. This is silly.' she concluded. Nevertheless, this missed call had spoilt some of the fun of the day.

Selene felt exhausted and went up to her room soon after dinner. She switched on the TV, but, after a few moments, she fell into a deep sleep.

CHAPTER ELEVEN

She was galloping through the woods, then, in a clearing, she saw an enormous swimming pool. She dismounted and approached the steps leading to it. But, as she looked into the water, she saw something hideous standing behind her. The reflection showed the protruding eyes and long fangs of Rangda, the bloodthirsty witch. The reflection opened her mouth and....

Selene cried out in her sleep, so loudly that she woke herself up. She was perspiring heavily and her heart was pounding as if she had been running a marathon. It was only a bad dream. She poured herself a glass of water, and then, to calm herself down, she watched the news from home on the BBC, the TV being still on from the previous night. The sun had already risen and promised another splendid day.

That morning, Selene lingered in bed, wondering at how her life had changed, and thinking of Michael Taun and of Gabriel. How different they made her feel. Michael Taun was light-hearted and laid back. She felt comfortable with him, maybe because he posed no threat to her equilibrium. Gabriel, instead, was the complete reverse. He had been kind to her, but in a polite, almost impersonal way. Sometimes, though, she had glimpsed a spark in his eyes when he looked at her and had felt the warmth of his sensuous lips on the back of her hand, when he kissed it. He made her feel vibrant and alive in a way no other man had ever done, and she was afraid for her peace of mind, because she knew that he had the power to make her suffer.

The ringing of the telephone interrupted her musing.

'Hello Selene,' Gabriel's voice reached her from the other end of the line, 'how are you?'

In a faltering voice, Selene answered, 'I'm fine. I'm enjoying myself. I'm having such a splendid time.' she babbled, 'and you?

Working hard as usual?' she enquired inanely.

'Yes, I've visited a couple of clients, but I'll be even busier after the weekend is over.' stated Gabriel, 'Where were you yesterday? I phoned, but Mei-Lin told me you were out.'

'Michael Taun took me to Senggigi. I had a wonderful time. We went snorkelling, then he showed me around town, and today he's coming to fetch me. I've been invited to a garden party his mother is giving.' she enthused.

'I see.' Gabriel's voice seemed to have become suddenly frosty. 'Well, take care, Selene, I really must go now.' and with that, he rang off.

'How strange.' thought Selene, 'what was all that about? Why the third degree?' He really was an impossible man. His parting words sounded as if she had phoned him, not the other way round. Men!

She was so annoyed that she was galvanized into action. The party was not until the afternoon, therefore she was going to have a go at the maze, take a leisurely stroll around the rose garden, then write a long email to her friend Vanessa, in which she would recount everything that had happened to her.

Selene had lunch on the patio and asked Mei-Lin what kind of clothes would be appropriate for her to wear at the party. 'Denek Bini Dewi Mas Majapahit likes to invite Sasak people and white people. She likes Sasak to wear traditional clothes, and white people in formal clothes.' Mei-Lin informed her, 'If Miss like, I do hair for her. I did hair for Miss Elizabeth.' she added.

Selene went to her room and examined the clothes she had brought with her. She was in a prevalently Muslim country, so she would wear something that did not emphasize her natural curves. In the end, her choice fell on a long, well-tailored, cream linen skirt with a ¾ sleeve-matching top. She made her face up, wore her emerald necklace with the emerald bracelet and earrings she had bought, and then called Mei-Lin to do her hair.

When she was ready, she gazed at herself in the mirror and held her breath. She looked like someone else. Mei-Lin had secured her hair up with ivory shell-shaped clips, revealing her slender neck and beautifully shaped ears. She had left some ringlets down, to frame her face, creating an effect of natural elegance that really suited her. Very pleased with herself, she slipped into a pair of 4 inches high-heeled sea-green leather sandals, with matching handbag and hat. She clipped on her gold watch and was about to exit her room when the buzz of the answer phone at the gate announced Michael Taun's arrival.

'You look ravishing.' exclaimed Michael Taun, admiringly, 'I could almost fall in love with you.' Selene laughed her embarrassment away. She didn't want Michael Taun to pay her those kinds of compliments. She had preferred the fraternal attitude he had displayed in Singgigi.

During the short journey to Dewi Kunta Villa, though, Michael Taun changed again into the carefree individual he had been on the previous day so that by the time they arrived, Selene felt relaxed and in high spirits.

A servant rushed to open the car doors then escorted them to the garden at the back of the impressive house, which had been built in the typical architectural style of the island. The main body of the house was over one hundred years old, but more recently it had been extended on both sides in a subtle way, betrayed only by the difference in the grain of the wood used.

When they reached the back of the house, Selene had the impression of finding herself on the set of a Hollywood-film production.

Two perfectly aligned rows of palm trees stood on both sides of the garden, a fitting frame for the splendour of the beach that could be glimpsed in the distance. The life-size statues of two Balinese warriors, aided by two lions, guarded the steps leading down to the impeccably kept lawn, where four long tables covered with beautifully embroidered tablecloths, made of the finest Egyptian cotton, were laid with ingeniously arranged fruit pyramids amidst a display of tropical flowers. Silver dishes of rice and *sate* or *satay* - diced and sliced chicken, goat, mutton, fish, and tofu - were served on skewers made from the midrib of coconut leaves. Other dishes of sticky rice and *pisang goreng* (fried bananas), were served as desserts, to titillate the guests' palate. Jugs of *santan* (coconut milk), pineapple, and orange juice stood next to tea sets of the best bone china, probably heirlooms from the host's family. Servants wearing sarongs of identical colour and pattern were close at hand to wait on the guests. Wicker chairs vied with wooden chairs, ornate with the most skilful of Balinese carvings. Last of all, turned towards Lombok's strait, there stood a 3-metre high statue of God Batara, who is said to dwell on Gunung Rinjani, the holiest of mountains.

On this fantastic stage, the guests mingled freely: the Sasaks, dressed in their colourful sarongs, - weaved with real gold and silver threads - discussed the latest international news, or exchanged titbits of gossip with the Westerners, clad in an assortment of formal dresses, all made by top designers. The main common factor that united them, though, was their wealth.

Selene was rather awed by this spectacular sight. She was so taken by all that surrounded her that she hardly noticed a very slim, beautifully proportioned, impeccably turned-out woman in a silk *songet ikat* (a traditional sarong with a design passed down from generation to generation), in a wavy pattern of gold and silver threads The woman was wearing precious handcrafted jewellery. In a firm, authoritative voice the woman said, 'Well, Michael Taun, aren't you going to introduce me to the young lady?'

'Mother, this is Selene Finch, Elizabeth's Duncan's niece. Selene, this is my mother, Denek Bini Dewi Mas Majapahit Fairchild.' Michael Taun could not have pronounced his mother's name more solemnly if he had introduced the Queen of England, considered Selene before uttering the conventional, 'How do you do?'

Michael Taun's mother looked at her with hauteur and slight

contempt, as if she had been a peasant gatecrashing a private party where only aristocrats had been invited. However, Selene did not let the older woman intimidate her and answered clearly and decisively all the questions that she was asked.

Mrs Fairchild left them after a few minutes, because, as she explained, she 'had to see to her other guests.'

Selene was relieved. She had felt an instinctive antipathy for the woman, the kind we all experience without any logical reason for it. It wasn't only the way Mrs Fairchild had looked down on her, but something more sinister and threatening. She would make a powerful adversary if displeased and Selene determined not to create any opportunities to unleash Mrs Fairchild's anger.

Selene found herself alone near one of the buffet tables, when Dewi Rinjani approached her. 'Hello, Selene,' she uttered in her usual off-handed manner. 'Did you enjoy yourself with Michael Taun yesterday? Isn't he fun to be with?'

'Yes, Dewi Rinjani,' replied Selene, disregarding the other girl's tone of voice. 'Your brother is a real extrovert and has a good sense of humour.'

'I'm pleased to hear it.' Dewi Rinjani continued, in a friendlier mood, 'I think you'll see a lot of him. He's very keen on you.'

'Not too keen, I hope,' remarked Selene, uneasily, 'I'm not one for holiday romances.'

'But you're not on holiday, surely. I thought you were going to settle here.' added Dewi Rinjani, as if she really cared what Selene would do.

'I haven't made up my mind yet. I still find it difficult to believe that *Inggris* will soon be mine.' said Selene, then excused herself, asked one of the servants for a glass of *santan* and ice, and hovered next to the sticky rice dishes.

'Good afternoon,' an accented female voice called out to her, 'You are Selene Finch, aren't you? You could only be Elizabeth's niece. You look so much like her.' Aware of the puzzled expression on Selene's face, the woman introduced herself. 'I'm Beatrice van der Meer. I was a friend of your aunt. We went to school together and were members of the same charity groups. I'm very glad to make your acquaintance. There are so few Westerners left on this island, it would be nice if you came to visit me.'

Selene relaxed and smiled. Beatrice van der Meer seemed very nice and she certainly needed a friend. Besides, thought Selene, she may be able to tell me what Aunt Elizabeth had been like. She followed Beatrice, who introduced her to all the fifty guests gathered there. Most of them could not disguise the curiosity they felt towards her, nonetheless some of them welcomed her warmly and exchanged phone numbers, with the promise to visit her or asked her to visit them at their homes.

It was a hot, sticky day, not marred by the daily rain that had accompanied Selene's sojourn on the island so far. Although her body was becoming used to the heat, Selene asked one of the servants where she could go and freshen up a little.

She had just stepped out of the bathroom, on her way back to the garden, when she heard her name spoken. Two people were sitting on a marble seat, in the conservatory. The top windows were open and it was through them that Selene heard Michael Taun and Dewi Rinjani's words.

'She likes me, but I'll have to move slowly, she is a bit skittish and I believe she hasn't had much practice dealing with men.' Michael Taun informed his sister.

At first, Selene failed to understand why Dewi Rinjani and Michael Taun were speaking in English rather than Sasak, but later she remembered Gabriel telling her that the brother and sister spoke English all the time, except when they were alone with their mother. It was a habit their father had imposed on them from a very early age. Besides, they obviously did not think any of the guests were inside the house. Intrigued by the words she had overheard, Selene stopped and listened to this conversation, which had a close bearing on her and her aunt

'Are you sure she hasn't got a crush on Gabriel?' enquired Dewi Rinjani.

'I don't think so. She was adamant that you could have him if you liked.' reiterated Michael Taun.

'That doesn't mean a thing.' went on Dewi Rinjani. 'She might have told you so, but she may still want to make a play for him.'

Come on Sis. Give me some credit. You know I'm an expert in how to please a woman, particularly if she is inexperienced.' Michael Taun reassured her, rather smugly.

'I don't care how you do it, but you must make her marry you. You know Mother. She won't stand another failure.' replied Dewi Rinjani.

'I know. But uncle said it was an accident, after all.' continued Michael Taun.

'An accident? I hope it was. Thank goodness Mother has the Chief of Police in Kunta Bay eating out of the palm of her hand.' remarked Dewi Rinjani, getting up from her seat.

Selene was aghast and felt physically ill. She had to exert herself not to utter a sound. What she had just overheard was monstrous. What they had said about her meant that they were plotting together to have her marry Michael Taun, but why? Their mother certainly disliked her and Dewi Rinjani had never shown any friendship towards her, rather the reverse. Moreover, the way Michael Taun had spoken about her showed that he had no love for her, yet he wanted to marry her. Anyway, she had to leave any further deliberations until she was in the privacy of her home, as the two of them were about to exit the conservatory and they would soon see her. Fortunately, she had removed her sandals before entering the house, so that she was able to walk quietly away.

When Dewi Rinjani and Michael Taun rejoined the party, Selene was talking to Beatrice and her husband and soon after, the three of them took leave, as Selene had managed to secure a lift back in their car. Before parting, Beatrice invited her to go and visit her in Mataram on the following Monday.

Selene needed to be alone, so she instructed Mei-Lin that she was going to put the answer phone on, because she did not want to be disturbed and that she and Komang could take the rest of the day off.

It was time to reflect on the events of the day. Little by little, scraps of conversation came back to her mind. What Dewi Rinjani had said about the loss of the piece of land sold to Aunt Elizabeth's adopted parents. How Michael Taun had 'happened' to be on the beach at the same time as her on her first trip there. How he had satisfied her every whim on their excursion to Senggigi. The way he had told her that he might fall in love with her. His mother's invitation to the garden party, despite the fact that she obviously disliked her and held her in contempt. Was it all part of a Machiavellian plan to regain what they thought of as their lost property? If so, why couldn't they buy it back from her? But, most important, was Gabriel part of this plot? And what about her Aunt Elizabeth? Had her death not been an accident? If not, how was their uncle involved? Dewi Rinjani had said that her mother had an ascendant on the Chief of Police. Had her aunt's death been too easily and rapidly dismissed as an accident, without any proper investigation having been carried out?

She needed to know more and, in order to do so, she needed to see Michael Taun again, as well as Beatrice and all the people who had known her aunt.

Therefore, when Michael Taun contacted her the following day proposing a trip to the traditional hand-weaving village of Sukarare, Selene readily accepted.

On the way, Michael Taun asked Selene if she had had a good time at the garden party and, taking advantage of this question, Selene answered that she had been amazed at the amount of people who had known her aunt and had been her friends.

'Acquaintances, Selene,' corrected Michael Taun, 'Mere acquaintances. The only true friends your aunt had were my family. As a matter of fact, she and my uncle were about to become engaged when your aunt had her fatal accident.' he added.

'Really?' exclaimed Selene, extremely surprised, 'Gabriel never told me.' she remarked.

'Gabriel didn't know. They wanted only the family to know, at first. You see she was going to be wedded to my maternal uncle, and you know how prejudiced people are about mixed marriages. Besides, the fact that my uncle is a high exponent of the Wetu Telu religion on this island and your aunt was a Christian didn't help,' reiterated Michael Taun. 'Particularly after the riots of 17th January 2000.'

'Oh, I see.' murmured Selene, quite amazed at Michael Taun's revelations. 'Where is your uncle now?' she enquired.

'He's in Jakarta with my father. They have business commitments there. That's why I was unable to introduce you to them yesterday.' answered Michael Taun, urbanely.

She mulled over this piece of news, but Michael Taun started talking about the ancient art of weaving and diverted her attention.

Once again, the day was spent pleasantly and Selene learnt a lot about the traditions linked with the *songets ikats*, prevalently made in the Sukarara village in central Lombok. Michael Taun also took her to Penunjak, which is famous for its colourful *gerabah* (traditional pottery), some examples of which Selene had seen at *Inggris*.

On the way there, they stopped at a *rumah makan* (a typical eating-place), where they sampled some *pelecing kangkung* (plain rice with water convolvulus, served with a chilli fish paste, tomato and lime sauce), under the shade of a huge banyan tree.

This time, they were caught in the rain, the wind mocking any attempt to use an umbrella. By the time they reached the car park, they were soaked to the bone. They returned to the eating-place where Selene changed into a *songket* that she had purchased earlier on. Her new outfit brought on admiring looks from Michael Taun and the other punters, even though it had no gold or silver threads and did not shimmer as she moved, unlike the one worn by Michael Taun's mother at the garden party.

'You're a real beauty, Selene. I'm crazy about you.' Michael Taun whispered in her ear.

'Please Michael Taun, stop it. I've already told you how you make me feel uncomfortable when you pay me compliments. Let's keep it light, shall we?'

'OK, Selene, but surely you must have had admirers in the past.' continued Michael Taun, 'You can't blame me for trying.'

'I thought I'd made it perfectly clear that at present I don't want any sentimental involvement with any man.' declared Selene, in a firm yet placating tone of voice.

After that, Michael Taun went back to being the carefree spirit he had shown her he could be in Senggigi, and the rest of the day went on smoothly.

'Tomorrow I'll take you trekking on Mount Rinjani.' Michael Taun told her when he stopped the car outside her home.

'Sorry Michael Taun, but Beatrice asked me to spend the day with her tomorrow, therefore Wayan will drive me to Mataram tomorrow morning, after breakfast.' Selene informed him to his dismay.

'Pity.' commented Michael Taun, 'Shall we make it Tuesday, then?'

'Maybe,' replied Selene with a smile, 'I'll let you know.' and she swiftly walked to the sanctuary of her home.

What Michael Taun had told her sounded plausible enough. Yet, those allusions Dewi Rinjani had made about her aunt's death not being an accident, and that her mother would not stand another fiasco, meant that whatever her aunt had felt for Michael Taun's uncle was no guarantee that he had felt the same.

That evening, Selene decided to broach the subject with Mei-Lin. When Mei-Lin brought her dinner, Selene asked her whether her aunt had had many friends and whether she liked Michael Taun's uncle.

'Your aunt very popular, Miss. Many visitors. People who liked things past. Miss Elizabeth gave money to charity.' was Mei-Lin's answer. But when it came to discuss Michael Taun's uncle, Mei-Lin shuddered, 'No good. He no good man. Miss not liked him,' was her answer.

This account differed completely from what Michael Taun had told her, and Selene decided to wait until she had spoken to Beatrice before making up her mind, although part of her was already putting more credence in Mei-Lin's words.

That night the wind kept on howling, creating a symphony of creaking noises, Selene had not experienced so far. It was as if a demoniacal presence had penetrated *Inggris* and was fighting with all its might not to be dislodged from the position it had gained.

CHAPTER TWELVE

Selene tossed and turned all night long and was up very early, feeling tired and frustrated. The wind accompanied her all the way to Beatrice's luxury penthouse in Mataram.

It was vast yet comfortable, with succulent plants and orchids everywhere. It was filled with soft furnishing and Dutch paintings, all blending in with a curious mixture of Indonesian ornaments and vases. A subtle smell of incense pervaded the whole apartment and mingled with the aroma of a coconut-based dish.

Beatrice was alone, her husband Vincent being at work but expected for lunch. Taking advantage of the situation, after having discussed the weather and her journey there, Selene took the plunge and asked, 'Please Beatrice, tell me about my aunt.'

Beatrice took out a photo album and started to tell her what a marvellous person her aunt had been. They had met at the same private school in Jakarta, and had become bosom friends. They had spent their holidays at each other's home and even when Beatrice had married and Elizabeth had gone to Stanford University to study Anthropology, they had kept up their friendship.

'Why Stanford University? Why not send her to Britain?' enquired Selene.

'Seen that, as you've just revealed to me, she had been adopted, the Duncans probably did not want to run the risk of her stumbling on the truth. They simply adored her and would have done everything in their power not to share or lose her affection.'

'What about the Fairchilds?' Selene said, rather emboldened by Beatrice's frank replies.

'At first, when her parents....Sorry, I keep on thinking of them as Elizabeth's real parents ....., purchased the land on which they had *Inggris* Villa built, they were on good terms with them. This might have been because they spent most of their time in Jakarta, where

Sir Charles Duncan worked as ambassador at the British Embassy. The acquaintance petered out, though, only revived, now and again, by an invitation to a formal dinner or lunch, whenever the Duncans happened to spend their holidays or the odd weekend on Lombok.' explained Beatrice, politely.

'What happened when Aunt Elizabeth returned from Stanford?' went on Selene, holding her breath with excitement.

'She went straight to Jakarta, where she helped out at balls and other social events at the Embassy. She was much sought after, because she was a beautiful and intelligent woman and she had quite a few proposals. But she had always been too independent to be tied down by a husband and children, consequently, after a while, she decided to do a PhD on tattoos and indigenous beliefs of what she called 'the forgotten tribes of Papua New Guinea'. She went to live in some remote areas in the rainforest for many years, but came home regularly to visit the Duncans. When Sir Charles Duncan retired, she returned to live on the island permanently.

Soon she developed a real interest in Sasaks' traditions and beliefs. In order to satisfy this new passion she asked Dewi Mas if she could introduce her to some of the oldest aristocratic Sasak families on Lombok. Dewi Mas was not very keen to do that, but delegated her brother Datu Raden Nuna. She convinced Elizabeth that he was truly interested in her research and wanted to help her. Your aunt was pleased with the arrangement, because she knew that a man could open doors on this island that no woman could. That was the main reason why the two of them spent a lot of time together.

At one stage, I asked her whether there was any romantic involvement between them, but Elizabeth always laughed heartily at the suggestion. She was grateful that he devoted so much of his spare time to furthering her knowledge of his people, and he was flattered when she thanked him for helping her in one of her publications.

Apart from her love of anthropology, Elizabeth and I became staunch supporters of a few charitable organisations both here and abroad. We campaigned against the exploitation of children by the big Western companies, who have them work for 16 or 18 hours a day for a few dollars a month. She also helped financially with the setting up of the Lombok Craft Centre and the Sembalun LoomWeavers.

Lately, too, Elizabeth had been championing the rights of women on the island. She was strongly against the practice of arranged marriages, particularly amongst cousins or members of the *gubuk* (cluster of male-related households). She opposed the practice of *kawin lari*, where a girl is willingly "abducted" and hidden by the man that wants to marry her. The man and the girl's family then negotiate terms. Once the parties have come to an agreement, there follows an official wedding ceremony. Elizabeth's revulsion and strenuous fight against these practices had been a cause of friction between her and Datu Raden Nuna.

A couple of days before the accident, Elizabeth had phoned me to say that she was coming to Mataram to see me. She wanted to tell me something that was worrying her, but she didn't tell me what it was. I have often wondered whether it had something to do with Datu Raden Nuna or the Fairchilds.' concluded Beatrice.

Beatrice's vivid narrative confirmed Selene's own suspicions on Michael Taun's mendacious affirmations. She was grateful of the insight Beatrice had given her on her aunt's personality and of the story of her life. Elizabeth seemed to have come to life through the appraising words spoken by her bosom friend, bringing this woman, this aunt, closer to her heart.

As the wind persevered, joined by squalls of heavy rain, Beatrice invited Selene to stay on for the rest of the week, with the lure of going on a shopping spree the following days. Selene enjoyed Beatrice's company very much. The older woman was fun to be with, the weather improved and the clothes in the shops were stylish and less expensive than in Europe.

During Thursday's dinner, Selene ventured to ask Vincent if he knew Gabriel, and what he thought of him.

'He's a very good man.' replied Vincent, without reservations, 'I've placed all legal matters in his hands more than once, and I've never regretted it. He's very upright and kind, and has a remarkable handicap on the golf course.' concluded Vincent.

Selene and Beatrice laughed. Trust a man to give such an accolade to another man just because the man in question was a good hand at golf!

There were many other questions that Selene was dying to ask, and, eventually, as the conversation reverted back to the Fairchilds, she was unable to contain her curiosity.

'What kind of job does Michael Taun do? Since I've been on the island all he seems to do is enjoy himself.'

'Good question,' fielded Vincent. 'He started off working for his father. Sir Edward Fairchild, Michael Taun's father, is the chairman of a world-renowned international bank and Michael Taun worked there as a financial advisor, after graduating from Oxford. Recently, however, he seems to be spending all his time running after the daughters of the wealthiest families from here to Tokyo.'

'Isn't his family already extremely wealthy?' Selene persevered, eager to know more.

'It was one of the wealthiest and most aristocratic families on the island, directly descendent from a prince of the Majapahit Empire. I won't bore you with the whole history, but Dewi Mas's title of Denek Bini shows that she comes from one of the most powerful branches of the ruling classes. Old money, you see.

Her father, though, started running into debts when he was still a young man, so that Dewi Mas's grandfather had to sell the land that now belongs to you, in order to pay them and avoid disgracing the family.

He forced Dewi Mas to marry Sir Edward, because of his noble birth and his position at the bank, in order to borrow more money to cover Datu Raden Nuna's extravagant expenses. Dewi Mas's brother has inherited their father's careless attitude to money and Michael Taun, too, seems to have come out of the same mould. Obviously, Selene, I'm telling you all this in the strictest confidence. The Fairchilds are a very powerful family and it wouldn't do to have them as enemies.'

Satisfied and disturbed by all that she had heard, Selene steered the conversation in a different direction and the rest of the evening was spent debating worldwide issues.

When she retired to her room that night, Selene wondered at all that she had learnt about her aunt and the Fairchild family. She also puzzled over the fact that, since she had been at Beatrice's house, she slept well, without having one single nightmare. It was as if Beatrice exerted a benign influence over her.

Friday, the day of Gabriel's return, was announced by a bout of heavy tropical rain. Selene had breakfast with Beatrice and Vincent, who invited her to stay and return to Kuta Bay with Gabriel.

'The two of you must still have some unfinished business relating to your inheritance, Selene, and it wouldn't make sense for you to call Wayan to drive you home when Gabriel has already hired a car.

As you know, women drivers are not approved in this country, and, for your own safety, I'd rather you had a man like Gabriel next to you on your journey back. Besides, we had already invited him to stay here for lunch before we met you.'

Touched by this sign of friendship, Selene accepted their invitation to protract her stay, and spent the morning listening to Beatrice's anecdotes on the days when she and Elizabeth were at school together. Beatrice had a dry sense of humour and had Selene in stitches more than once.

CHAPTER THIRTEEN

As the time grew near for Gabriel's arrival, Selene felt increasingly nervous. She had butterflies in her stomach like when she had waited to go onstage at the end-of-year play at school. Her whole body seemed to become attuned to the ticking of the old grandmother clock Beatrice had brought from Holland. Her nerves were as tense as the strings of a violin and near to breaking point, so that when Gabriel finally walked into the sitting room, it was almost an anticlimax.

He greeted Beatrice first, then turned a surprised look on Selene and regaled her with one of his bewitching smiles.

'Hello Selene. What an unexpected pleasure,' he said, 'have you come to see Beatrice?'

'Yes.' replied Beatrice. 'We met at Dewi Mas's garden party and it was friendship at first sight.' added Beatrice, in a jocular mood.

'Well, I'm very pleased for you Selene,' continued Gabriel, looking at her. 'You have chosen wisely. Beatrice is one of the nicest persons I know. You couldn't find a friendlier or more caring person on this island and beyond.'

'Stop it, flatterer, or you'll make me blush. Now, stop chattering, sit down, and relax. What about a nice cool drink?'

'Thank you Beatrice. Let me have one of your iced lemonades and I'll be your servant forever.'

'Such gratitude, and so well expressed, may I ad,' replied Beatrice, impishly, before hurrying out of the room.

'You look wonderful,' Gabriel complimented Selene as soon as they were alone, 'You have a light gold tan that really suits you.'

'You look tired, Gabriel,' Selene blurted out, seeing the lines of fatigue on his forehead and the bags under his eyes.

'Thank you, Selene. You really know how to boost a man's ego.' laughed Gabriel. 'You wouldn't look too good yourself if you had

had to endure the marathon of meetings and travelling I've been through this past week.'

'Sorry, Gabriel. I didn't mean to be so blunt. But you do look as if you need a holiday.' Selene told him, apologetically.

'Great minds think alike. I've taken two weeks off and I'm going to spend them on the island.' Gabriel informed her, 'Once we are through talking about the loose threads of your inheritance, I'm going to show you the beauties Lombok has to offer.'

Selene's eyes reflected her happiness at this piece of news. It sounded like heaven. Two weeks together with him on this paradise island!

'To go back to business, I've wonderful news. All the initial paperwork has been completed. You are now joint owner of everything that belonged to your aunt on this island. Obviously for you to become sole owner, you'll need to wait at least another year.'

'Thank you, Gabriel. I'm still not sure whether this is not a dream from which I'll soon wake up. It seems so unreal.'

'Well. It's very real instead. You're now a free agent and can do anything you like with your life.'

Just then Vincent arrived home from the office, so they all sat down to lunch. It was a lively, happy affair. Selene had never felt so good in her life. Afterwards they had coffee on the terrace, which had comprehensive views of the city and its minarets.

Both couples parted with the understanding that they would soon see each other again, and then Selene found herself alone with Gabriel. He was the first to speak.

'Selene, if you agree, we will stop at Sembalun, from where we can join the trekking expedition to Mount Rinjani. I thought we could tour Rinjani and the National Park. It would take roughly a week. How do you feel about it?'

Overcome with elation, Selene was unable to answer for a few minutes, and noticed that Gabriel's expression was changing into a cold mask, 'Unless, of course, you'd rather go there with Michael Taun,' he added, bitterly.

'Certainly not.' Selene blurted out, 'As a matter of fact I need to discuss Michael Taun and his family with you, but not just yet. I'd love to go trekking with you.' She sounded so sincere and determined, that Gabriel brightened up considerably.

'You'll have to let Mei-Lin know that you won't be back for a week and to ask her if everything's all right at *Inggris*. I've booked two rooms at the Oberoi Hotel in Mataram for tonight, so you can phone her from there.'

They arrived at the hotel by taxi, Gabriel having hired a Suzuki jeep for their journey to Sambalun Lawang. On the way up from reception, Selene told Gabriel to go and rest. He would need all his strength for the trekking expedition. 'You're such an extraordinary person, Selene. No other woman would understand my needs better.' He brushed his sensuous lips on hers and walked along the corridor to his room. Selene went to the hotel's shops and purchased some warm clothes for the trip, as, apparently, the temperature in the Mt Rinjani's area was similar to the temperature one encounters during a skiing trip on the Alps. Then, once in her room, she phoned Mei-Lin. The latter seemed a little perturbed.

'Miss, Mr Michael Taun ring every day. He ask me where you are. He angry. He say I must tell him.'

'No, Mei-Lin, don't say anything to him. Anyway, you don't know where I am now, therefore you won't be able to answer his questions. I'm staying out another week, you can tell him as much. I'll phone him when I'm back. Meanwhile, you and your family can take a break. Goodbye.'

Selene was flustered. That evil Michael Taun and his family! Well, she wasn't acquainted with his father and, as far as she knew, he might be a very nice man, completely in the dark about his family's designs on her (or her estate!)

She quickly recovered and started daydreaming about Gabriel. She now realised how much she had missed him. Selene was very pleased with his reaction when she had failed to answer him promptly about the trekking. He sounded positively jealous. And she had to admit to herself that she had developed a major crush on him.

That evening, Selene decided to let Gabriel sleep and had a tray sent up to her room, together with a leaflet about Mt Rinjani. After having got herself ready for the night, Selene picked up the leaflet and read on, curious to know what to expect.

'There are over twenty villages around Mt Rinjani and there are many routes up the mountain, but the main access is from Senaru, in the north and Sembalun Lawang to the east. The challenging three-day Rinjani Trek route from Senaru to the crater rim (Plawangan), down to the stunning crater lake then on to Sembalun Lawang, is considered one of the best treks in South East Asia.'

'How fantastic,' she thought. 'Only two months ago I was battling against the cold and wet English weather, doing a fairly dull job in a poky office, and now, here I am, living like a queen and worrying only about my next pleasure trip.'

No, this was not quite true. She had worries. What had really happened to her aunt? And what was she going to do in the near future? But not tonight, not tomorrow, not for the whole of next week, she promised herself. And on that note, she fell asleep.

The following morning, Selene woke up early, looked out of the window and her heart sank a little. The wind was blowing gustily, but at least the rain was holding off. She showered, had breakfast, then packed a rucksack where she had placed the clothes she was taking with her, the rest having been handed over at reception to be collected on the way back from Mt Rinjani. Then she dialled Gabriel's room number. Gabriel's deep baritone answered her and her heart missed a beat. Yes, he was ready and had just been on the point of coming to knock on her door when she had rung. No sooner had she replaced the receiver, than there was a knock on her door. She picked up her rucksack and opened the door.

Gabriel smiled, brushed his lips softly against hers and said, 'Thank you Selene. I really needed the rest. I feel like a new man. If you're all set, let's go.'

Selene had never felt better or happier in her life. She was sitting next to him, in one of the most amazing places on earth and he looked so relaxed and at one with her. Everything was forgotten. She lived only for this moment.

The traffic, which had been chaotic at Mataram, soon petered out as they drove through the Monkey Forest, which linked Mataram to Pemenang directly bypassing the coast. The road meandered up and down through the forest but there were few proper stopping places. There was a considerable amount of trucks on the road, which created a hazard and Gabriel needed to concentrate fully to avoid a collision.

While Gabriel's attention was on the road, Selene was diverted by the impressive number of monkeys in that part of the rainforest, mainly small long-tailed macaques, although she discerned some black monkeys, too.

The drive took them through coconut palm groves and they passed by clusters of small villages and huts, with adjacent subsistence farming on the rather dry hillsides.

Now and again, Selene spied a goat. But what they encountered most were small herds of water buffaloes, which, as Gabriel explained, were a characteristic sight in that part of the island.

Once they were north of Pemenang, the area became greener and crossed by small rivers. Here they found paddy fields and more open fields. Selene was so thrilled with everything she saw that she asked Gabriel to stop several times as she wished to keep a photographic record of their journey.

The area along the north coast was the driest they had come across, with no paddy fields and dusty open hillsides and scrub, and yet it was inhabited by large numbers of people. The northeast was the least populated area, with scrubby dry forest reaching the sea and covering large tracts of the Rinjani foothills.

The entire region skirting the main road across the island was densely inhabited, with more paddy fields, coconut palms, banana groves, and tobacco plantations.

As they went further along, Gabriel had to drive even more carefully, in order to avoid the cows that had been tethered too near the road and others that had managed to come loose and wandered off, becoming a hazard for drivers.

On their journey to the north, they drove through the villages of Bengal, Gindang, Obel-Obel and many other Sasak hamlets. When they arrived at Bayan, Gabriel turned southwards, so that they could visit the amazing waterfalls at Sindang Gila, Tiu Kelep and Betara Lenjang.

They took pictures of each other with the stunning backdrop and some of them together, Gabriel holding her by the waist or with his arm on her shoulders. Those were perfect, relaxed moments of pure joy for both of them.

Eventually, they stopped to change and eat at the Rinjani Trekking Centre, situated at the trailhead above Senaru, a traditional village. The temperature had gone from muggy to cold, and Selene was glad of the warm clothes she had brought with her.

At the Centre, they found information and displays on the trek, the National Park, the Sasak culture and on the full range of activities available in Senaru.

'I'd like very much to go and visit the village,' pleaded Selene, 'before we carry on with our journey.'

'Your wish is my command,' replied Gabriel, in an indulgent mood, so, without wasting any more time, he escorted her to the village at the foot of Mt Rinjani, which was hidden by the clouds.

As they walked to the village, Gabriel took Selene's hand in his and the warmth that simple gesture produced, spread through her body, bringing a sparkle to her eyes.

'Happy?' murmured Gabriel in her ear.

'Very.' responded Selene, her spirits soaring.

He stopped, wrapped his arms around her and gave her a tender, lingering kiss, which produced a surge of powerful emotions within her. She fought for a few moments to regain control, then slowly pulled away from him, her head whirling, overwhelmed by her own response.

In the village of Senaru, they went to see the handloom weavers. Gabriel confirmed what Beatrice had told her about the Sembalun Loom-Weavers. They were women her aunt had helped to form a co-operative, which, not only brought them the money they needed to make a decent living, but also allowed them to maintain alive the ancient skills of their ancestors. They mainly wove cloth for religious ceremonies or weddings, but also produced a wide range of artefacts.

Gabriel bought her a tastefully designed bag, with a jasmine motif, because, he whispered to her, 'You taste of jasmine.' And Selene bought him a belt decorated with the flora and fauna typical of that area, to remind him of the wonderful hours they had spent and were going to spend there.

Satisfied with their purchase, Selene and Gabriel headed back to the jeep, ready to carry on with their journey, which would take them to Sembalun Lawang, the base from where their trekking adventure was to begin.

CHAPTER FOURTEEN

During their journey, Gabriel entertained Selene by telling her all that he knew about Mt Rinjani. 'The last big eruption,' Gabriel explained to her, 'was in 1847. Since then, there have been minor eruptions in 1901, 1994, 1995 and1996, which caused the formation of a small cone in the centre of the caldera where the flow entered the Segara Anak Crater Lake. The latest eruption took place in 2004. The clear, green waters of the lake are surrounded by hot sulphur vapour emissions.

The Sasaks and the Balinese people consider this volcano sacred. Every year, on full moon nights, the pilgrims bring their offerings of flowers, fruits, and gold trinkets to the gods residing on Mount Rinjani, in a ritual called *pelekan*. The pilgrims believe that the water from the hot springs around the lake has healing properties, particularly for the skin.

'How romantic,' enthused Selene, looking at him with wistful eyes.

'I thought that would capture your imagination,' said Gabriel, gazing into her eyes briefly, before concentrating back on the road.

They were now on the Round Rinjani Drive. From there, the road ascended the Rinjani forest reserve to reach the plateau at Sembalun Lawang as well as the nearby villages, in the northeast of the island. It led them through the verdant rainforest and open country, crossing part of the rhododendron zone and mountainous grassland before reaching a hill between Gunung Rinjani and Gunung Nangi.

'Look, Gabriel, look!' shouted Selene, filled with excitement, 'monkeys!'

'You're lucky, Selene. They are *javan lutung* or leaf monkeys. They are rather shy creatures, difficult to spot.' remarked Gabriel, in a half-laughing, half-mocking voice at her spontaneous child-like glee.

From that point, the road descended to the southern side of the island, passing through the rainforest again. The road surface was much better than the one of the roads they had travelled up to that point, so that, within a short time, they reached the Rinjani Volcanology Centre, a handful of kilometres from their port of call.

They stopped at the Centre, where Gabriel asked about the latest activities of the volcano and was reassured on that score. This was encouraging, as they had planned to go as far as the caldera in the next couple of days and he did not want any unpleasant surprises.

After they left the Centre, the sturdiness of the jeep became an asset on the dirt track, when the road started ascending the plateau at Sembalun Lawang. The terrain became rugged and full of potholes. After a bumpy ride, they finally reached their destination. Gabriel removed their equipment, including the bottles of water he had bought at Mataram and carried all of it to the hotel where he had booked their rooms.

After dinner, Gabriel and Selene met the other members of their trekking party as well as the head guide. The latter informed them that they would leave early the following morning for the crater rim. They would walk from their level of 1,156m to 2,639m. It was going to take them nearly eight hours, with various stops at different rest camps on the way.

'The trek is not difficult, nor is it dangerous.' The guide informed them, 'you don't really need a guide to find the way, but it is better to have guides and porters, because they will provide tents, sleeping bags, stoves and all the equipment needed. They also will protect you from the risk of being attacked by bandits as there have been robberies over the past couple of years, some of them involving episodes of brutality and violence.' concluded the guide.

After the meeting, they retired for the night. For all the party concerned this was going to be the last night they would spend in a proper bed. For the next four days, they would live rough. This meant that that was the last time they would be able to have a good wash until the trek was over, so Selene spent a long, leisurely time in the shower.

Selene had imagined she would find it difficult to sleep because of the excitement of the days to come as well as the thought that Gabriel slept in the room next to hers, with only a thin wall between them. He had been so attentive, so tender towards her. They had shared moments of absolute perfection. They had discovered that they had a lot in common. Both of them liked to be in the open air, close to nature and that they respected the people of this island. Before parting, Gabriel had taken her in his arms and had given her the longest, most sensual kiss he had dared so far. At first Selene had responded, but then she had been seized by that feeling of panic she had experienced at Senaru. This feeling made her push Gabriel away before rushing into her room, and locking it behind her. She went to bed but she kept on thinking at the way her body responded every time Gabriel kissed her or merely brushed against her and she felt scared. She didn't want to be the slave of the passion this man aroused in her. She didn't want to be hurt again. In the throes of emotions evoked by such thoughts, she tossed and turned all night, only falling into a dreamless slumber just before dawn.

After breakfast all the porters and mountain guides arrived, around sixteen people in all. The porters carried bamboo poles from which hung food, sleeping bags, water, cooking utensils, as well as the tents and a First Aid box, filled with medication. A special rescue team was organized for emergencies, equipped with radio connection. The trekking party assembled ready to leave for the RTC Office where they had to register. After registration, all the participants received a blessing. This was part of the Sasak tradition of *meloqak*, carried out by the village elder of Senaru. Now, they were set for a real adventure.

Natives aside, the rest of the party comprised backpackers – mainly boys and girls on their gap year – as well as businessmen from Australia and New Zealand, an assorted group of Europeans, Americans, and Indonesians of various ages and backgrounds. Their head guide, named Segara Anak (child of the sea), gave them a few more instructions before setting off. He warned them that sometimes there were sudden, severe electric storms. When these occurred, they had to take shelter, avoiding prominent ridges. He told them to beware of snakes, stinging insects, and poisonous plants. He finally advised the trekkers to watch out for leeches, which were a real nuisance during the wet season.

The first part of the trail led them through grassland, which turned into a lowland rainforest after about a two-mile walk. The guide called a halt and they ate, drank water, and had an hour's rest. The air was crisp and filled with oxygen, which penetrated the pores and gave a feeling of elation and wellbeing. They spotted a chestnut-backed thrush and some white-rumped kingfishers, which satisfied those of the group who were keen birdwatchers. They started back on the trail, which proved to a fair climb, as it ran uphill all the way. Some people, appreciating the difficulty of the climb decided to head back, the steep slopes awaiting them seeming too difficult or tiring to tackle.

Since they were in the mountains during the rainy season, they expected quite a bit of rain, and the slippery paths led to some entertaining acts of faulty equilibrium. Whenever there was an incline of any degree, the slick, clay-like mud seemed to claim at least one victim. Initially Selene was quite good at sliding, almost losing her balance, yet somehow finding a way to stay on her feet with Gabriel's assistance, but an unseen small pointed rock among the mire tripped her up, and she fell, landing on her derriere, for the amusement of the onlookers. Wounded only in her pride, Selene put on a brave face and even joined in the general merriment at her expenses.

After a few more amusing episodes of the sort, involving other members of the party, they eventually entered the cloud forest where rhododendrons and oak trees predominated. The guide pointed out the Auk Kalgan Hot Springs, which they would go and visit the following day. The guide also showed them a landmark, which consisted of a banyan tree where the paths from Sonar and Sembalun met. With a wide space on the lower part, this tree looked like a person standing up, legs apart. It stood next to one of the forest's entry gates to the First Camp on the Rinjani Trek. This made it an easy landmark to recognize if, for any reason, any of the slower, less experienced hikers were left behind.

At an altitude of about 1,000 meters, the forest became more open, gradually turning into mountain scrub. As they neared the crater rim, they glimpsed at some long tailed grey macaques, which the natives called *keri*.

Selene was exhausted, but had enjoyed the climb and was now looking at the valley below. Gabriel came up to her and put his arm round her shoulders, pointing out rivers and birds. They had arrived at the Plawangan, Rest Camp II, where they were to spend the night. Here was the second landmark, the *Bate Penyesalan* stone.

The porters set up the tents and lit a campfire round which everybody hastened to settle, seeking for warmth. Selene was fascinated to note how important bamboo was to the natives of the island. That day, as well as the ones that followed, they drank tea that was boiled in bamboo. The rice they ate was steamed in bamboo. They drank out of cups made from bamboo. They used spoons, and other utensils also made from bamboo, and ate soups flavoured with bamboo shoots. It was incredible to see how people who were used to living off the land had adapted bamboo to their needs. Because bamboo is hollow but each section is sealed, it is ideal for holding liquid. To make tea, they filled a large, fat stalk with river water and set it upright in the fire. Then tealeaves were added, and half an hour later, they had a wonderfully aromatic and flavoured drink. In another stalk of similar width, Segara placed two sections of bamboo on the fire. The bottom section was once again filled with water. A small hole covered with banana leaves was placed inside. He then poured an enormous amount of dried rice into the remaining section of bamboo on top of the leaves. Perhaps half an hour to an hour after placing this bamboo in the fire, a large quantity of deliciously steamed sticky rice overflowed the top of the bamboo "pot". In addition to bamboo, the large, strong, broad banana leaves often assisted at mealtime. They served as makeshift mats when they sat down for meals, as filter when steaming rice, oven mitts when handling the heated bamboo, and as packaging material when storing leftover sticky rice.

That first night, after dinner, one of the boys from Australia took out a panpipe and played a few tunes. The sky above was filled with stars. It was a magic moment, one that would remain embedded in their souls forever.

'Oh, Gabriel, thank you. Thank you,' Selene whispered softly to him, her head resting on his shoulder. 'This is the best moment of my entire life. Thank you for sharing all this with me.'

'I should be thanking you, Selene,' he replied, moved by her words, 'I don't think I would have enjoyed this day as much with anyone else.' Then, he added, 'You are a very sweet girl, Selene, and I like you very much.'

Selene's heart sank. "Like?" That was not what she wanted him to say. She wanted him to love her with the same intensity of passion with which she loved him. 'Yes,' she thought, 'it's not a crush I have for him. I fell in love with him the first time I met him.'

Troubled by what she had discovered about her feelings for Gabriel, Selene found it impossible to sleep. At one stage she felt so restless that she left the tent and sat outside looking at the stars.

It was a perfect night for stargazing. In the total darkness that surrounded the camp, the sky was like a black velvet cloak, filled with myriads of sparkling diamonds, which clustered into constellations she found difficult to make out, as they merged with millions more Selene had never seen before.

After feasting her eyes for a while on the cosmic spectacle above her, her neck started to hurt and this, together with the cold night air that was seeping through her clothes, made her seek for the shelter her tent afforded. Selene retreated there, as if a haven, for the remaining hours of the night.

The sun had barely risen when the trekkers were woken up by their guide. After consuming a breakfast of pineapple pancake complemented by a mango and banana fruit salad, washed down with green tea, they set off for the last part of the trek to Mt Rinjani. As they reached the top, their eyes were met by the spectacular view of the crescent-shaped lake and the post-caldera cone -2,351m high -, called Gunung Baru (New Mountain). They were also able to admire the trio of volcanoes in the east of Bali - Agung, Abang, and Batur, the Gili Isles, and the island of Sumbawa. As they continued their trek, they occasionally spied a rusa deer along the Rinjani trail, and met a constant flow of local people carrying firewood on their heads.

Gabriel had brought field glasses, which he handed to Selene whenever something interesting presented itself. When the occasion arose, he put an arm around her and, with his other hand, he pointed to the object of interest. At one point, he directed the field glasses towards the Gunung Rinjani National Park. He handed the binoculars over to Selene and explained that the park lay within the Wallace transition zone, where the flora and fauna of South East Asia make a dramatic contrast to that which is typical of Australasia.

The Park, Gabriel explained afterwards, had been developed with the New Zealand Government's assistance since 1999. It represented a unique partnership of the National Park, of the tourist industry and of local communities. This partnership had been forged to manage and protect the rich variety of plants and animals around Mt Rinjani.

'You seem to have a sound knowledge of Lombok and its inhabitants,' exclaimed Selene, impressed.

'That's because I've had the opportunity to visit extensively both the island and Mount Rinjani on my previous journeys here.'

A suspicion arose in Selene's mind, 'Did you go on your own during these expeditions or did you have someone with you who knew the island?' she asked, holding her breath.

'As a matter of fact I went on several trips with Dewi Rinjani and on some with Michael Taun.'

On hearing the other girl's name, Selene felt as if all the breath had been knocked out of her. Her knees buckled under and she fell on the ground, stunned.

'Are you all right?' enquired Gabriel, solicitously.

Selene took a couple of gulps, then stuttered, 'I....I lost my balance for a moment. No please, let me go. I'll be back on my feet in just a minute.' She could feel him hesitating and turned away from him, pretending to tie up the laces of her boots, her eyes smarting with tears, behind her thick eyelashes. How was it possible that she could suffer so much? The mere thought of Gabriel and Dewi Rinjani together was devastating to her. She had to curb these feelings for her own survival.

Selene had never felt more alone in her life. All the fears about her aunt's death, her worries about the Fairchilds' machinations to try and coerce her into a marriage that would return to them the land they had lost, mingled with her uncertainties about the future. She had wanted to discuss them all with Gabriel, ask for his advice, but now she realised that it was impossible. He had shown to her that he had a long-standing relationship with the very people she had to fight against, that he might even be in love with Dewi Rinjani, so how could he believe a virtual stranger's words against theirs?

The bubble of happiness that had lifted her spirits up in the past few days had burst, leaving her bereft. How was she to endure the days she still had to spend with him?

As if sensing her mood, Gabriel left her side and spent the next few hours talking to the guide.

The trekkers arrived at the Lake Camp Area by mid afternoon, in the midst of a typical tropical downpour, which was over in less than an hour. The porters set up the tents, whilst the party decided to go to the Aik Kalak Hot Springs, where they had a regenerating soak in their healing sulphurous waters.

There were three caves in this area, Goa Susu, Goa Payung, and Goa Manik. The group decided to go and visit the Goa Susu or Susu Cave, as Senara called it. The cave had a narrow entrance, and the legend went that people with unclean minds were not able to enter. There was water inside, dripping from the tip of a stone, which looked like a nipple. It was alleged that this water had healing powers, and that it tasted differently from any other water. Senara led them inside the Susu Cave. It was hot there, like in a sauna. There was a lot of smoke, which looked like cooking steam, so that people called it *mengukus* (hothouse). Senara pointed out that a great number of pilgrims visited the cave all year round, chanting mantras and asking the gods for favours.

Gabriel tried unsuccessfully to recapture the friendly camaraderie they had shared, but Selene fended his overtures off with a cool detachment she was far from feeling and eventually he desisted.

Selene felt numb inside, as if her very soul had been ripped from her. The tenderness he had weaved around her, she now considered as his modus operandi with any female who happened to be available when he wasn't with Dewi Rinjani, the girl he really loved. She was torn between her love for him and the fear of the power he had over her. Her grandmother's words came back to her, 'You must be absolutely sure of a man's feelings before letting him make love to you, or you may regret it for the rest of your life. Love is built on trust.' She couldn't trust him. Not when she had seen him kiss Dewi Rinjani the way he had kissed her the first night they had arrived on the island.

From that moment, Selene tried to avoid any situation that would place her in too close a proximity to Gabriel. He noticed her withdrawn expression, the way she flinched every time they accidentally brushed against each other and Selene felt his quizzical brooding gaze on her for the rest of the day.

While negotiating yet another particularly slippery slope, Selene found herself next to a young man of more or less her age, who helped her up. His name was Patrick Tierney and he introduced her to his sister Jessica. Apparently, they were the son and daughter of a famous Australian architect, who was inspired by Aboriginal art, while their mother was one of the top piano players in Sidney. Patrick had just graduated in IT, while Jessica was in her gap year, which she had taken in order to decide whether she wanted to study Japanese or Aboriginal Art. The brother and sister were nice, friendly and laid back, and Selene discovered that she enjoyed their company.

CHAPTER FIFTEEN

The trekking party spent most of the following day on the banks of the lake, fishing, diving, or exploring. The porters meanwhile, picked mushrooms as they hiked from spot to spot as well as tender bamboo shoots growing along the lake. They used their findings to flavour the soup they all enjoyed for lunch. In the evening, they reached Montong Satas, their last camping place before the five-hour walk to the Rinjani Trek Centre, where their journey would end. They camped in a large, open area for cooking and lounging, sheltered from the rain, and rich with fresh river water. At dinner they ate the excellent grilled fish, which some of the trekkers and the porters had caught at Segara Anak, dipped in a mouth-watering chilli sauce, then finished off the evening singing old American cowboy songs, sitting round the campfire, under the light of a full upside down moon.

Having made friends with Jessica and Patrick, the brother and sister from Sidney, Selene, contrary to her reserved, cautious nature, invited them to go with her and Gabriel to tour the Gunung Rinjani National Park and then to spend a few days with her at *Inggris*. They accepted readily and Selene felt relieved that she would not have to endure a long journey alone with Gabriel.

'He's gorgeous,' commented Jessica, giving Gabriel a long look of appraisal, 'but a bit too old for you, Selene.' She concluded from the wisdom of her 18 years.

'He's lethal,' were the only words Selene was able to utter, before changing the subject.

Patrick was a likeable gregarious person, full of fun and laughter and kept the two girls entertained for most of the day.

Half way to their destination, Gabriel came up to her and asked, 'What's wrong Selene?'

She darted a swift glance in his direction and replied, in a voice she just about manage to keep steady, 'Nothing's wrong. Can't you see I'm having fun with my friends?'

'OK, Selene, have it your way.' His mouth set in a grim line, Gabriel turned away and Selene was greatly relieved.

'What was that all about?' enquired Jessica, inquisitively.

'Nothing to worry about. He has set out to be my babysitter, but I'm old enough to look after myself,' replied Selene, a smile on her lips, but shards of ice in her heart.

Noting her uneasiness, Patrick kept on diverting her attention by calling out every time he spotted a bird or a monkey amidst the foliage of the dense primary rainforest that covered the steep slopes of the mountain. The party proceeded for a while in silence, savouring their last moments in these spectacular surroundings.

All of a sudden, the peace that had settled around them was broken by the alarm call of the smaller *kijang* (barking deer), with its distinct dog-like bark. This sound caused some sulphur-crested cockatoos to take flight, to the delight of the birdwatchers of the group. This seemed to set the mood for the rest of the day as everybody got their cameras out, ready to capture any movement in the proximity of the trail.

The Rinjani Trek Centre was only an hour or so away when the party was caught in a frightening electric storm. Lightning crashed all around them, zigzagging its way from the sky to join the ground through the fastest possible medium. The guide shouted to them to stay away from the ridge of the crater and to take shelter away from the trees. Selene, scared out of her wits, looked around her, but could not see Gabriel anywhere. Patrick, who was standing next to her, made her lie down prone on the ground and put an arm round her, protectively. The smell of charred wood and sulphur was everywhere, as the storm unleashed its power.

Fortunately, this show of nature did not last long and within a short time it was all over. 'Thanks, Patrick,' Selene uttered with a smile, 'I've never been so scared in my life.'

‘That’s all right, Selene,’ Patrick comforted her, helping her back on her feet, ‘I’m so used to my sister’s reactions to this kind of storms, that it’s second nature to me to deal with frightened females,’ and with that, he gave her a fraternal peck on the cheek. Selene turned round just in time to see Gabriel frowning, his eyes like thunder.

Patrick having run ahead to attend to his sister, Gabriel came up to Selene and said, frostily, ‘You are doing well, Selene, first Michael Taun, now Patrick. It seems that no member of the male population is safe when you are around.’

Shocked by the accusations as well as by the tone of voice in which they had been delivered, Selene gave him a haughty, contemptuous look, then walked away. To think that she fancied herself in love with this brute, this…this… monster! Selene was fuming inside. ‘Thank goodness for Patrick and Jessica.’ she thought. ‘One more day alone with him and I would have murdered him.’

Soon they arrived at the Rinjani Trek Centre, where they said their goodbyes to the guide, the porters and the rest of the group with whom they had shared this marvellous adventure.

They spent the night at the base of Gunung Rinjani in a village called Batu Koq where there were a number of comfortable *losmen* (inns), where the food was great and the price was low. Theirs was called Puncak Senaru. The food that was served there was excellent and the view over the Sendang Gila waterfall offered great opportunities to observe birds and monkeys in their spectacular habitat.

Before they retired to their rooms, Gabriel told them that a guide would come and collect them in a jeep the following morning, as he had handed in the one he and Selene had travelled in to Sembalun Lawang.

What a glorious morning! The sun was out, the wind had dropped, and the company was in high spirits. The guide, a short middle-aged Indian looking man, called Raj, took them along a well-beaten track, then stopped the jeep and they continued on foot.

'Look here. The ground has been disturbed by the *babi hutan* (wild pig), foraging.' he remarked. 'Be on the alert for *bodok* (leopard cat). If you are very quiet, you may be able to see the *ujat* (palm civet). Look, over there you can see a *landak (*porcupine),' whispered Raj, pointing to the left. Then he added, 'Sometimes, early in the morning, it's possible to see the rare black ebony leaf monkey, known locally as *lutung*.'

Selene spied a purple heron standing on one leg, looking majestically aloof, whilst scanning for food an impressive pond filled with water lilies. Further along, Patrick spotted a yellow wagtail, while the sound of the oriental pipit accompanied them during part of their visit to this magnificent area.

'Many of the forest-dwelling animals, insects, birds, civets and monkeys owe their survival to the *beringin* (wild fig tree) as a provider of food and shelter.' Raj told them, knowledgeably. 'The pine-like *casuarina* species, *cemara*, are a feature of the grassy higher slopes, while orchids are also a feature of the grassland areas, as is the edelweiss growing above the tree line. It is a beautiful icon of the Park and one of our best-known sub-alpine plants.'

It was yet another memorable day, thought Selene, one of many she had spent on this dream island. If only she could have trusted Gabriel, it would have been perfect.

The hike took them through the pleasantly shady bamboo forest. Lush ferns, spiralling vines, and tall shoots of bamboo surrounded their path, and ended with a thrilling view of a small cascading stream.

Their visit to the park lasted well into the afternoon. This meant that they had to spend the night at another *losemen*. Like the previous night, Selene shared a room with Jessica and had another of those horrible nightmares. This time, in her dream, she was being dragged near the swimming pool by a man in a mask. She tried to get away, but her efforts were carried out in slow motion. The more she tried to struggle, the slower her movements became.

She woke up in a cold sweat, but not wanting to awake Jessica, she lay there, motionless, trying to calm herself down. Her pulse was racing and she felt a bout of nausea assail her. She felt terrible and was glad that she would soon be back at *Inggris*.

A wet, windy day greeted them. They took their time over breakfast, none of them in a particular hurry to brave the deluge.

Their guide had been dismissed the evening before as all the members of the group had decided it would make a change to travel by *bemo,* the converted passenger-carrying minivan used on Lombok for long-distance journeys.

After haggling with the son of the *losemen* for some time, a price was agreed and they jumped onboard the vehicle with all their equipment. As the *bemo* drove off, the rain stopped and regaled them with the beautiful sight of three rainbows arching over the rainforest that they were leaving behind. A handful of macaques peeped at them from a *beringin* (a banyan tree*)*, while some children ran behind the van, vociferously uttering their goodbyes.

The *bemo* soon reached the main road, which effectively cut Lombok into two halves through the most populated area of the island. It sped by Lombok's characteristic terraced hillside paddy fields. Then it turned southwards, heading for Praya, Sade Awang and, finally, Kuta Bay.

Gabriel, his face still betraying his thunderous mood, had chosen to ride at the front with the driver, leaving plenty of room for Selene, Jessica and Patrick at the back.

'What an amazing holiday,' sighed Jessica,' but I'm dying for a shower.'

'Yes, Jessica. And a nice soft bed.' added Patrick.

'Hear, hear,' agreed Selene, and she thought within herself that she needed time away from Gabriel. She had been away from *Inggris* only for a couple of weeks, but it felt like years. All she wanted to do for the next few days was rest and think of the future.

CHAPTER SIXTEEN

When they were a few miles from *Inggris*, Selene took out her mobile and phoned Mei-Lin to warn her of their arrival. It was the first time she had used the ultra modern mobile that she had bought in Singapore, conscious of the unwritten law of the island, which stated that the indiscriminate use of mobile phones was not tolerated.

Mei-Lin was waiting for them at the door, as she had been that first evening Selene had arrived on the island, except that this time her husband Komang was there, too. Patrick helped Selene out of the *bemo* and she bestowed him a warm smile of thanks, before going up to Mei-Lin and hugging her, so happy was she to see her again. She then introduced Jessica and Patrick. Last of all, she turned to Gabriel and asked politely, 'Will you stay for lunch, Gabriel?'

'No, thank you. I have a lunch engagement with the Fairchilds.' was his curt reply, his forehead set in a frown.

For a moment she was struck dumb, then, sullenly, she said, 'See you around then.' 'Good riddance,' she told herself, but why was her heart aching so?

'Goodbye.' he replied, including Jessica and Patrick in his farewell, then the *bemo* left and Selene and her friends gathered in the hall.

'Now Jessica, I thought you could sleep in the bedroom next to mine in the east wing, while you, Patrick, can have one of the two bedrooms in the west wing. You can go and freshen up, have a rest, then come down and have lunch on the patio. Is that all right?'

'Fine.' they both said in unison. Then Komang, helped by Patrick, picked up their luggage and showed him and Jessica to their rooms, while Selene retired to hers. She undressed and moved to the bathroom, turned the Jacuzzi on and slowly let the warm invigorating jets bring new life to her aching body.

'I needed that,' she murmured wrapping herself up in the soft towelling robe. She walked back into her bedroom and switched the laptop on. There was an email from Vanessa telling her how pleased she and Darren were that she had had a bit of good luck at last. Selene answered her immediately, explaining everything that had happened to her, including the conversation she had overheard. She poured out all her fears and doubts, as well as giving her friend a detailed account of her trekking holiday.

Feeling much lighter, after having finally managed to unburden herself to her long-standing friend, Selene put on a baggy T-shirt and trousers, picked up a little something she had bought for Mei-Lin and her family, then made her way downstairs. She entered the kitchen and, finding Mei-Lin there, she handed over her gifts, while she asked her if she had had a nice break.

'Very nice,' answered Mei-Lin. 'But Miss, Mr Michael Taun phoned and phoned. He come here, too, asked for you. He angry with me. I think him angry with you. I don't like Mr Michael Taun. He very bad.' Mei-Lin looked at her with concern in her eyes.

'Don't worry, Mei-Lin. He can't do anything to me. And why should he be angry?'

'I don't know. His uncle was same with Miss Elizabeth. When she not here, he very angry.'

Once again, Selene was confronted with what she thought of as 'the Fairchilds' problem'. If she had been on good terms with Gabriel, she could have discussed it with him, but seeing the way he was behaving, together with the suspicion that he might be in love with Dewi Rinjani, it was out of the question. She was expecting Vanessa to give her some advice and she could talk to Beatrice. Maybe she could discuss it with Patrick and Jessica, although she had only known them for a very short time and that went against her reserved nature. But maybe talking to them would be a good thing. They were not involved. Beatrice had known her aunt and the Fairchilds, Vanessa was her bosom friend, but the brother and sister had had no time to become involved, therefore they would be able to assess the situation in a more detached manner.

Taken up by these thoughts, Selene had wandered by the pool, still uncertain on what to do, when a cheerful voice addressed her, 'A penny for them.'

'Oh, hello Patrick. Have you had a good rest?'

'Yes, thank you Selene. This place is fantastic. That beach, down there, looks perfect for surfing.'

'It is, particularly early in the morning.' remarked Selene.

'You haven't answered my question, though. You looked miles away just now.'

'As a matter of fact, there is something bothering me, something I wanted to talk to you and Jessica about, but not right now.'

'All right. Whenever you're ready. Jessica's just coming.'

'Good. Let's sit over there.' Selene instructed, leading him to the patio.

Jessica joined them and, after a lunch of fish and boiled rice, they sauntered off to the beach. There were more local people assembled on the beach than Selene had ever seen, but none of them spoke English, so she was unable to understand the reason for such gathering. The sight of all that crowd had put them off bathing, but Patrick was set on climbing up the huge rock on the east side of the beach, and that is what they did. It was hard work. The weather was hot and muggy, so they stopped several times. Fortunately, they had carried bottled water with them, which helped them against dehydration. Once they reached the top, a wonderful view met their eyes, and it was agreed that the following morning they would climb up there to see the sunrise.

On their way back home, Selene saw Michael Taun approaching them. She had barely the time to whisper to Patrick and Jessica to observe him carefully, that he was upon them.

'Selene,' he cried out and made to fold her in his arms, when she stepped back and coolly said, 'Hello, Michael Taun. You look well.'

'So do you. You look splendid. But you left without saying a word. I was worried about you.' he replied, trying to take her hand.

'I told you I was going away to see Beatrice, and then I decided to take a few days off trekking.' Selene went on in a flat, detached voice.

'Yes, I know. Gabriel has been entertaining us with your adventures on Mount Rinjani.' He gave her an ingratiating smile, which didn't quite reach his eyes.

'Really?' went on Selene, putting on her haughtiest manner, 'Then let me introduce you to my friends Patrick and Jessica Tierney.'

After the introductions were over, Patrick asked Michael Taun the reason why so many local people had assembled on the beach.

'In a week's time there's going to be the traditional festival of *Bau Nyale*. This is a festival when hundreds of Sasaks gather on the beach to catch the *Nyale Fish* (a sea worm or eel). A good catch is a sign that the rice harvest will also be good. It's an annual ceremony held here, at Kuta Beach, and it's related to the legend of Princess Mandalika. '

'I've never heard of this princess before.' stated Jessica, 'Can you tell me the story?'

'All right. I'll tell you the essentials. Princess Mandalika was a beautiful well-mannered girl, with many virtues. She was an expert spinner and weaver. Many princes sought her hand in marriage. Unfortunately, her rejection of any of them would bring about a bloody war. This made it difficult for the princess to choose.

After many days of deliberating, the princess finally made her decision. She informed her suitors that, on the 20th of the tenth month of the Sasak calendar, on the seashore, she would announce the name of the man she had chosen. The man who would have the right to own her.

When the time arrived for her to announce her decision, she told her parents, her people, and the princes that she was going to become a Nyale, so that everybody could enjoy her.

That's why this festival is also a courtship ceremony, where young men and women gather merrily along the beach to collect the *Nyale Fish*, teasing and flirting with each other in the process.' Michael Taun ended, looking at Selene with soulful eyes.

'Is it always celebrated at this time of the year?' enquired Jessica.

'No, it's not. It takes place when the moon, the wind, and the tide come together at a particular conjunction and thousands upon thousands of sea-worms (the *Nyales* or small eels) of many different colours are washed ashore. A local priest scoops up a handful of worms. He then proceeds to the ceremony of 'reading the worms', after which he tells the community their fortunes for the coming year. Once the future is told, the people collect the worms for a special annual feast. And with the feast there is a festival where boys and girls meet and there's plenty of music and dancing.' concluded Michael Taun, 'That's why the beach is and will be full of natives for the next few days. They're preparing for the festival.'

'How exciting!' enthused Jessica. 'I can't wait to see it.'

'It will be a pleasure to accompany all of you.' asserted Michael Taun.

'Thank you Michael Taun.' said Selene, 'and now, If you'll excuse us.' She turned towards the steps and started climbing them before he could utter another word. Patrick and Jessica followed her and the three of them headed towards the Japanese garden.

'What do you think of him?' enquired Selene, after they had entered the garden.

'I don't trust him,' replied Patrick, looking her straight in the eye.

'I'm not sure. He's so polite and he's extremely good-looking.' said Jessica, tentatively.

'He behaved towards you as if you were his long lost lover,' added Patrick, 'and he didn't like it when you repulsed his overtures.'

'So, what's your verdict on Michael Taun?' insisted Selene.

'I wouldn't trust him at all. He seems to be a playboy who thinks all girls are fools and easy prey to his masculine charms.' was Patrick's honest remark.

'Yes, he does fancy himself, but he's got the looks and, I guess, the money. His clothes were certainly not 'off the peg', besides he has that air about him of wealth and power.' declared Jessica. 'He clearly fancies you. I can't understand why you gave him the cold shoulder.'

'Well, maybe now is the time for me to tell you a bit about my aunt and about myself.' And Selene narrated to them all the events regarding her aunt's death. She also described Michael Taun's behaviour towards her, the conversation she had overheard between him and Dewi Rinjani and what she had learnt from Beatrice and Mei-Lin.

'Wow!' exclaimed Jessica, 'This is some story. No wonder you're so much against him. What a snake.'

'Does Gabriel know?' asked Patrick, evenly, 'After all he's your solicitor.'

'No, he doesn't. I can't tell him because I don't know whether he's involved in this or not.'

'Why do you think he might be involved?' asked Patrick, looking even more interested.

With a heavy heart, Selene related to them about the relationship she thought existed between Gabriel and Dewi Rinjani, about the ties that appeared to unite the two families and the fact that Gabriel and his family had known the Fairchilds for years.

'My, you're in a spot.' blurted out Jessica, 'what are you going to do?'

'I don't know. That's why I've told you all this. I was hoping you would help me find a solution.' cried out Selene, who felt close to tears of frustration and unhappiness.

'Don't worry, Selene,' promised Patrick, 'we'll help you.'

'Thank you Patrick. I feel so lost, so alone.'

'I understand Selene. We haven't known each other long, but I can tell you're a very nice girl and you do need friends around you just now.' said Patrick, putting a consoling arm round her shoulder.

Jessica grabbed her hand and said, 'We'll stay with you for as long as you need us. I like you Selene. Don't be afraid to ask.' She squeezed her hand, and then the three of them headed back to the house.

They ate a light lunch of fruit and coconut milk, and then they went up to their respective rooms to have a rest. They would meet at teatime and set down a plan of action.

Selene had left the laptop on and noticed that she had received mail. It was Vanessa telling her that, in her opinion, Selene should leave the island and go and stay with her and Darren until she had made up her mind about what to do. Her heart filled with a mixture of joy and sadness. She was lucky to have such a good friend. Unfortunately, this solution was out of the question, because she had to reside on the island or she may lose the property. She sent an email back to Vanessa, thanking her for the offer and explaining the reasons why she could not accept her kind invitation. She did invite her and Darren over, if they were free to come.

'What about Beatrice?' she thought, 'She and Vincent may like to come over for the *Bau Nyale*.' She was uneasy, almost scared at the predicament she found herself in, and felt that she needed people she could trust around her. Without wasting any more time, she called Beatrice. Unfortunately the maid answered that Beatrice was out. Selene could only leave a message to be called back. After that, she lay on the bed and closed her eyes.

CHAPTER SEVENTEEN

Selene was walking towards the swimming pool when someone grabbed her from behind. She tried to fight off her assailant, but she was too weak. Soon enough she was dragged to the edge of the pool, then a mighty hand pushed her head under the water and kept her there, gasping for breath. She was about to succumb when...

There was a light tap on the door and Selene woke up. She looked at her watch, it was ten minutes past four. She had slept for nearly three hours! She jumped up from the bed and saw that a white envelope had been pushed under the door. She picked it up, went to the little desk by the window, and opened it.

The writing was unfamiliar to her, but when she looked at the signature, she couldn't believe her eyes. It was from Michael Taun. She started perusing its contents and an uncontrollable anger surged within her, coupled with a cold sense of dread. He was incredible. He made it sound as if the few hours they had spent on the beach the day they had met and the day they had had in Senggigi had been a prelude to some kind of engagement, which had his mother's blessings. He went on to say how distraught he had been when she had disappeared for almost two weeks without a word and how hurt he had been by the coolness of her reception of him on the beach that morning.

'This is too much,' Selene was beside herself with anger, 'The man's insane.' Her heart was racing as if she had been jogging up a steep slope, her throat was dry, while her body was hot as if she had a fever. 'I must calm down. I mustn't let him get to me.' she kept on telling herself. She almost ran to the shower and turned it on full blast, letting the cold-water jets hit her like a whip until she felt numb. Having calmed down a little, she patted herself dry, donned a pale green and blue caftan, tied her hair up into a knot, picked up Michael Taun's letter from the carpet where it had fallen, then rushed downstairs.

Patrick, sitting on one of the sun loungers by the side of the pool, saw her first and noticed her troubled features. 'What's up?' he asked, getting up and moving towards her.

'Here. Take a look at this.' She handed him the letter and sat down, waiting for him to read it.

'Is he mad? Does he think we are in the Middle Ages?' were Patrick's first utterances, when he had completed his perusal.

'We might well be. Don't forget where we are. Think of the way women are treated in this society. He's from an influential aristocratic family. They probably want to force me into marrying him against my will.' And with that, Selene burst into tears.

'Selene, don't cry. It's no good upsetting yourself like this. We'll find a solution to this problem, and fast. I understand how worried you are. Please Selene. Here, take my handkerchief.' Patrick handed her a clean cotton handkerchief, all the while stroking her back as he would have stroked a child's, whispering soothing words in her ear.

Little by little, Selene's sobs subsided. She blew her nose and looked at Patrick with gratitude. At that moment, Jessica joined them and she, too, read the letter.

'What's to be done?' she asked when she had finished.

'The way I see it, Selene, you have three options: option one, you leave the island and go back to England; option two, you give up the property; option three, you find someone who will marry you only in name, so that you will be free from Michael Taun's clutches.' concluded Patrick.

'Unfortunately, Patrick, I don't have any of those options. You see, if I leave Lombok, the property will no longer be mine. As for giving it up, it would seem a dreadful slight on my aunt's last wishes. And lastly, whom will I find in such a short time that will be willing to marry me?'

'I will, of course.' answered Patrick, in earnest.

'What?' cried both Jessica and Selene. 'You can't mean it, surely.'

'Why not?' persisted Patrick, 'I'm single, I can work from anywhere in the world, as long as I have a computer or laptop. Lombok is not very far from Australia, so I would be able to pop over there any time I need to. Besides, we won't be married forever, just long enough for you Selene to be able to acquire ownership of the property and move on.'

'Thank you, Patrick, for your extraordinarily kind offer, but I need to think about it.' replied Selene, gratefully.

'Take all the time you like,' Patrick reassured her, 'meanwhile, some other solution may crop up.'

'You've given me food for thought, but now I'll try and get in touch with Beatrice again. The more friends I have around me, the happier I'll be.' Selene left the siblings to have a race in the swimming pool, whilst she went back to her room to phone.

This time she was lucky. Beatrice had just returned from one of her charity meetings, and was very happy to hear from her. She was delighted with the invitation, which she readily accepted. She wasn't sure whether Vincent would be able to leave his work and come with her, but she would be there on the following day.

Relieved at the news, Selene felt more optimistic about the future than she had been for a long time. She walked down to rejoin the others with a lighter step, when she heard the sound of a car drawing up outside the front door. Someone slammed the car door and rang the bell. Anxious that it might be Michael Taun, Selene stepped into the sitting room. She heard Mei-Lin open the door, then Gabriel's voice. What was she to do? She didn't have the time to think of a place where to hide, as Mei-Lin opened the sitting room door and announced him.

'Hello Selene,' greeted Gabriel in a grave tone of voice. He looked drawn, his forehead furrowed, as if he was preoccupied about something.

'Gabriel.' Selene greeted him, in a voice that did not betray the turmoil his sight had created.

'I need to talk to you about a disturbing piece of news that I've just heard.' said Gabriel.

'Oh, and what has this to do with me?' she replied, tartly.

'It's everything to do with you. For heaven's sake, Selene, is it true that you are engaged to Michael Taun?' cried Gabriel, his voice rising.

'Of course not. Where did you get that idea? I hardly know him.' answered Selene, heatedly. This was a nightmare. She could not believe Michael Taun's audacity in spreading this rumour.

'Well, he and his family seem to think so.'

'They're mad. I've barely spoken to Michael Taun four times. He has always seemed friendly and easy going, but there has never been any talk of love or marriage, at least... not from me.'

'What do you mean 'not from me'? Didn't I warn you about the customs of this country? Have you forgotten that Michael Taun's family are directly connected, through their mother and uncle, with the leading exponents of a very powerful branch of the Wetu Telu religion?'

'What about it? I've never given Michael Taun any indication of being partial to him. As a matter of fact, I've kept him at arm's length ever since the garden party.'

'Why, did anything happen at the party?' probed Gabriel, his frown deepening.

'Nothing I wish to discuss with you,' Selene was getting more and more upset. Upset about the lies Michael Taun had been spreading, about Gabriel's betrayal with Dewi Rinjani, about her world falling apart. How she hated this island right now, these awful people, the fact she couldn't wear what she liked, couldn't drive a car. She felt stifled and close to tears. She wanted to go back to England, to her old tranquil life.

'Look Selene, you'd better tell me everything that has happened between you and Michael Taun if we want to avoid unpleasant surprises.'

'What surprises?' Selene was really worried now, 'anyway, I don't trust you. You're on their side. You're getting married to Dewi Rinjani.' As soon as she had uttered those words, Selene rushed out of the room and nearly collided with Patrick, who had been looking for her.

'Selene, what's wrong?' Selene dropped down unconscious at his feet. He was about to lift her up when Gabriel pushed him aside. He swept Selene's limp body into his arms and carried her delicately, as if she were made of the finest fragile porcelain, into the sitting room, where he deposited her, very carefully, on one of the settees. He told Patrick to go and fetch a glass of water. He took her tiny cold hands into his warm ones and rubbed them gently, to try and restore circulation. Selene opened her eyes to gaze into a pair of deeply concerned cobalt blue ones.

'How are you feeling Selene?' Gabriel asked her in a tender voice.

'I'm all right. What happened?'

'You fainted.'

Patrick came in carrying a tray with a jug of water and a glass. Gabriel took it and helped Selene sip a few drops. 'I'm OK, now. I just want to rest.'

'All right, Selene, but we need to talk.' said Gabriel with determination.

Selene felt totally drained and surrendered into the arms of Morpheus.

CHAPTER EIGHTEEN

She was standing by the pool. There was someone with her. They were arguing about something. She was becoming agitated. She felt someone's hands pushing her. She fell into the pool. It was then that she hit the bottom. Her screams jolted her out of her dream.

At first Selene, still distressed by her nightmare, couldn't remember where she was, then, little by little, the events of the day unfolded and she sprang up, only to be overcome by a spell of dizziness. More slowly, she got to her feet, then held on to one of the little side tables. Where was Gabriel? Was he still there? Was he engaged to be married to Dewi Rinjani? She needed to know for sure, so that she could wipe him completely out of her system.

She walked out of the sitting room and headed for the pool. As soon as she reached the French windows, she heard voices outside, on the patio. They were all sitting there, Patrick, Jessica, and Gabriel. They seemed to be getting on well, by the sound of it. As she walked out towards them, they turned their gaze on her. Gabriel and Patrick got up at the same time and got hold of her, one on each side, as if she were an invalid that needed support. 'Let me go. I'm fine. I can walk on my own. Please, this is ridiculous.' But her pleas went unheeded. They carried her to one of the chairs, adjusted some cushions behind her back, and only when she looked as if she was going to explode with frustration, they returned to their seats.

'Now, let's have it.' said Gabriel in a brisk, business-like manner.

'What do you mean, "let's have it"?' responded Selene.

'The whole story. I've been pumping your friends all afternoon, but they haven't said a word. They wouldn't disclose to me what you've told them in confidence, and I appreciate their loyalty. But, if I am to help you, and God knows you need help to extricate yourself from the mess you've got yourself into, I need to know the whole sad story from beginning to end.'

'But I can't tell you. You'll soon be part of the Fairchilds' family and you're bound to be biased.'

'Once and for all, Selene, I am not engaged to Dewi Rinjani, I've never been engaged to Dewi Rinjani and I have no intention of ever becoming engaged to her. She means absolutely nothing to me. Is that clear?'

'But you kissed her. You're their friend. You told me yourself that you've been to trips around the island with them and that your family and hers have been friends for years.' Selene could not help reminding him.

'First of all, I've never said that my family and her family are friends. If I recall correctly, I told you that my father and her father are friends. I've been coming to the Far East and to Lombok for years. As I've already explained to you, I'm responsible for a large portfolio of clients in this area of the world. As Dewi Rinjani's father and my father are friends, it's normal that I have been invited to stay with them and that Sir Edward has taken me to visit the island, together with his son and daughter. Finally, to answer your other accusation that I kissed her, I'd like to point out that she kissed me, and that a kiss does not make an engagement.'

'Well. I've never kissed Michael Taun, but he seems to think that we're engaged.' Selene stressed, rather relieved, yet not completely satisfied with his explanation. She still did not trust him, even if what he had said made sense. She didn't know what to do. Her heart was pulling her one way, while her brain pulled her in the opposite direction, or, at least, advised caution. Unable to make up her mind, Selene decided to talk to Beatrice first and then, with her approval, she would reveal her suspicions to Gabriel.

'I know there are some questions I need to answer, Gabriel, but I'm not up to it right now. Do you mind if we postpone this interview till tomorrow?'

'Fair enough, but, remember, the sooner you tell me everything

I need to know, the easier it will be to put a stop to Michael Taun's claims. Goodbye Selene, for now at least. Goodbye Jessica. Patrick.' Selene got up and accompanied him to the door.

'If you change your mind and want to talk to me sooner, you can call me at this number. Room 12. Take care, Selene.' He took her hand and kissed her, and then he was gone.

Selene walked back to the patio. She joined Patrick and Jessica and asked them if they believed what Gabriel had said.

'He sounded very convincing,' exclaimed Patrick, 'Besides, I liked him. I've liked him from the time of the trekking expedition. He always seems so positive, so much in control. He's certainly very fond of you. There is a spark in his eyes when he looks at you.'

'I agree,' put in Jessica, 'he seemed genuine in what he said. I think I'm in favour of telling him everything.'

'I've always been cautious,' confided Selene, 'all my life I've been warned against men, and I've had first-hand experience of how callous and egotistical they are.'

'Thanks for the vote of confidence, Selene,' commented Patrick, half-serious, half-mocking.

'I don't mean you, Patrick. You've such an open, honest face you couldn't fool a baby if you tried.' Selene said soothingly.

'I hope it's a compliment.' laughed Patrick, and, with this final repartee, they went indoors to prepare dinner, as Selene had given Mei-Lin leave to retire early.

Dinner was fun. Patrick, a white paper hat on his head, shooed them out of the kitchen, stating that he was the chef and they were not to invade his territory. The two girls laid the table in the breakfast room, went outside in the rose garden, and, scissors in hand, cut some yellow roses. Jessica arranged them in a vase that she used as a centrepiece for the table. Selene found some matches, and some green scented candles in a cupboard and placed them in the crystal holders next to them. She put them on the table and lit them. Through the panoramic window, they could see the sun setting and they savoured every minute of it, until they heard a gong. Dinner was ready.

Patrick wheeled in the meal, which consisted of Vegemite sandwiches, followed by Lamingtons (sponge cubes covered with chocolate and coconut).

'I should have known, 'laughed Selene, 'Once an Aussie, always an Aussie, but I'm glad we're not having rice for once.'

'Patrick's ability in the kitchen is restricted to sandwiches, mash potato and mince, spaghetti and mince and chips.' added Jessica, highly amused.

'There's no pleasing the ladies. I've been slaving away in the kitchen all day, and that's all the thanks I get.' declared Patrick in an injured tone of voice.

'You've been great. The sandwiches and Lamingtons taste delicious. My compliments to the chef.' praised Selene.

The banter went on throughout the meal, which was followed by fruit salad and coffee. The girls did the washing up, while Patrick went hunting for some beach mats.

'We're off to the beach.' Patrick announced when the girls had completed their task. They fetched their swimming costumes, retrieved the golf cart from the garage and off they went.

It was a wonderful night. The sky was glittering with millions of stars, while the salty sea air teased their nostrils. Selene had put all cares at the back of her mind and enjoyed the simple pleasures nature dispenses to all living beings.

'Tell me, Patrick,' quizzed Selene, looking up at the moon, 'How come the moon looks different here? I've been meaning to ask people that, ever since I arrived.'

'Well, Selene, you should know. After all, you're named after the moon. Selene being the Greek name for it.' replied Patrick, laughing.

'Stop fooling around, Patrick and answer my question.'

Clearing his throat and taking on a lecturing tone, Patrick

stated, 'In the northern hemisphere the moon travels from left to right. It is the opposite below the equator, where the moon travels from right to left and, of course, it's upside down compared to the way you see it in countries above the equator.'

'Thank you Professor Tierney. You've given me a clear answer. I'm duly impressed.' Selene burst out laughing at his imitation of a pompous professor.

'Now you know what I have to put up with.' echoed Jessica.

As they neared the beach, they noticed people walking westward along the shore and heard a magical, melodious percussion music coming from that direction. Filled with curiosity they headed that way, too, and what spectacle met their eyes!

There was a wide circle of people sitting on the sand. Some were Sasak musicians, playing tunes with their bamboo flutes *(suling)*. Others accompanied them, by beating their double-ended drums *(kedang)*.

'They're performing the *Legong Trunajaya*, the dance of love and emotions,' murmured Patrick.

In the middle of a circle, there stood two beautiful young women, dressed up as men. The women wore a *destar* on their head -a headgear normally worn by men- and an unusual loincloth called a *kancut*. They were dancing together in synchronous movements to the mesmeric sounds of the *gong kebyar*, a fast, rhythmic beat, which accompanied the harmonious movements of the dance.

Dewi Rinjani danced, her legs half-bent, elbow raised and lowered in a gesture that displayed the suppleness of her hands and fingers, her torso shifting in symmetry with her arms. Her *kancut* was deep red silk interwoven with gold threads, her lips were like ripe cherries. Her beautiful blue eyes, ablaze with passion, under gold eyelids were fixed on Gabriel. Gazing back, his eyes intent, his body poised like a panther's about to spring on his beautiful pray, sat Gabriel, his lips slightly parted.

Selene couldn't believe her eyes. 'That's men for you,' she thought.

There was the man who only a few hours earlier had protested, so vehemently, that Dewi Rinjani was nothing to him, looking at her as if she were a goddess.

'I'm going home, she told Patrick and Jessica. I've had enough of this place and of Mr Gabriel Hart.' And with that, she stormed away from the scene. Her friends caught up with her and Jessica blurted out, 'I can't believe the man. He sounded so sincere, so honest, and now this.'

However, Patrick had different views, 'He was probably invited by the family and couldn't say no.' he reasoned.

'Did you see the way he was looking at her? Did he seem like someone who wasn't interested?' cried Selene, frowning.

'Well, it was a very charming dance, and the clothes were impressive.' remarked Patrick.

'Men!' shouted out the girls in unison, 'They're all alike. They see a pretty face and lose it.'

'I'm glad we're having an early night,' said Jessica, 'Don't forget we're climbing up the giant rock just before dawn tomorrow.'

'You two go,' uttered Selene, determined, 'I really do need to speak to Beatrice, and I want to put down a plan of action.'

'If you're sure,' replied Patrick.

'I am. Please, take the time and go surfing as well. Enjoy yourselves.'

By then they had reached the house and after a kiss from Jessica and a hug from Patrick, they went their separate way to their bedrooms.

After closing the door behind her, Selene let herself flop down on the wicker chair by the window. She had been crazy to think that Gabriel had been truthful with her. He had probably gone there to find out what her plans were so that he could report his findings to the Fairchilds. She felt a lump in her throat at the thought of how he had tried to deceive her. Her mind recalled all those brooding glances he had shot in her direction. Selene's mind lingered on the way Gabriel had kissed her hand, on the spark she had glimpsed in his eyes. She reflected with bitterness that all he had done had been a mere ploy. It had all been part of a plan to make her feel safe and loved, while all the time he had been after her aunt's land and house for the people who really mattered to him, namely Dewi Rinjani and her family. But she would show him. She would show to all of them that she was not a pushover. She had become wise to their plotting and scheming and tomorrow, with the help of her friends, she would find a way to counteract their machinations.

CHAPTER NINETEEN

She was on the edge of the swimming pool. She was arguing with a man. He pushed her. She fell into the water and struggled to get out. He kept her head under the water until her lungs were on fire. She couldn't breathe. Her eyes were popping out of her head. Now she was sinking. Before she reached the bottom of the pool, she jolted herself awake.

'What a horrible nightmare.' Selene was panting, rivulets of sweat rolling down her back. It was nearly four o'clock in the morning, but it was still dark outside. Selene had a shower and wrapped herself up in a silk dressing gown that she had bought in London, and then sat down on the bed. Why was she having those horrible nightmares? Was it her aunt trying to reach her from the great beyond? 'Don't be a fool.' She chided. It had all to do with what she had been told about her aunt's death, to what she had discovered about Michael Taun's plans, not to mention Gabriel's behaviour. All those factors put together had fired her imagination, which her brain translated into the recurrent bad dreams that had been plaguing her.

Somewhat reassured, she switched on the TV and watched an old film on the Australian channel. Her mind, though, kept on replaying the scene she had witnessed the night before. In her mind's eye she could still visualise the way Gabriel had been staring at Dewi Rinjani and a sudden pang of jealousy rippled through her body.

She heard Jessica leave her room and tiptoe downstairs. She and Patrick would be heading for Hard Rock, then to the beach. She, instead, would get dressed and wait for Beatrice's arrival.

Selene, wearing a long white dress, her hair off her face, under a wide brimmed straw hat, walked about in the Japanese garden. It was an oasis of peace, with its little bridges, its incredible floral display, which attracted a variety of colourful and exotic birds and insects. Every step she took was accompanied by the tinkling of wind chimes, by the soothing sound of the water trickling down from bamboo pipes. Little waterfalls cascaded happily into deep blue pools where gold fish mingled with their colourful cousins among large and beautiful water lilies. The sound of the birds singing and twittering in the trees could be heard against the background of billows breaking in the distance. Selene sat there for some time, lost in thought. She thought back at her childhood days, and then moved on to consider all that had happened to her in the last few months and in recent weeks. Her mind lingered particularly on her fabulous trip to Mt Rinjani.

Beatrice found her there, staring into nothingness, a frown on her face. 'Hello, my dear. You do look glum.'

'Hallo, Beatrice. I didn't hear you coming. Have you had a good journey?' Selene asked her friend, after having given her a peck on the cheek.

'Yes, thank you. But let me look at you. You have a lovely golden tan. I'm positively envious. You've lost some weight, though. But tell me, how are things between you and Gabriel?' the older woman wanted to know.

They sat there, talking for what seemed hours and Beatrice's expressive face showed all the gamut of emotions that went through her at the unfolding of Selene's narrative.

'It's preposterous! How dare Michael Taun spread such nonsense? And Gabriel, I would never have thought him capable of acting in this way. My poor, dear Selene. We must consult a local solicitor and see what he has to say. Vincent knows a lot of influential people. He will take care of it. I'll phone him as soon as we're back at the house.'

The two of them started walking towards the house only to see Gabriel advancing in their direction. He looked cool and handsome in his white linen suit and light moccasins. When he saw them, he smiled.

'Good morning Beatrice, good morning Selene. How lovely you both look.'

'You don't look too bad yourself,' replied Beatrice. 'But what brings you here just after breakfast?'

'I need to speak to Selene. Hasn't she told you about Michael Taun's claim?'

'We both know he's talking nonsense, but he shouldn't be allowed to go about spreading this kind of rumour.'

'Precisely! That's why I want to sort this out once and for all.' Gabriel shifted his eyes on Selene and said, 'We have to talk Selene.' He looked so appealing, so open, even caring, and Selene was nearly lost in the warmth of his gaze. But then she remembered the way he had looked at Dewi Rinjani the night before, and her lips set in a thin determined line.

'Sorry, Gabriel. Vincent is going to be acting for me from now on.'

Gabriel looked stunned for a moment, then asked, 'Why Selene, don't you trust me?'

'Let's say I have my reservations. Besides I feel I need someone who was a friend of my aunt and who had always her interest at heart, to champion my cause.'

Gabriel's eyes turned into two icy pools. 'I see,' he stated through clenched teeth, 'well, there's nothing more to say then.'

'No, there isn't. From now on, I'll be speaking through Vincent. Goodbye Gabriel.' And with those words, Selene got up and left them.

She fled into the house, ran upstairs, and threw herself onto the bed. Powerful sobs racked her body, she felt so full of despair. How hard it had been to keep her cool in front of Gabriel! She still felt this incredible attraction, this love for him, but she could not trust him, and it was tearing her apart.

Exhausted, she fell into a dreamless, fitful sleep. She was awakened some time later by a light tap on the door. She shouted, 'Just a minute, please.' She ran into the bathroom, splashed some water over her face, tidied herself up a little, and then opened the door.

Beatrice walked in and sat on the bed, 'My dear child, whatever is the matter? You love him, don't you?' she asked, patting Selene's hand.

'Yes, I do love him' she whispered. There was no point in denying it. She already knew that she had loved him from the first time she had set eyes on him.

'Why did you let him go, then, without an explanation?' asked Beatrice, kindly.

'Please, Beatrice. Don't make it worse. I've told you everything that has passed between us, therefore you must understand that I have lost all faith in him.'

'You might be making a mistake, though. I've never heard a word said against him and there may be some mitigating circumstances to his acting the way he did.'

'I can't cope with this at the moment. Please, Beatrice, for the time being, don't mention his name to me again.' pleaded Selene.

'All right, my dear. I only hope you won't regret it.' were Beatrice's parting words.

Immediately after Beatrice had left, Selene had a shower, put on a long pale green linen skirt, with matching top, used foundation to hide the havoc the tears had caused to her face, and blow-dried her hair. When she was ready, she went downstairs to join the others.

Jessica and Patrick had had a wonderful time at the beach, after viewing what they called, 'the most sensational' sunrise they had ever seen in their whole life. 'The surfing here is brilliant,' enthused Patrick. 'The waves are just how I like them, challenging without being dangerous.'

Noticing Selene's downcast look, they enquired if anything new had distressed her that morning. Once Selene had filled them in, they all went to have lunch on the patio, where Patrick, once again, reiterated to Selene that he was prepared to marry her if this would make things easier for her.

'I don't think I approve of such an idea,' objected Beatrice, 'although it might help to stop Michael Taun from saying that they are engaged. It would obviously put an end to any plans he has about marrying you in order to recover the land his family have sold. However, before we get carried away and make a rush decision, let's wait and see what my husband suggests.'

A kind of apathy seemed to take hold of Selene, who merely picked at her food. She was overcome by a lassitude she had never experienced before. Let Michael Taun do what he liked, she could not be bothered any more. But then a little voice inside her said, 'Aunt Elizabeth would have wanted you to fight, and to find out how she had really died.'

Feeling in a more belligerent mood, Selene lifted her chin up and looked at her friends. 'I can't wait for Vincent to come. I've got plans.' She announced to an incredulous audience, 'Excuse me, will you? I'm going to write down the strategy that has just come into my head.' Then she got up and left the table.

She walked into the study, took pen and paper, and wrote down a plan and some notes, ready to submit them to Vincent once he arrived. It was all so simple, she could not understand why she had not thought it up before? 'Because you were mooning about, thinking of Gabriel.' she reminded herself.

Pleased with the solution she had reached, Selene decided to go for a ride. Beatrice, who was a keen horsewoman, was happy to join her, while Jessica and Patrick went to the tennis court for a game. Selene brought her mobile with her, to make it easier for Mei-Lin to contact her the moment Vincent arrived.

The weather was getting drier by the day, the monsoon season being almost over, but the breeze was still blowing, making the ride more exhilarating, and her hair looking like the fiery tail of a comet. They had pushed the horses into a competitive gallop towards the beach, when the pretty baroque tune of her mobile warned her that Vincent was there, so they turned back and raced towards the pool, coming up a few metres short of it.

Selene jumped lithely off her mount and handed the reins to Wayan, who had been their escort and was now to take the horses back to the paddocks. Beatrice walked up to her husband and started to kiss him playfully on the chin, when he turned it into a proper kiss, full of passion and longing. Selene stood by watching them with envious eyes. They had been married for twenty-six years, yet they still looked like a couple on their honeymoon.

'Welcome, Vincent. Sit down and Mei-Lin will bring you something to drink. What would you like?' asked Selene.

'A cool Bintang beer would be nice, thank you Selene.'

Selene asked Mei-Lin to serve the same to everybody, then introduced Patrick and Jessica who had joined them and they all sat down and sipped their beer in the shade of a large umbrella, listening to the pleasant sounds around them and making idle conversation.

After half an hour, Selene asked, 'Vincent, would you like to go and freshen up before we start?'

'No, thank you Selene. The quicker we tackle this situation, the better it'll be for all of us.' he replied in a business-like manner.

'Let's adjourn to the study, then,' proposed Selene. The two of them got up and headed for the study, whilst the others remained seated, waiting to hear the outcome of the discussion.

'Before you tell me about your plans, Selene, let's consider what we have to deal with,' started off Vincent, 'Number one, there is this tale Michael Taun is spreading around of an engagement between the two of you.' As Selene was about to say something, Vincent lifted up his right hand to check her and said, 'No, let me finish, please Selene, I'll give you plenty of time to talk once we have laid everything down clearly. Secondly, there is the problem of what you propose to do with this property. Last, but not least, we have your lack of trust towards Gabriel. Am I right, so far?'

'Yes, Vincent. There it is, in a nutshell.'

'Good. Will you tell me please why is Michael Taun saying to all and sundry that you two are engaged?' asked Vincent, with an encouraging look.

Selene explained to him what she had already told the others and added, 'It seems to me that his uncle had tried to do just the same with Aunt Elizabeth, that something happened and she died. Now I'd like to find out whether it was an accident, if she was really alone or if someone was instrumental to her death. For this reason, I'd like you to engage a good detective. It won't matter about the cost, but I must know once and for all.'

'All right, Selene, I'll do that. So you feel that the family are after this property, do you?'

'It would appear so. I've told you what I overheard at the garden party, and marrying me would be the easiest and quickest way of getting the land back. Now, this is my plan. You should get in touch with Mr Denpasar and tell him that I want to sign over to him the official document, the statement that I relinquish any rights I may have to this property. I want *Inggris* to become a co-operative with Vikram Depansar and you at the head, with the proviso that the property will be run as a hotel, with Mei-Lin and her family as managers. The income generated should serve to pay their salary, while the remainder should go to the Lombok Craft Centre and the Sembalun Loom-Weavers. My ultimate goal is a self-sustainable organisation run by local people, where decision-making and distribution of profits is controlled by the potters' and weavers' groups. Vikram Denpasar can retain a 2% fee to oversee all this and you, Vincent, can decide on a percentage for yourself.' explained Selene enthusiastically.

'My dear Selene I am truly honoured, but have you thought this out carefully? You mean you want to give away nearly three million pounds of you inheritance?' exclaimed Vincent amazed.

'Yes. You see, I shall still be a millionaire, and this project will help to carry on what my aunt started. I've learnt from Beatrice and from other sources how dear such a project was to my aunt's heart. Beatrice told me of the love she had for the people of Lombok, particularly the women. I'd like these women to be as independent as they can possibly be, so that they and their children may be able to have a better future.' asserted Selene, determination written all over her face.

'Well, my dear, this is very commendable. I know how keen your aunt was to achieve just that, and, if you are absolutely sure that this is what you want, I'll be delighted to help you and will do it for free, in memory of the ties of friendship that bound Beatrice and me to Elizabeth. As for Vikram, I've known him from the time he was a toddler and can vouch for his integrity and business acumen.' Vincent's voice conveyed to her that she had risen in his esteem and felt proud within herself to have obtained the approval of this kind, caring and capable man.

'However,' continued Vincent, 'this won't stop Michael Taun from pursuing you and wanting you to be his wife. He's after the rest of your inheritance, not only the property on this island.'

'Yes, I realise that. Now, you know that Patrick has said that he would be willing to marry me, just to get Michael Taun off my back. We could, therefore, tell everybody that I'm officially engaged to him and, once the papers are signed over to make you and Vikram Denpasar joint managing directors of the *Inggris Co-operative*, I'll be able to leave the island and this bogus engagement will die its own death.'

'That would certainly help. But, before we proceed with it, are you absolutely sure that Patrick is acting out of friendship for you and has no other ideas in his head?'

Selene smiled and said, 'Patrick is a peach. He wouldn't say boo to a goose. Really he's a nice harmless boy, but you're welcome to find that out for yourself.'

'There's just one last item on our list.... Gabriel,' added Vincent, frowning slightly. 'I know you've told me about what you saw and heard, but believe me Selene, Gabriel is not that kind of man. I've known him now for twelve years. I know his father, his mother and his brothers and I can assure you Selene that there isn't an ounce of malice in him. He's level headed and upright and I've never known him to trifle with a girl's affection. He's the kind of man I wouldn't have minded having had for a son-in-law, had Beatrice and I ever had a daughter. I'll act on your behalf out of respect for you and your aunt, but I beg you to reconsider your opinion of him. And now, if you're ready, let's go and announce to the others what conclusions we have reached, as we'll need their help as well.'

'Wait. Before we leave this room, I want you to give me your word of honour that you won't breathe a word to Gabriel of what we've discussed.'

'I disagree with you, but I do give you my word of honour. Only remember that I'll need to inform him of your intentions with regard to *Inggris*. All the papers relating to your inheritance are still in his hands.' Vincent reminded her.

'I know it can't be helped. But please just tell him the minimum required.' urged Selene.

When Beatrice learnt what Selene planned to do with the property, she was really moved and hugging her proclaimed, 'You're the true heir of your aunt. She would have been proud of you.'

Jessica, too, spoke highly of her decision. Patrick congratulated her about her projects for *Inggris*. As far as his involvement in the plan to thwart Michael Taun's scheme, he just said, 'When are we getting officially engaged then?'

'We'll announce our engagement in the Jakarta Post, the New York Times, the Times and other top newspapers. Please, Vincent, see to it. I hope that that will put a stop to Michael Taun's assertions. As far as relinquishing my claims on *Inggris* in favour of the Co-operative, I want it to be done before the *Bau Nyale* festival.'

'That doesn't leave me much time,' exclaimed Vincent. 'I'd better go and get in touch with the papers and with Vikram Denpasar immediately.'

'What you're about to do, dear Selene, calls for a celebration,' cried out Beatrice, 'Let's get some champagne. I know Elizabeth kept some for very special occasions.'

'Yes, let's. Afterwards we can go and try out the mini golf. I've wanted to do that ever since I arrived, but I've never had the chance so far.' commented Selene.

The wine was kept in the building next to the garage, in a room adjacent to where Selene had seen Mei-Lin ironing and where the temperature was kept constant. Vincent went to retrieve a bottle, which he opened with expert hands.

Afterwards, Beatrice, Selene, Patrick, and Jessica had a lot of fun playing mini golf, while Vincent went to freshen up and to place the important calls Selene had asked him to make. After a while, tired out, the mini golf players went back to sit by the swimming pool, watching another spectacular sunset. Eventually, they all retired to their room to shower and change for dinner.

Once they were sitting round the dinner table, Vincent reported that the Jakarta Post had been duly contacted and the announcement would come out the very next day. As the weekend was near, he was going to email the Times and other important international papers, which would probably announce her engagement at the end of the following week. He had also tried several times to contact Vikram Denpasar, but getting no answer had left a message on his mobile. Finally, he had spoken to Gabriel, telling him to come over the following morning.

'Bravo, Vincent,' exclaimed his audience.

When dinner was over, Beatrice signalled to him to go and sit next to her on one of the sofas in the sitting room, where they sipped their coffee.

They spent a pleasant evening. Vincent was talking to Patrick and the women were having a game of Scrabble when the phone rang. It was Vikram, returning Vincent's call.

The conversation went on for several minutes and everyone held their breath, waiting. 'It's all right,' declared Vincent, exultantly replacing the receiver, 'Vikram will come back next week to settle things. He wants to meet you, of course, but he said that, with a little money given to the right people, the matter should be concluded quite speedily and to everyone's satisfaction.'

'Hurray!' shouted Selene. I can't wait to go back to England, start a normal life, and drive a car again.'

'You must come with us to Sidney first,' suggested Jessica, 'You might as well have a look at our part of the world before you go back to your fabulous English weather.'

Patrick excused himself, 'I must contact my parents and fill them in about our bogus engagement. I'll never live it down otherwise. Mother would be on my back constantly about her being the last to know etc., etc. You know what mothers are like.' he remarked with a laugh.

At one point Vincent asked Selene if she could follow him to the study and there he told her that he approved of Patrick and that he had contacted the newspaper with a light heart. After that, the evening wore on with talks about who should visit whom, of holidays to come, of places to be explored, and of many other interesting topics.

That night, Selene went to bed a happy girl. A detective would come soon to investigate her aunt's death. In a week's time she'll be rid of *Inggris* and, best of all, she would score a tactical victory on Michael Taun and his family.

CHAPTER TWENTY

The morning chorus awoke Selene from her slumber. It was another cloud free day and the temperature was already climbing. She got out of bed and opened the windows wider, letting in the fragrance of the flowers and the distance sound of the surf. She felt at peace with the world. The previous day had been a milestone in her newfound life and from now on she was going to live to the full, no more mooning around. After she had showered and dressed, she walked to the stables and asked Wayan to accompany her. They rode all around the property and by the time they returned, she was simply starving. Mei-Lin greeted her with a smile.

'Miss up early,' she pointed out, 'Miss sleep well?'

'Like a log. I'm famished. What's for breakfast?'

'Rice fritters, pineapple juice, mango slices and coffee.'

'Perfect. By the way, Mei-Lin, Mr Vincent will need to talk to you and your family soon. Don't worry. It's good news.'

'Yes, Miss. Thank you Miss. When Mr Vincent talk to us?'

'Oh, here he comes. He'll tell you himself.' concluded Selene, picking up another rice fritter.

Beatrice joined her soon after and told her that Patrick and Jessica had gone surfing and would be back for lunch.

A short time later, Vincent joined them, followed by Mei-Lin and all the members of her family who had wanted to thank her personally. Selene told them how good and kind they had all been towards her, how grateful she was for the way they had looked after her, and how she hoped they would find fulfilment in their new jobs.

When they were alone, Vincent warned her that Gabriel would be coming soon and that he had sounded like a bear with a sore head over the phone. 'He must have read the announcement of your engagement to Patrick.' commented Vincent.

Patrick and Jessica came back early, claiming that the crowd on the beach had spoilt their surfing. 'By the way, we saw Michael Taun, but he didn't notice us. He was chatting up a pretty, local girl. So much for being engaged.' revealed Jessica.

'He probably hasn't read the papers yet, or he'll be contacting me about a breach of promise.' Selene said dismissively with a shrug.

As if on cue, someone rang the bell and after a few minutes, in strode Gabriel, his eyes glaring with pent up anger. He looked at Selene as if he wanted to strangle her and was almost rude to the others who greeted him and politely enquired after his health. 'May I have a word with you?' he asked Selene, aggressively.

'Wait a minute,' interrupted Patrick, possessively, 'Don't use that tone with my fiancée.'

'Well, I need to speak to your fiancée about legal matters, if you don't mind.' snorted Gabriel, 'I'm still her solicitor.'

'Very well,' replied Selene, her hackles rising, 'follow me to the study.'

'How dare you come into this house and be rude to my friends and fiancé.' she upbraided him as soon as they were in the study. 'Who do you think you are? I've already told you that Vincent is my spokesman as far as anything legal is concerned, therefore I object to your charging in here like a bull in a china shop.' She was really angry now. Her green eyes were ablaze, her hair streamed on either side of her cheeks like leaping flames, her cheeks on fire. She was so beautiful Gabriel closed the distance between them, clasped her in his arms, and kissed her with such passion and longing that Selene felt her knees turn to jelly.

Her response was overwhelming. She clung to his lips like a limpet to a rock. Sensations she had never experienced before were unleashed, and she responded to him in a way she would never have thought possible. The kiss seemed to go on forever, became deeper and more demanding. 'No, you mustn't. Let me go,' she cried, pushing him away.

'Selene, what...' Gabriel was panting as if he had been running. His heart was thudding against his ribs. His eyes were slumberous and filled with a hunger she hadn't seen before.

Little by little, he regained control over himself and said, 'Why did you get engaged to him if you can respond to me like this? Are you a teaser, Selene? Is this what you did to poor Michael Taun, too? The poor boy is so upset..'

'I bet he is,' sneered Selene.

'What's that supposed to mean?' enquired Gabriel, his voice rising.

'Why don't you ask him? After all, you're the family's friend.' Selene replied sarcastically, angry to have made a fool of herself, and afraid of having revealed too much of what she felt for him.

'Why don't we stop this guessing game and you tell me what's bugging you? You've blown hot and cold ever since we met. Isn't it time you put me in the picture?'

'I've nothing else to say to you, Mr Hart. Please leave this room right now. I don't want to see you again.' Selene opened the door and kept it open for him to go. 'Vincent will come to talk to you at your hotel. Goodbye.'

Gabriel made as if to speak, but the hardness in her eyes and the finality of her speech made him change his mind and he left, slamming the door behind him.

Selene ran upstairs and sobbed as if her heart would break. He was heartless, he was impossible, but she knew, in her heart of hearts, that she had never loved anyone as she loved him.

Selene cried her heart out, until she had no tears left, then she eventually composed herself. She must go down to her friends. She had a lot to do. She was going to act her part as Patrick's loving, devoted fiancée for all the world to see. On Monday the detective was flying in from London. Vikram Denpasar was also coming to meet her, but first of all, she had to tell Vincent about the fact that he was to meet Gabriel at his hotel, not at *Inggris*. Never again would Gabriel cross the threshold of her aunt's home if she could help it.

When she went out, she saw Vincent reading the paper, with Beatrice next to him, lying on one of the sun loungers, reading a novel. Patrick was swimming in the pool and Jessica was sunbathing.

'Hello, Selene. How did it go with Gabriel?' asked Vincent.

'Not well. Not well at all. Please Vincent, go and see him at his hotel. I don't want Gabriel to come back here ever again.'

'That bad, was it? What did he do to upset you?'

'I'd rather not talk about it. Let's say we didn't see eye to eye.'

'Well, I'd better phone him, then. He's leaving in two days' time and I definitely need to speak to him before he goes.'

'Where is he going?' asked Selene, feigning indifference.

'He's going back to London. He's decided to cut his holiday short.' Vincent answered.

'Maybe he has some pressing business to attend.' replied Selene, stricken. Gabriel was leaving. What about Dewi Rinjani? Her leave and the Easter vacations would soon be over and, if not flying back with him, she surely would see him in London. Despite his protestations, Selene was sure that Dewi Rinjani would waste no time to hold him in her clutches. Well, good luck to them. She, instead, would probably die an old maid, like her aunt. She would spend her life alone, her heart filled with the pangs of unrequited love.

'A penny for them.' a friendly voice asked.

'They're not worth that much,' replied Selene, smiling.

'Come on then, fiancée, let's go for a stroll on the beach.'

'Why not?' said Selene, brightly, 'Let me fetch my hat.'

Patrick was a real dear and fun to be with. He made her feel like a little girl again, enjoying simple things, like looking for shells on the seashore, or running in the sand with him in hot pursuit. They climbed up Hard Rock. Afterwards they hopped onto a *bemo* and went to visit Rembitan and Sade, two traditional Sasak Villages. There he bought her a fan made of sandalwood, and a *suling* (bamboo flute) for himself. They stopped to watch a *legong*.

'What's a *legong*?' asked Selene.

'It's an individual dance, which has no connection with other dances. It has no story and was specifically created for welcoming and entertainment purposes.' explained Patrick, pulling her hair familiarly, 'Pay attention when your teacher speaks to you, young lady.'

'Yes, Sir. Whatever you say, Sir.' she replied, sticking out her tongue. They both laughed, like two naughty kids playing truant from school. They visited the open market, full of colour and odorous with spices. Selene selected a ripe avocado and a passion fruit.

They were walking away from the market when it started to rain and they asked a young man if they could take shelter in his hut. There, they were offered the best seat, drink and food the family could afford. It was the kind of hospitality, which used to be popular in Europe a few centuries ago. Selene and Patrick did not offer to share what they had purchased for fear of offending them, not sure of their customs. Instead, they handed the fruit to the children, who were playing outside, once the rain had stopped. In the *bemo* that they hired on the way back, they commented on how kind and generous humble people were, compared to the egotistical attitude of those living in Western societies.

They asked the driver to drop them off near Kuta Beach and, hand in hand, they walked on the sand. The beach was fairly empty at that time of day, but Selene spotted a rough looking man who followed them with his eyes. She felt a cold chill run down her spine and shivered.

'What's the matter, Selene?' asked Patrick, putting a protective arm around her.

'Nothing.' murmured Selene, 'I guess I'm a bit tired. It's been a wonderful day and I've really enjoyed it, but now I'd like to go home.'

Someone was looking at her. She could feel his eyes boring into her back. She turned round and saw Gabriel's grim face. He was looking at the way Patrick's arm was wrapped round her shoulders. 'He couldn't be jealous, could he?' Selene asked herself, and at the thought, her heart missed a beat.

That night Selene thought hard about Gabriel. Who was he really? The warm, kind, considerate, even sensuous companion he had shown her he could be, or the two-timing louse, so similar to Simon? It was a hard puzzle to solve. Meanwhile, time was ticking on and he would soon be gone.

The following day Selene and her friends had just had their lunch, when the phone rang. 'Miss Dewi Rinjani for you Miss,' Mei-Lin announced.

'All right, I'll take the call, thank you.' Selene's heart sank. She knew instinctively that it was going to be an unpleasant exchange. 'Selene speaking...Oh, hello Dewi Rinjani, how are you?' At the other end of the line Dewi Rinjani told her in very angry tones what she thought of her, and of the shameful way she had treated her brother. Selene's blood pressure climbed notably under the onslaught, while her voice took on such an icy cutting edge she found it difficult to recognise it as her own.

'Now Dewi Rinjani you know as well as I do that your brother has started a rumour that was never true and will never come true in a million years. Therefore keep all this so-called indignation of yours to yourself as, anyway, we don't have an audience to impress. I don't want to hear any more of this nonsense your brother had thought fit to spread around, no doubt with the intention of forcing me into a marriage I had and have no intention of entering. Furthermore, if I hear any more gossip on this subject, I shall see no option but to consult my lawyers about suing him, you or anyone else involved, for slander. Is that clear?' Instead of answering, Dewi Rinjani slammed the phone down. What a beastly family! She was glad the detective was coming to see her later on that very day, thought Selene, fuming with repressed ire.

'Come, Beatrice,' she urged, 'let's go for a ride.'

'Gladly, my dear.' Beatrice replied enthusiastically.

Free, Selene felt wonderfully free, her hair flying around her face, her body brushed by the sea breeze, her eyes sparkling. She felt free and alive. She was giving herself up to the moment, enjoying every minute of it. And it was like that, shiny-eyed and with a heightened colour on her cheeks that Gabriel saw her. He was standing by the steps leading up to the property and looked surprised yet pleased to see her. She brought the horse to a halt, and then asked, archly, 'What are you doing here, Gabriel?'

CHAPTER TWENTY-ONE

'Please, Selene, I need to talk to you. Don't say no! It's important.' Gabriel pleading was a new experience for Selene, who was taken aback and even moved to see this new side of him. Still, she wouldn't give an inch away.

'I thought I'd made it clear, I don't want to talk to you.' she answered.

'I know, but give me this last chance. I'm leaving tomorrow and may not have this opportunity again.' Something in his voice touched a chord in Selene's heart, which she found impossible to ignore.'

'Oh, all right then. Let's get it over with. Beatrice, will you excuse me? Wayan, please take my horse back to the stable, Mr Hart and I will walk back to the house.'

Beatrice looked from one to the other, but seeing the earnestness in Gabriel's eyes, after nodding her 'goodbye,' she turned her mount round and galloped off towards the stables.

'First of all, let me tell you how much I admire what you have set out to do. Your aunt would have been so pleased.' Gabriel began and, before she could stop him, he quickly continued, 'There's something else I want to tell you. Please listen. I love you Selene, I've loved you from the first time you walked into my office. Please believe me. I've never loved like this before. I want to marry you.'

Selene could not believe her ears. Gabriel loved her. He had always loved her. Was it possible or was it just a ruse? And if he loved her, how could he have looked at Dewi Rinjani with such intense interest?

'Look, Gabriel, please don't mock me. I've already suffered in the past through another declaration like yours. I suffered deeply and it has made me weary of men. I beg you Gabriel, if you are as true and upright as Vincent seems to think, don't tell me that you love me if you don't mean it.'

'Of course I mean it. I've never been more in earnest in my whole life. Please believe me.' He looked straight into her eyes and his voice and manners seemed to betray only emotion and sincerity.

'Oh Gabriel,' cried Selene, bridging the gap that separated them, 'I love you, too, with all my heart.' He swept her into his arms and kissed her as if there would be no tomorrow. Then his lips, which had been greedy and full of need, became tender and longing, so that she melted in his arms and lost all track of place and time.

'We must talk.' he whispered against her lips, then he put his arm round her waist and they headed for the Japanese garden.

'Now Selene, tell me why you had that absurd announcement placed in the Jakarta Post about your engagement to Patrick?' asked Gabriel, sitting on a bench and pulling her close to him. And Selene told him everything she had wanted to tell him for some time about the Fairchilds' family.

'You poor darling.' exclaimed Gabriel, holding her and kissing her, 'But now I'm here to protect you. We'll get married at the British Embassy in Jakarta. We'll have Vincent and Beatrice as witnesses. Then when we return to England, we'll get married properly in church. I want my family there to see you make an honest man of me.'

'Don't forget Patrick and Jessica. They've become my best friends.' added Selene, excitedly. 'And I want them at my wedding.'

'I'm your best friend.' emphasized Gabriel, possessively. 'You know, when I saw you with Patrick, I wanted to kill him.'

'And I wanted to kill Dewi Rinjani when I saw you looking at her so intently at the *Legong Trunajaya*,' confessed Selene.

'But I wasn't looking at her. I was watching Michael Taun speaking to a rough looking individual. I was wondering why he was speaking to a man like that. He looked like an ex-convict or a Malaysian Pirate.' replied Gabriel.

'Are there such things as pirates in this day and age? I thought they were a figment of some film director's fantasy.' asked Selene, relieved at Gabriel's explanation.

'No, they are very real. It's like the bandits we were warned about by the guide on Mount Rinjani.' said Gabriel with a serious look about him.

'Wait a minute. I saw a man like that yesterday at Kuta Beach. He was following me with his eyes, or so it seemed to me.' Selene told him, a shiver running down her spine.

'I wonder whether it's the same man. Maybe Michael Taun is up to something. I feel sorry for Sir Edward. I don't think he's aware of his children's behaviour. Dewi Rinjani has been after me for years, but she seems to have surpassed herself lately. Since she's met you she has kept on throwing herself in my way. She doesn't know that my heart was taken as soon as I set eyes on you.' A long pause ensued, when Gabriel showed Selene just how much she meant to him.

'Oh dear,' murmured Selene. 'We must stop the papers.'

'What do you mean?'

'The announcement of my engagement to Patrick will be published in all the major international newspapers, if we don't do anything about it.'

'Don't worry. Vincent only contacted the Jakarta Post with the announcement, and that was only meant to expose Michael Taun's claim for the lie that it was, but he had no intention of committing you to the international press.' Gabriel reassured her. 'You see, he and Beatrice have your happiness very much at heart and he acted in *loco parentis*. But now, before we face our friends, I want you to try this for size.' He took a small box out of his trousers pocket and handed it to Selene. When she opened it, she found the most fabulous ring she had ever seen. The central piece was a flawless emerald, surrounded by sparkling diamonds, set on a platinum band. She tried it on and it fitted her perfectly.

'How did you know it would fit me?' she asked, her eyes filled with happiness.

‘Do you remember when you went shopping with Beatrice? You stopped at a jeweller’s shop in Mataram....’

‘And she prompted me to try some rings, just for the fun of it....I can’t believe it. I’m the victim of a plot.’ cried Selene, pretending to be cross. ‘I feel like refusing you just to wipe off that smug expression you’ve been wearing since I accepted your proposal.’

‘Impossible. It’s too late. You have committed yourself to making me a very happy man for the rest of our lives.’ He hugged and kissed her again, to show he was in earnest.

When they returned to the house, they discovered that the others, forewarned by Beatrice, had set up an impromptu engagement party and had fetched a few more bottles of champagne to celebrate the event. Selene hugged all her friends, tears of joy in her eyes and whispered to Beatrice, ‘You’re impossible. But I forgive you this time.’

Laughing and crying Beatrice confessed, ‘I’m an incurable romantic. I immediately saw you were made for each other and acted accordingly. I wish you every happiness.’

‘Well, that’s a letdown,’ sighed Patrick, ‘here I was, proclaimed a fiancé by the papers only yesterday and today I find myself single again. Life’s not fair. If you have a change of heart I’ll be here waiting.’ he proclaimed, kissing Selene on the cheek.

‘Put my fiancée down, Patrick. I’ve suffered enough heartache on your account.’ growled Gabriel.

‘Well done, girl.’ Vincent hugged and kissed her on the forehead. ‘It gives me great pleasure to see the two of you together.’

‘And me.’ joined in Jessica, hugging them both.

Mei-Lin, Komang, and Wayan put *leis* (garlands) round their necks, Polynesian style and sang their best wishes in their native tongue.

The detective showed up soon after. His name was David Links and he was the same detective that had been employed by Gabriel to find her. Selene was pleased. He already knew about her family and the least people were involved, the better it would be, she argued with herself.

David Links busied himself straight away, interviewing Mei-Lin and her family. Next, he talked to Beatrice, Vincent, and Gabriel. He recorded everything, transcribing all the statements in his laptop.

'I've engaged a local man I had already employed on another assignment for a previous client on this island,' he told Selene, 'the reason being that people tend to talk more to someone they know, rather than to a foreigner. I'm staying at the same hotel where Gabriel has a room, and I'm pretending to be a tourist. I won't come to the house again. I don't want people to know you know me. I'll get in touch with you on my mobile phone as soon as I have news. I'll walk back to my hotel now, taking a different route from the one I took when I walked here earlier on, so that if I'm seen, I'll say that I was having a look around the area and got lost. I'll contact you the moment I discover something important. Goodbye for now.' David Links left the house through the side door.

'He's very professional,' declared Vincent, admiringly, once the sleuth had left them, 'he certainly doesn't waste time.'

'No, he's really good. He's helped us a lot in the past to trace people like Selene, who didn't know they were the heirs of lost relatives or friends. The client he mentioned is one of ours. I introduced him to this client and he was very satisfied with the work David did for him.' added Gabriel.

'Well, that's one ball set in motion, now we have to think about the meeting with Vikram and alerting the English Embassy about your wedding.' commented Vincent.

'True,' agreed Gabriel, 'when did you say Vikram's coming?'

'I had a call from him this morning, informing me he'll be in Mataram around lunchtime tomorrow. I made an appointment with the notary for tomorrow afternoon.'

'That was fast work.' Gabriel complimented him.

'You know what money can do, if you are in a hurry.' replied Vincent, rather smugly, 'Therefore, I thought, you, Gabriel, Selene and myself will ask Wayan to drive us to Mataram tomorrow morning. We'll have a leisurely lunch at my favourite restaurant, and then we'll go to the notary's office where we'll sign all the documents. With a bit of luck we should be back here by dinner time.'

'Excellent planning.' agreed Gabriel, patting the other man on the back, approvingly.

'I'll feel such a relief when all this bureaucratic formalities are over!' exclaimed Selene, sliding her arm into Gabriel's and regaling him with a warm smile.

'I won't feel easy until I've married you, darling. I'm so afraid you may change your mind.' She put her arms round his neck and the others disappeared, giving them the privacy the moment required.

After dinner, Gabriel and Selene decided to take the golf cart and wander around the property. 'Won't you miss it?' asked Gabriel, looking at her tenderly.'

'A little. But we can still come back for holidays, can't we?'

'Yes, of course, darling. I just meant, won't you miss being the owner of it?'

'No, Gabriel. I'm looking forward to a normal life back in England.' was her prompt reply.

'What do you mean by "normal"?'

'Driving a car whenever the whim takes me. Wear smart clothes that show my figure, rather than be forced to wear these baggy, unflattering dresses. Go dancing, drink a glass of wine in a public place with my friends, you know, all the things we take for granted.'

'Has it been that bad?'

'No. Of course it hasn't. Probably because I've always thought of this house as a holiday place, not as a permanent home.' It felt so good to voice her feelings to him.

'When we return to England, you'll be my wife and we'll live in an old mill, which I've had recently renovated. It's a six-bedroom house now. All the rooms have an ensuite and there is an annex for visitors. There are stables, paddocks, and tennis courts. I think you'll like it.' he murmured, clasping her waist and kissing her, 'You're so sweet, I can't have enough of you. I could go on kissing you all day and all night.'

Selene couldn't help smiling. She felt so incredibly happy she could have burst. Only a week now, the time to have all the documents ready, and they would be married. What bliss awaited her?

They had just reached the steps that led to the beach, when Selene had a glimpse of something glinting in the sunset coming from Hard Rock. There was someone up there looking through a pair of binoculars. The light of the setting sun illumined this tall, rugged figure and Selene cried out, 'Over there. Look Gabriel! It's that man again. The one I saw looking at me the other day.' But by the time he looked, the man had disappeared.

'Why is he stalking me?' asked Selene, suddenly filled with fear.

'I don't know and I don't like it. Pity I didn't have a chance to see whether it was the same man who was talking to Michael Taun. After what you've told me of the conversation you overheard, I've been feeling a bit uneasy. Maybe we should ask David to check him out.'

'What do you think Michael Taun's intentions are?'

'I don't know. He's certainly sore at not having won you over, but from that to having a man stalk you... No, it's ridiculous. His father would be furious if he ever tried to pull some kind of stunt on you.' concluded Gabriel, reassuringly.

The evening was spent in a convivial mood. Despite the age gap, Vincent and Beatrice fitted in well with the others, and could discuss any subject under the sun with intelligence and humour. It was very late when a rather reluctant Gabriel was driven home by Wayan. 'I wish he could stay here with me.' thought Selene, 'But then,' Selene consoled herself,' I'll see him again tomorrow and soon I'll see him every day and every night.' At that thought a languorous, exciting feeling spread through her body, leaving her with a longing she had never experienced before.

CHAPTER TWENTY-TWO

A knock on the door awoke her the following morning. Mei-Lin had brought her breakfast in bed. 'Miss, time to get up.' smiled Mei-Lin. Mr Gabriel and Mr Vincent ready.' Selene couldn't believe her eyes. It was half past nine, the latest she'd ever awoken since all this business of the inheritance had started. She had slept right through, no nightmare troubling her dreams, and she felt better for it. She thanked Mei-Lin, jumped out of bed , showered, put on an emerald green skirt and blouse, to match her engagement ring, drank her coffee and ate her rice cake. She did all this in less than half an hour, and then dashed downstairs to the pool, where they were all gathered waiting for her.

Gabriel hastened by her side and gave her a sweet good morning kiss. That brought a sparkle to her eyes and they all commented on how good she looked. 'I've had a good rest, and the first peaceful night in weeks,' she observed, 'no nightmares.'

'What nightmares?' asked her Gabriel, frowning.

'Oh, nothing. I'll tell you later.' she replied dismissively, with a laugh. But Gabriel wasn't satisfied and, during the journey, she told him about the dreams that had plagued her since she had been told how her aunt had died.

'Don't worry, my love. It's obvious that all this business has been playing on your mind, but it'll soon be over and I'm sure you won't have any more bad dreams.' he reassured her confidently, holding her hand, an arm round her shoulders.

On the way, they stopped to visit the Pura Meru in Cakranegara, Lombok's biggest Balinese temple. 'This temple is dedicated to the Hindu trinity of Shiva, Brahma and Vishnu.' explained Vincent, 'It was built in 1720 by Anak Agung Made Karang, and has three courtyards. As you can observe, three pagoda-like places of worship stand in a line from north to south in the innermost courtyard. The one on the north side is dedicated to Vishnu and has a roof with nine tiers. The central one with two tiers on its roof was built to celebrate Shiva, and the southernmost one, with a roof of seven tiers, is dedicated to Brahma.' concluded Vincent.

After leaving Pura Meru, Gabriel suggested stopping at Taman Mayura, once part of the royal palace. They accessed the splendid artificial lake set in the middle of the park through a raised path, which led from the side of the pond to a pavilion built in the middle of the lake. 'In former days,' Gabriel told her, 'justice was meted out here, and religious rituals were performed in this open-sided pavilion.'

Selene started to laugh, rather amused, 'It seems to me that since I arrived here, every man I've been out with has been wonderfully knowledgeable about the places I've visited. I'm beginning to wonder if you've all followed a course on "everything you've always wanted to know about Lombok" in order to impress the ladies.'

'The only lady I want to impress is you, darling.' answered Gabriel, squeezing her hand.

Despite the detours, it was merely twelve o'clock when they were deposited outside Vincent and Beatrice's penthouse. Wayan was given the notary's address, so that he could come back for them at five. In the interim, he was to take the time off, to do whatever errands he might have in town.

Selene was glad that she was able to freshen up. The sights she had visited had been fantastic, but the heat had increased lately, so she enjoyed a nice, cool shower. She wanted to look her best for the momentous task of signing away her claim to her aunt's property. She also wanted to be her best for Gabriel's sake, a little voice whispered to her. In the end, they had lunch at the penthouse, where they were soon joined by Vikram Denpasar.

He was a tall man in his late thirties. Like the majority of the people living in Lombok, he was a mixture of Indian, Chinese and Sasak. His smile reached his eyes, which looked straight at her. His handshake was firm, his voice pleasant. He had a look of honesty and earnestness about him that Selene liked. They sat together for a time, speaking of the island and the things that could be done to make it a better place. Then, when the time came, they went to the notary and, once the formalities were over and she had no longer any claim of ownership on *Inggris,* Selene was able to breathe a sigh of relief.

'I've decided to use my fees to attract more people into the project through advertising, and I want to invest the profits we'll make in such a way that the business will continue to grow.' promised Vikram.

'That's more than I could ask of you. You're making my dream come true.' Selene thanked him warmly. ' I'd like you to come to our wedding,' she added, looking at Gabriel for approval.

'I was going to ask you that, too. We would be honoured if you and your wife came.' echoed Gabriel.

'I'll be delighted. Let me know when the ceremony takes place and we'll be there.'

'It will be at 11 o'clock on Saturday 11th April.' replied Gabriel. 'I received an email this morning. The ambassador won't be back from his annual leave till the 4th April. He explained that the 11th April is the earliest day he can fit us in.'

Vikram looked in his diary, and then said, 'Saturday April 11 will be fine. I'm so pleased I've met you Selene and it will be a pleasure for my wife and children, too. Thank you both for inviting us to your wedding. Now, I'm afraid I must take my leave of you. If you'll excuse me, I'm going home to my family.'

Once Vikram had left, Gabriel said, 'I'm sorry, Selene. I meant to tell you this morning. But I was so intrigued with your talk of nightmares, that it went right out of my mind.' murmured Gabriel, contritely, brushing her forehead with his lips.

'Don't worry, darling. So much has happened lately that I, too, don't know whether I'm coming or going half of the time.' she reassured him.

Vincent was very pleased for them and, in high spirits, they waited for Wayan to come and collect them.

They arrived at *Inggris* just as the sun was being swallowed by the sea in a pageantry of fire. As it became darker Venus appeared near the crescent moon, which Selene always looked at with wonder, even after Patrick's explanation on the differences between the sky viewed in the northern and the southern hemisphere.

As they entered the house, they were met by the sound of laughter. Patrick, wearing a sheet sarong style, and a towel draped round his head, was attempting to dance by bending his knee and twisting his body, his face expressionless. Balinese music was issuing from the CD player, while Beatrice and Jessica were giving him instructions jokingly, hoping to make him lose his balance. However, he kept up his stance, unperturbed, until Gabriel gave him a friendly push. Patrick sprawled down onto the wooden floor with a thud, and everybody, himself included, burst out laughing.

Gabriel kept Selene close to him all evening and told her how increasingly difficult it was for him to part with her at night. Of how he ached to have her in his arms and make love to her. When the others gave them some moments alone together, their kisses became deeper and more demanding, but Gabriel always managed to pull away in time, conscious of Selene's inexperience and of the trust she had placed in him.

'Don't forget that tomorrow night there's the festival of *Bau Nyale.*' Selene reminded them all, 'I'm really looking forward to it.' she added, longingly.

'So am I,' echoed Gabriel, 'I can't wait to show everybody on the island that I am your fiancé, not this handsome Australian.'

'Thanks for the compliment, pal. This doesn't mean you're forgiven for sweeping my fiancée off her feet.' responded Patrick, slapping Gabriel on the back.

After Gabriel had left, Selene excused herself with the others and went up to her room to email Vanessa, inviting her and Darren to the wedding. 'I know it's short-notice,' she typed, 'but I've only found out about the date this morning.' Then, dancing for joy, she went to bed to dream of Gabriel.

It was pitched black. Selene was scared. Her heart was racing. She was trapped somewhere and she was becoming claustrophobic. She could hear people talking near her. Then someone laughed a horrible crazy laugh and she felt her throat tighten...tighten... Selene screamed.

'Selene, wake up, wake up.' Someone was shaking her awake. Beatrice stooping over her, her hair down, her nightgown sweeping the floor. 'Selene,' she was saying now, in a soothing tone of voice, 'it was only a bad dream. Now, dear, calm down.'

'I was so scared, Beatrice,' she croaked.

'I know, but now it's all over. Here, have a glass of water. It'll make you feel better.' Beatrice helped her to sit up, and plumped up the pillows, while Selene sipped the water.

'It wasn't the usual nightmare,' she explained, 'I was kept captive in a horrible dark place and someone was laughing like a mad person. It was really horrible.' Selene shivered.

Beatrice wrapped a blanket round her, then sat down and held her hand. She then uttered silly, soothing words, as if Selene were a child in need of comfort.

'Thank you Beatrice,' Selene said, truly grateful, to her friend, 'I feel much better now. I'm so happy you're my friend.' And she gave Beatrice a peck on the cheek, then sent her off to the room she shared with Vincent. The room that had been her aunt's. When she was alone, Selene switched on the TV and after a while drifted off to sleep.

Gabriel came to breakfast. He looked absolutely gorgeous. All dressed in white, his tan showing off his perfect profile and cobalt blue eyes. As soon as he saw Selene, he smiled and immediately headed in her direction. Vincent laughed, 'Isn't it incredible how love turns even the best-mannered gentleman into a rude cave man. Here we are, all sitting at the table and he can't even see us, his eyes are all for the object of his love.'

'Thank you Vincent,' scolded Selene with a mock-angry expression, 'but I'm no object. You're right, though, he has become rather rude.'

'Thanks for your support, wife-to-be,' put in Gabriel, his eyes reflecting his happiness, 'I can see I'll have to show you who wears the trousers in this partnership.'

This brought about gasps of protest from Selene, Beatrice, and Jessica and the three women ganged up together to put a stop to any other untoward macho remark.

After this piece of bantering, Jessica, Beatrice, Selene, and Patrick decided to have a tennis match, Patrick and Beatrice challenging Jessica and Selene, whilst Gabriel and Vincent looked on and talked.

CHAPTER TWENTY-THREE

Vincent noticed that Gabriel looked at Selene with concern.

'What's up, old chap?' he enquired, in a low voice.

'I'm worried, Vincent. David slipped a note under my bedroom door and I'm afraid, it contained some disturbing news.'

'Want to discuss it with me?' urged Vincent, becoming grave.

'Yes, but not here. I don't want Selene to hear. She told me she had another nightmare last night, and I don't want to add to her distress.'

'What about telling them that we're going to have a round of mini-golf and talk about it then?' suggested Vincent.

'Excellent. Let's do that.'

Once they were alone, Gabriel disclosed to him that David had heard that a tall, rough-looking man had been seen talking to Michael Taun on several occasions. This man had apparently spent five years in prison in Bali for piracy, extortion and kidnapping. He had been released from prison only six months before. Datu Raden Nuna, Michael Taun's uncle, had also been seen with him a month prior to the death of Selene's aunt.

'This is alarming, indeed,' exclaimed Vincent, frowning deeply.

'Particularly as Selene has lately seen a man more or less of this description stalking her.' added Gabriel, in a concerned manner.

'What do you intend to do?' asked Vincent.

'I would be grateful if you and Beatrice could take her with you to Mataram, until the day of our wedding.'

'We'll be delighted to take her with us. You know how fond we've become of her. Anyway, we're due back in town tomorrow.' replied Vincent, his face brightening.

'Thank you Vincent. That's a load off my mind. I want to stay here for a while, to see what else David can uncover.' sighed Gabriel, highly relieved.

Having given Mei-Lin and her family the day off to partake of the *Nyale* festival celebrations, Selene and her guests ate a light lunch, after which they headed for the beach. There were crowds of people everywhere enjoying the performances of several artists.

Walking along the beach, they came across a folk war dance called *presian dance*, where two young men, standing on a wide square of red cloth were duelling with rattan sticks and shields made out of cow leather. A group of traditional musicians provided the musical background.

Farther along, they watched the *rudat*, a folk dance from West Nusa Tenggara, influenced by the Islam religion. The dance was accompanied by four people playing the *kendang* (double ended drum beaten by hand), with a singer providing rhythmic religious chants.

It was while they were intent in watching this performance that they were approached by Michael Taun and Dewi Rinjani. Noticing Gabriel's arm circling Selene's waist, Michael Taun said, with a sardonic air, 'Hello Selene. What's this? Yet another fiancé? What's happened to Patrick?'

Bristling with anger, Gabriel replied, 'No, Michael Taun. I'm Selene's fiancé. There was a misunderstanding with the Jakarta Post. Patrick's going to be best man at our wedding in a few days' time. Not that it's anything to do with you.'

'Congratulations, I'm sure. She'll make a lovely bride. So finally you'll put your dirty paws on our land.' sneered Michael Taun.

Gabriel was going to hit him, when Selene intervened, 'No, Michael Taun. I have rescinded all claims of ownership of *Inggris*, so put your heart at rest on that score.'

Michael Taun's face contorted with hatred. 'What do you mean you've renounced possession of *Inggris?*'

'The property has now become a co-operative run by a very capable businessman born in Lombok and by Vincent.' reiterated Selene, challenging him with her eyes.

'I don't believe it.' barked Michael Taun.

'Neither do I,' echoed Dewi Rinjani, her cheeks turning a bright red.

'But it's true,' butted in Vincent, 'I was at the notary's with them and signed the papers.'

'You slut,' shouted Dewi Rinjani, throwing herself at Selene and trying to claw her face with her long, sharp, crimson nails. But Gabriel was quicker and grabbed her wrists in a vice-like hold.

'Stay away from her. Both of you.' growled Gabriel in a deep angry voice, 'If you ever go near her again. If you dare touch her or speak ill of her you'll have me to deal with. Furthermore, I'm going to tell your father about your disgraceful behaviour. I believe he'll be at the celebrations tonight. Now go away. Leave us alone.'

'You haven't heard the last of us yet, Mr Hart. You'll live to regret it.' were Michael Taun's parting words.

The cold threat contained in Michael Taun's words had chilled Selene. She looked at Gabriel with anguished eyes and he, putting a protective arm around her, whispered, 'Don't worry, darling. There's nothing either of them can do to you. I've already discussed it with Vincent and you'll be leaving for Mataram with him and Beatrice tomorrow.'

'What about you?' she murmured, huskily.

'I'll stay on for a few more days. I want to keep in touch with David.' He told her, reassuringly, 'but I'll come to Mataram in two days' time. Don't worry. I'll speak to Sir Edward. He'll take care of Michael Taun and Dewi Rinjani.'

This encounter spoilt the pleasure Selene had felt, therefore she asked Gabriel if he would take her back to the house. She excused herself with the others and urged them to stay on and watch the performances.

Walking hand in hand with Gabriel, she reached the house. She still looked shaken and Gabriel made her a cup of sweet tea, then brought it to her in the sitting room, where she was curled up on one of the sofas, her feet hidden under her folded legs. Selene looked so ethereal, so helpless that Gabriel sat next to her, pulling her close to him. She looked at him with dreamy, slumberous eyes, her veins filled with the fire he kindled in her. Selene put her arms round his neck and her lips parted of their own volition, allowing him to probe every moistened part of her mouth with his tongue. Her head was spinning, her breath was laboured under the passion he was unleashing and she moaned her pleasure, heightening his response. He had started a slow, sensuous exploration of her body and she was beginning to melt in his arms when, suddenly, the telephone rang and rang. Gabriel swore under his breath, and Selene slowly surfaced from the sensual rapture she had experienced and looked at him from the deep jade pools of her eyes.

'Who is it?' barked Gabriel, 'Oh, hello David. What? Are you sure? Yes, yes, of course. No, nothing. Don't worry. Thank you.' He put the receiver down and looked at Selene with a shocked expression in his eyes.

'Who was it? What's happened?' she asked, hesitantly.

'It was David. He was watching a programme on the local TV when there was a newsflash. It announced that Sir Edward and his brother-in-law Datu Raden Nuna Sasakan died in an air crash about an hour ago. They were flying to Lombok from Jakarta in a small private plane. Nobody knows yet the dynamics of the accident, but it happened twenty miles off the northern coast of Bali. The plane plunged into the Bali Sea. There are no survivors. I have to inform my father, and then phone my condolences to Dewi Mas.'

'Do Michael Taun and Dewi Rinjani know about their father and uncle?' asked Selene, also shocked by the news.

'No. But David informed me that he saw one of the servants scouring the beach looking for them.'

'Will you go and see Dewi Mas?'

'Much as I dislike her, I'll have to. After all her husband and my father were at Harrow together.' While he was telling her all this, he picked up the phone and dialled his father's number. 'It's nearly four here, so it'll be eight o'clock in the morning London time... Oh, hello father.....'

While he was talking to his father, Selene went to the kitchen and made some more tea. She made a cup of jasmine tea for herself and one of Earl Gray for Gabriel. 'How awful,' she thought. She had never met Sir Edward, but Gabriel had always spoken highly of him. He must have been a good man. Datu Raden Nuna, on the other hand, was another kettle of fish. Still, she would not wish death on her worst enemy, she mused. 'I wonder what will become of them now?' she said to herself. Sir Edward, as far as she understood, had been at the helm of the family, trying to keep Michael Taun and Datu Raden Nuna out of mischief, but now, with no one to watch over him, what will become of Michael Taun? And what about Dewi Rinjani? Whatever happened, Selene was glad she was leaving *Inggris* and would soon be back in England. She was so engrossed in her thoughts that Beatrice's voice made her jump.

'Hello Selene. Are you feeling better, dear?'

'Much better thank you. But we've just had some shocking news.' And Selene related what had happened to the older woman who was also horrified. Beatrice told her that she had met Sir Edward on several occasions and had liked his fair play and uprightness. Vincent, Patrick, and Jessica soon returned from the beach, and this item of news had to be disclosed to them as well.

It was agreed that Vincent, Beatrice, and Gabriel would go and pay their respects to the widow and children of the man they had known and respected. Selene would write a note conveying some words of comfort in their bereavement, while Patrick and Jessica would either stay at home with her or go back to the festival, seeing that they had no links at all with the Fairchild family.

Patrick and Jessica declared they would stay with Selene, but she did not want to spoil her friends' holiday and urged them to go and observe the celebrations, which, later, they could describe to her. She still had not recovered from the encounter she had had with Michael Taun and Dewi Rinjani and thought that after dinner, when the others had gone, she would go upstairs to her room, read a little, pack her bags, then have an early night.

She had started her packing when she felt a desire to look at the view once more. Selene opened the French windows and stepped onto the balcony. It was a beautiful night. A light sea breeze caressed her cheeks, tantalising her nostrils with the fragrance of jasmine, cinnamon, and vanilla, which mixed with the scent of orchids, frangipani and magnolia from the garden. Selene passed her tongue over her lips and tasted the saltiness of the briny sea. Distant chants and music reminded her of the festivities taking place on the beach. In the sky above her, a huge tropical moon was illumining the Japanese garden, its silver rays tracing a path to the paddocks, the beach and on the shimmering waves. The noise coming from the beach contrasted with the peace that shrouded Selene like a mantel.

Selene had removed her necklace, ring and earrings, but had not changed for the night yet. All her senses were filled with the spectacle around her. 'Will I ever experience something so perfect again?' she asked herself.

CHAPTER TWENTY-FOUR

Selene was still lost in thought when she heard the bell ring. Who could it be? Maybe Beatrice and Vincent were back already. Was it possible that Jessica and Patrick had decided to return so early? The doorbell chimed again. Mei-Lin was out. She was alone in the house. She got up and stepped lightly downstairs. She turned the light on and went to open the door. She had barely opened it a few inches when two masked men pushed it right open. She tried to struggle, but her mouth and nose were covered by a hand holding a rag oozing with chloroform. Immediately her head started to spin and blackness engulfed her.

Darkness. Everywhere around her was darkness. Selene tried to get up, but her feet were tied. She tried to scream, but only a muffled sound came out of her mouth, covered by a rough thick cloth, tied at the back of her head. Her arms were twisted behind her back, her hands bound with rope. She had a foul taste in her mouth and her head throbbed. An overpowering stench of fish assailed her nostrils and she felt like retching. It was the nightmare again. The latest one, the one with the maniacal laughter.

Slowly, memory returned. This was no nightmare. She had been chloroformed and kidnapped by two tall masked men. Panic pervaded every fibre of her body. Where had they taken her and why? Who were they? Did the man she had noticed following her, stalking her, the one who had been watching her through binoculars have anything to do with this? Were they going to kill her?... No. If they'd wanted to kill her they would have done it immediately, not taken the trouble to sedate her and move her here, wherever "here" was. 'Stay calm. Think!' She urged herself.

The first thing she had to do was to familiarise herself with her surroundings. Little by little, as her eyes became accustomed to the darkness, she could see a strange shape about two feet away from her. Selene peered at it more carefully. It was a very unusual shape. It seemed to stem from the floor and rise up towards the ceiling, which appeared to be a long way away. The object was rather knobbly. From her foetal position, it was a bit difficult to calculate its height. What could it be? Then, a glimmer of faint light penetrated the darkness and she understood. She was in a cave and what she had been staring at was a stalagmite! Now she realised why the floor had felt so hard and uneven under the coarse jute sack on which she was lying.

It felt damp and cool in the cave, the air around her carried the briny smell of the sea. Where was she? They must have taken her to some secluded place, somewhere where nobody came. There were so many caves on the island. Would she ever be found?

She couldn't let her emotions have the better of her. She fought bravely against them. It was no good panicking. She had to keep a cool head if she wanted to survive this ordeal. After all, she had a lot going for her.

Her captors wouldn't harm her. She had very good, powerful friends in Vincent and Beatrice. And she had Gabriel. Gabriel! At the thought of him, her heart nearly gave way. She had been so happy. Only yesterday, before that unwelcome phone call, she had been closer to paradise than ever before in her life. They were due to get married in less than two weeks' time. Will they ever get married now? David!

Of course. Gabriel would ask David to find out what had happened to her. She didn't trust the police in Kuta Beach, after what she had heard from Dewi Rinjani's and Michael Taun's lips, but David was a force to be reckoned with. Gabriel had already asked him to check on the rough looking man and she was sure that he was one of the two bandits who had kidnapped her.

But why would they kidnap her? Money! She kept on forgetting that now she was a multi-millionaire. Gabriel had told her that he had seen the man talking to Michael Taun. But Michael Taun had just lost his father. Besides, was it really possible that someone who had appeared so carefree, so charming, would resort to such degrading criminal methods to achieve wealth? Then she remembered the words he and his sister had uttered at the beach, the previous night. The implied threat, the evil look Dewi Rinjani had sent her way, the inhuman iciness in Michael Taun's menacing tones.

They must have been planning this for a while, too. After their uncle's failure to secure a marriage between himself and her aunt, it had been Michael Taun's turn.

The casual encounter on the beach must have been carefully staged. Their excursion to Singgigi. He must have thought he had made headway there. He had been so cock-sure of himself, when discussing his prospects with his sister.

His mother's invitation to her to go to the garden party. It had all been carefully thought out. Then, when Michael Taun had seen his scheming thwarted, when he had read the announcement of her engagement to Patrick, he must have realised that their Machiavellian plan was in jeopardy and had resorted to taking drastic measures. She still remembered how angry the two of them had been when she had told them that she was no longer the prospective owner of *Inggris.* And Gabriel's news that they were to marry soon, had been the catalyst that had led to her abduction. Although, she recollected, the rough man had been following her for some days before yesterday.

Yesterday? How could she be sure it was only the night before that she had been kidnapped? ... Her clothes. They did not seem very dirty, only creased.

She was getting somewhere now. She had been kidnapped the previous night and taken to a cave. Gabriel and her friends might not be aware of her disappearance yet, because she had told them she was going to have an early night.

She had been due to leave with Beatrice and Vincent this morning after breakfast, therefore they would discover she was no longer at *Inggris* in an hour or so. Once they had realised that she had been taken, they would call Gabriel and he, in turn, would ask David to find her. Besides, Michael Taun must have instructed the bandits who had kidnapped her to get in touch with Gabriel promptly, and ask for a huge ransom.

While she was mulling over all this, Selene tried to move. It was extremely difficult. Her arms and legs ached because of the position she had been in all night. Her neck and shoulders were stiff. But she was twenty-four years old and a fighter.

Using her right shoulder as a lever, she rolled onto her bottom. She pushed her torso forward and she reached a sitting position. That was much better. The coarse jute sack no longer rubbed against her cheek. She leaned backwards and came into contact with the hard rock, which constituted the walls of the cave. She was now sitting upright and what she saw filled her with wonder. In front of her there was a small entrance from which some rough steps had been hewn out of the rock. They were leading to the sea, barely visible below. The sun was rising, and its rays illumined some of the objects within the cave. There were some boxes to her left, with fishing nets strewn over them. The cave wall to her right was in darkness, but she could hear water trickling down, probably through a fissure in the rock above. She couldn't tell what path the little rivulet took, but it probably ended in the small lake that had formed near the centre of the huge cave, with a couple of stalagmites in the middle.

Selene felt very thirsty. Her tongue was sticking to her palate. She had to do something or she was sure she would die of thirst. She was contemplating how she could quench her thirst, when one of her abductors climbed up the steps and approached the spot where she was sitting. He was carrying an oil lamp in his left hand, and was holding a jute sack in his right. At the light of the oil lamp, Selene could see that the sack was bulging out. The man stood there for a moment, looking at her.

Selene was very uncomfortable under his gaze. Why was he looking at her that way? Was he going to kill her? All the fears that had assailed her when she had first realised she had been abducted coursed through her body once again, and she could not hide her trembling limbs from her captor.

He walked up to her, bent slightly towards the pile of boxes that Selene had made out of the darkness earlier on. He removed the fishing nets, made the boxes more stable, and then placed the oil lamp on top. He picked up a pitcher, which was standing near what she now realised was a boulder, took off the cover that had hidden it from view, and poured some water into a cup made of coconut shell. Slowly, he walked up to Selene, removed the gag with a rough twist of the hand, and then helped her drink the water. Selene drank greedily, looking at him with grateful eyes.

When the cup was empty, he took a mango out of the sack he had now secured round his waist, cut the fruit into small pieces, then fed them to her. Selene felt the juicy fruit slide down her throat with pleasure. She was immediately more optimistic about managing to extricate herself from the predicament in which she found herself.

This man was no cutthroat. He just looked poor and was probably doing all this to earn money to provide for his family. She had no ill feelings against him. It was Michael Taun and Dewi Rinjani she really despised.

At this precise moment, they were probably being commiserated because of their loss, while they were still harbouring thoughts of greed and vengeance.

She closed her eyes for a second. When she opened them again the shadow of the man seemed to leap into existence at the light of the lamp and reminded her, with a sudden shiver, of her most recent nightmare. She could not help but wonder if it had been a premonition.

The man spoke roughly to her in the strange language of the island. When he realized she could not understand him, he pulled her up to her feet, loosened the rope that bound her wrists, so that she was able to bring her arms forward. He then proceeded to tie up her wrists again, and then loosened the rope round her ankles. Once she was able to move, he signalled to her to go round a boulder where she would have some privacy. Selene massaged her ankles, stretched as much as she was able, feeling pain and relief as part of her circulation started back. She half-walked, half-hopped until she found a dark, secluded spot where she was able to satisfy her body's needs. After that, she looked around her and found a small pool of water where, the bonds round her arms and hands allowing her, she knelt down and washed her face. After a few minutes, her jailer came round the boulder, grabbed her wrists, and pulled her back to where the jute sack lay. He tightened the rope round her wrists and ankles once more, making sure that she could not free herself. He then gagged her, and then pushed her down in a supine position. He picked up the oil lamp, which he extinguished and placed onto the floor of the cave, near the steps leading down to the beach, and left.

Some more light now filtered into the cave and Selene looked around to see if she could find a way to free herself and escape. The sound of the waves pounding onto the shore reverberated through the cave. The briny saltiness of the sea played on her lips, the smell of algae reaching her quivering nostrils. She could hear the continuous 'drip' of the water, filtering through the roof of the cave then falling all the way down onto the rough, uneven floor. It acted as a constant reminder of the dripping tap she had left behind in her flat in England.

Selene closed her eyes and remembered how easy it had always been for the characters of her favourite action films to extricate themselves from this type of situation. How far those long, lonely evenings she had spent on her own, watching the TV, after her mother's death, appeared to her now!

She recalled moments of her life as a happy child, then as a lonely teenager, because her grandmother had made her lead a sheltered life. She understood now why she had isolated her from boys and girls of her own age, trying to protect her from making the same mistake she and Selene's mother had made. But at the same time, her grandmother had prevented Selene from living her own experiences, whether good or bad.

Selene remembered how lonely, forlorn, and lost she had felt. How children had mocked her at school, because she did not join in their games. She was never invited to parties, and nobody chose her when the teachers asked the pupils to work in pairs.

This state of affairs stopped when Vanessa became her classmate. Vanessa had understood her immediately. Vanessa. Jolly, kind, extrovert Vanessa. She had always been ready to cheer her up with her laughter and good humour. Vanessa had taken her under her wing and, as she was popular for her achievements on the tennis court, the others had left Selene be. Selene, who had built an armour around herself, in order not to be hurt, had opened her heart to hope. She had finally made a friend. Someone she could confide in. Someone who helped her and her mother come to terms with their loss when Selene's grandmother had died.

Unfortunately, Vanessa had not been there when Simon had come along. She had been at university in Aberdeen. At that time, Selene's grandmother had been even more protective of her granddaughter.

That was probably why Selene had been captivated by Simon, by his freedom to be himself, as much as by his easy charm and good manners. But after the great hurt that she had experienced, she had clammed up. She had become a real introvert. Not even her work experience had managed to break through the tight control that she had on her feelings.

After Simon, the only other time her guard had slackened was when she had encountered Gabriel's mesmerising cobalt blue eyes.

Selene had finally come to terms with the fact that she had fallen in love with him the very first time that she had set eyes on him. That was why she had had such a strong reaction every time she had seen him with Dewi Rinjani. She had been jealous! Yet what changes the love that she had for him had brought to her life. Selene could not believe how quickly she had made friends with Beatrice and Vincent first, then with Patrick and Jessica. Her whole personality had changed. From a lonely introvert she had now become a caring, friendly extrovert.

This train of thought was not helping her to find a way out of the fix in which she now found herself. Was there something, anything she could do? And even if she managed to free herself where was she to run? She was probably in one of several caves around the island or even on another island. She remembered Michael Taun telling her that Lombok was one of an archipelago. All of those islands were dotted with secluded beaches and caves.

Still, Selene could not stay in this cave, passively waiting for events to happen. She needed to do something for herself. At least she had to try.

God only knew how long it would be before David and Gabriel found her, if ever. It was nerve wrecking to think of what exorbitant claims Michael Taun was going to make before he let her go. Worse still, he may try to force her to marry him, claiming that he had abducted her with her consent, following the tradition of *kawin lari*. What if Gabriel believed him?...No, she had to find a way out of here and soon.

Selene looked at the floor and at the walls of the cave. The section of the cave where she lay was fairly smooth, but about three or four meters away she could spy a rugged segment of rock jutting out of that part of the wall. She tried to wriggle, but did not make much headway. She tried to slither, but only managed to excoriate her legs and her arms. She was on the verge of tears of frustration when all of a sudden she had an idea. The floor of the cave sloped marginally downwards towards the place she wanted to reach, so she attempted to roll there.

It took time and an exhausting number of attempts, but she eventually managed to achieve her aim. Once she reached the protuberance, she tried to sit up and, pushing with her feet and her bottom, Selene reached the jugged bit of rock against which she rubbed the rope that tied her wrists.

After what seemed hours, the rope gave way and her hands were bleeding but free. She removed the rough jute cloth that covered her mouth, and then worked on the piece of rope that tied up her ankles. This proved more laborious and frustrating than she had thought, so much so that Selene had to lie on her back, place her feet on either side of the bulging rugged rock and move her legs up and down, rubbing the rope against the rough edge until eventually it snapped.

Selene felt extremely tired. Every bone in her body ached. Her skin was chaffed where the rope had cut into her flesh, and her excoriations were burning and bleeding. Yet the thought of her captors' return galvanised her into action.

Feeling thirsty again, Selene walked up to the pitcher and drank some water. Once sated, she walked down the steps towards the entrance of the cave.

When she reached it, she carefully peered outside. What she saw filled her with dismay. It was high tide and the sea reached almost up to the entrance of the cave. It was a rough, billowing sea, which precluded any attempt of her leaving the cave from that side. Was there another exit somewhere else? Selene climbed back up the steps and stopped to think.

One positive outcome was that the rough sea, while proving an obstacle to her escape, meant that the men who had kidnapped her could not reach the cave too soon. This would give her time to explore the cave, to see whether she could find another way out. Before she started on her exploration, though, she needed a light.

There was the oil lamp that the man had left, but how was she going to light it? She opened up the boxes, but all she could find were fishing utensils and some jute sacks.

Well, she had rope, she had the wood from the boxes and she had jute. Surely she could make a fire, or at least she could try. Unfortunately, despite having watched all those programmes on survival on TV, and putting into practice what she had learnt, nothing happened. Selene had to desist, but decided to explore the cave anyway.

As she went deeper into the bowels of the cave, the darker it became and she stumbled and fell more than once. Suddenly she felt something fluttering near her. Her heart pounding, she stopped on her tracks alarmed, wondering what it could be. Then flying creatures brushed past her from all sides and she realised that she had disturbed a colony of bats that lived there.

Shaken in body, yet still determined to find a way out, she carefully treaded her steps, keeping close to the walls of the cave. As she proceeded, she felt colder and colder. The walls and floor of the cave became slippery and more treacherous. She could not see what lay ahead or behind her. She felt helpless, without any kind of control on her surroundings, and she realised how awful it must be to be completely blind for life.

For what seemed ages, she advanced slowly and precariously into the recesses of the cave. As she stumbled forward, she could not help thinking that she was probably walking towards her death, either by falling, or by breaking a limb, or by starving to death. She had almost resigned herself to a bleak outcome to this adventure, when she felt a draught coming from her left. She turned towards it and after a couple of hours, she saw a faint light and started to make out the floor of the cave immediately ahead. Little by little, everything became clearer as a shaft of light beamed down from the roof of the cave. The walls felt drier under her palms, the closer she came to the aperture up above.

Fortunately the walls of the cave leading upwards were rather close, with spikes of rock jutting out here and there, enough for her to find purchase for her hands and feet. Slowly and painfully Selene climbed up, her progress made uncertain and more dangerous by the rain that had started to fall copiously from the angry sky. She had to stop several times to rest and to stem the flow of blood that poured from her head, which she had bumped against a rock during her ascent.

Selene's determination paid off. She reached the top just as the rain had stopped. She climbed outside and threw herself on to the wet, mossy grass, panting with fatigue, her hair covering her face and pricking her eyes. She felt as if she had climbed Mount Everest and so exhausted was she that she would have lain there and fallen asleep had not the fear of being found by her kidnappers given her a surge of adrenalin.

She dragged herself up and looked around. All she could see were miles and miles of rainforest. Her heart sank, but the feeling only lasted a second. She was free. She would find a way to return to those who loved her. Her last thought before she set off was for Gabriel.

CHAPTER TWENTY-FIVE

Selene took her first hesitant steps towards the luscious greenery of the rainforest. There was no path she could follow, so she had to tread her way through a tangle of trees, bushes, hanging roots and leaves. She was particularly careful not to step on some snakes that she was sure had their home in the rich undergrowth

It was very hot and humid and she discovered, to her horror that leeches were sticking to her legs sucking the blood that oozed out of the already painful scratches and grazes, which she had procured herself in the cave. Selene desperately tried to pull them off, tears streaming down her face. She tore some wide leaves from the trees and grabbed at the leeches, pulling hard. But for every leech she managed to remove from her legs, more took its place.

Seized by an uncontrollable panic Selene started to run, stumbling against the giant roots of the trees, or stabbing her toes against some stone or the fallen branch of a tree. Eventually she lost her balance and tumbled down a slope, her already battered body throbbed and weakened as more bruises and excoriations were added in her fall. There seemed to be no end to her bumpy descent, when all of a sudden Selene hit her head against a large, flat stone and lost consciousness.

CHAPTER TWENTY SIX

When Selene came to the first time, she ached all over. Her legs were on fire, her teeth were chattering, her whole body was hot yet wrecked by uncontrollable shivers. She tried to open her eyes, but the light made them hurt so much that she closed them right away. She felt a light hand put a damp cloth over her forehead, and then someone held the back of her head and helped her to drink some water.

She must have fainted again because when she regained consciousness the second time it was pitch dark. She was still shivering and felt extremely weak and tired. She went through a period of fitful slumber, interrupted by brief periods of consciousness in which she heard voices speaking in a strange tongue and, on a couple of occasions, she thought she heard a baby cry.

The next time she struggled back to reality, someone was again placing a wet cloth over her forehead. She opened her eyes and she saw a young woman bending over her. When the young woman saw that she was awake, she smiled at Selene, and uttered some words in her native tongue. Selene tried to say something but it came out as a weak grunt. The young woman went to fetch some vegetable soup, which she spoon-fed to her. The soup revived Selene a little and she smiled back at the woman.

A long time went by before Selene felt less weak. As soon as she was up to it, Selene looked about her. She must be in a fisherman's hut. It was a typical bamboo hut, with a thatched roof made of reeds. She was lying on a bamboo bed, which was surprisingly comfortable despite it not having any padding at all. Some fishing nets hung from the ceiling, while part of the walls was covered with pretty, colourful mats. Light was filtering through a small square opening in one of the walls, next to the door of the hut.

Through this opening, coming from outside, Selene heard the

sweet sound of birds, twittering a merry tune. She could hear the waves crushing onto the shore and the scent of tamarind and vanilla in the air.

She looked at the young woman and asked in a croaky voice she barely recognized as her own, 'How long?' But the young woman shook her head. 'How many days?'

Selene tried again, pointing to the sun, then mimicking sleep and the sun again. This time the girl showed her her open hands four times. Then she showed Selene three more fingers. Selene was shocked. She had been in and out of consciousness for twenty-three days!

Selene tried to lift her head, but it started to spin, and she felt as if all semblance of strength had deserted her. Even lifting a finger to ask for a drink seemed too much of an effort. The young woman understood, though, and brought her some water, which she helped her to drink. Selene swallowed a couple of draughts, and then fell back onto the bed.

Twenty-three days! She had been away from Gabriel and her friends for an incredible length of time. Now that she had run away from her gaolers and had been saved and brought here, would David be able to find her? The young woman or her husband must have found her where she had fallen and must have carried her to this hut. Maybe someone had seen them doing it. Maybe her kidnappers already knew where she was and were waiting to pounce on her again. This train of thought was rather alarming and only made her feel more tired...So tired that she fell into a deep, restorative sleep.

The next time Selene woke up, she felt hungry. She looked around and saw the young woman at the loom, weaving. She was sitting with her back straight and her legs under the loom. She had a baby in a *kain* (cloth). The woman wore the *kain* like a sling, tied over her right shoulder. On her back, inside the *kain*, Selene could see the baby sleeping quite happily. He was not at all troubled by the fast forward and backward movements his mother made while pressing her feet against the forward brace of the loom to increase the tension.

Selene looked on, fascinated. After a while, the young woman looked up and, noticing that Selene was awake, she smiled. She got up from the loom, scooped up some rice from a pot, and placed it into a bowl. The woman then walked up to where Selene lay, helped her to sit up, sat down beside her and aided her to eat. It was plain boiled rice, but Selene thought she had never tasted anything so good in her life. After a few mouthfuls, though, her stomach felt full and she refused the remainder with a smile.

Restored by the meal, Selene did not lie down again, but looked at herself. The first thing she noticed was that she was wearing different clothes from her own. She had on a white cotton blouse over an orange *kamben* (a 2.5 metre sheet of batik). She felt clean and comfortable and she knew she owed it to the young woman, who was now squatting on a mat on the ground, and was breastfeeding her baby, whom she had moved to the front of the *kain*. The baby was suckling contentedly and his mother looked at him with such tenderness that Selene felt a lump in her throat. How simple this woman's life was! Yet how fulfilled she looked. When he had had enough, the baby fell asleep again and the young woman took up her position at the loom once more.

It was pleasant in this bamboo hut with the reed-thatched roof. The waves were lapping under it and Selene realised, to her surprise that the hut was standing on stilts. It was what the locals called a *bugis.* She remembered reading in one of her aunt's books that the raised floor served to allow the breeze to lower the hot tropical temperatures. It elevated the dwelling above the collection of storm water and mud. This kept people, goods and food free from dampness and moisture.

In fact, now that she was recovering, after her harrowing sojourn in the cave, she discovered that she was enjoying her permanence in the hut.

After a while, the baby woke up and the mother bathed and changed him, then placed him back into the *kain*. She started singing a mantra and the baby listened, his eyes looking at the specks of dust dancing in the sunrays, his head resting on his mother's heart.

The sun was setting when the woman got busy preparing the evening meal. It was initially shocking for Selene to see how the woman picked up a fish and just chopped up every bit of it into bite-size pieces before throwing it into the *tom yam soup* - eyes, mouth, tail, and bones included. Seaweeds were added to the soup and although Selene was not sure about the ingredients, the mixture somehow did smell good and she understood that it must make a very nourishing meal.

Once dinner was ready, the young woman fed and changed her son again. She then helped Selene wash.

The young woman helped Selene up, and walked her slowly to a curtain on the far side of the hut. Behind the curtain, there was a large water jar made of fired clay. Once Selene was under it, the woman first rubbed Selene with soap, and then she pulled a wooden plug out of an opening near the bottom of the jar. Water squirted out and washed the soap away, down a hole in the floor of the hut.

Once the ablutions were over, the woman helped Selene back to the bed, and combed her hair.

When the woman was satisfied that Selene was comfortable, she went behind the curtain to wash and tidy herself.

Soon after, two men and a youth entered the hut. It was obvious that they were related. The older men must be brothers, as they had the same nose and eyes. The youth was probably the son of the elder of the two men, as he had the same mouth and chin as his father.

The younger of the two brothers kissed the woman and picked up the child out of the *kain* with pride. Selene assumed that he was the woman's husband and the baby's father. After having spoken to the woman for some minutes and after having looked in Selene's direction, the men sat and had dinner. They ate and talked. Now and then, they looked in her direction and after a while, their talk turned into what sounded like a heated discussion. The woman's husband appeared to be angry at something the other man was telling him, while the young man ate and looked at the baby, who had started to cry. After a short while, the older man got up and left the hut in a huff.

The family seemed to have found back their equanimity and even the baby, who had started crying at all the noise generated by the raised voices, calmed down and resumed his playful examination of a wooden rattle the young man had given him.

After dinner, the woman's husband and his nephew went out.

Washing up was an easy task, as the men had eaten out of the same bowl and plate with their hands. The woman poured some water from a container into a basin, washed the plate, bowl and glasses, and then, after having fed Selene, sat down and had her dinner.

Her repast over, the woman swept the floor of the hut. She took the baby from her back and laid him down on a bamboo bed to sleep. The men soon returned and Selene pretended to be asleep. They extinguished the flame of the oil lamp, and retired for the night.

When she was sure that everyone was sleeping, Selene tried to rise from her bamboo bed. Her head started to spin and she realised that she was still too weak to attempt to leave the hut, therefore she sensibly lay down again and closed her eyes. She had to make a plan. She had to find out how long the men were out each day in order to establish a pattern. She also needed water and something to eat to take with her. She had no idea where her kidnappers had taken her or how far away she was from *Inggris*. All she knew was that she had to go before her captors traced her to this hut.

Selene had come to the conclusion that enquiries had been

made and that the older man was keen to give her away for money. The young woman's husband had shown himself to be averse to the idea. Selene had gathered this by the way the two men had argued. She thought that, in a few days, when she was strong enough, she would make her escape. Maybe she could persuade the woman to help her. After all, she seemed such a nice, gentle creature. Meanwhile her aim was to regain her strength as soon as possible. Exhausted by all this planning, she let sleep claim her.

The following morning, after the men had left, the woman helped Selene to wash, then handed her a *kamben* and a white cotton top with sleeves down to her elbow, which smelt clean and freshly laundered. Slowly and a little shaky on her legs, Selene took off the clothes she had slept in, and wrapped the sky blue-coloured *kamben* with pink and yellow flowers round her waist. She then wore the white cotton shirt and, using the last bit of strength that she had left, pulled up her long, flame-coloured hair into a knot. The effort it took brought back a bout of dizziness and she had to sit back on her bamboo bed.

She caught her breath back, then, pointing a finger towards her breast said, 'Selene.' She pointed that same finger at the woman who answered, 'Meme (mother).' Selene felt pleased with herself for having established a link, even if the young woman, following Lombok's tradition, had not disclosed her name. Maybe the following day or even that same day, she could ask Meme to help her to contact Gabriel.

As Selene felt strong enough to remain in a sitting position, Meme brought her a breakfast of day-old sticky rice wrapped in a banana leaf and some snake soup, observing her with a satisfied look, while her guest ate and drank by herself.

Selene had to make a great effort to swallow the snake soup. She managed to drink it all by thinking that that soup was what made up the diet of most poor people in that part of the world. She also told herself that she had to build up her strength if she wanted to go back to her friends and to the world that she knew and only now started to appreciate.

While she was completing her breakfast, the baby started to cry and Meme left her side to attend to his needs. Meme was a good, attentive mother and Selene started daydreaming about having a baby boy who would have Gabriel's incredible cobalt blue eyes.

The baby having been fed, Selene signalled to Meme that she would look after him while the woman carried out her everyday chores. Uncertain, at first, Meme made sure that Selene followed Lombok's tradition, which dictated that a baby's feet should not touch the ground until he was at least 210 days old.

Meme nodded when she saw how gently Selene lifted up her baby out of the *kain,* how the baby laughed when she tickled his tummy and how mesmerised he looked while tugging at Selene's stray wisps of red hair.

When the men came back, they were astounded to see Selene taking care of the baby and some words were exchanged between husband and wife. The men had brought back chicken feet and liver, which would serve to prepare *tum yum chicken* and rice for the evening meal. Meme seemed to have won the battle over having Selene as baby-sitter and soon after lunch, the men left again.

The rest of the day was spent with Meme carrying on with her daily tasks and by Selene keeping the baby occupied and amused.

Before the men returned, Selene used a very basic type of sign language to ask Meme what was the name of the baby. Meme, however, kept on shaking her head, unhappily. Oddly, it seemed that Meme did not want to disclose her boy's name to Selene.

After wondering if she had done something wrong, Selene finally remembered reading that, on the islands of Lombok and Bali, a child had to be a certain age before he was given a name.

'Never mind', Selene told herself. 'Even if Meme will never tell me what name she's chosen for her baby, or even her own name, she seems to like and trust me.'

Selene felt more positive and thought that, in a few more days, she might be able to secure Meme's help.

CHAPTER TWENTY-SEVEN

The following day started under good auspices. Meme was the first to get up, as usual, as, according to custom, rice had to be cooked in the kitchen by sunrise. She had to put tiny pinches of the newly cooked food on small folded coconut leaf trays (*banten jotan*), and place them in front of the various house shrines as offerings. After that, she had to sweep the dirt of the previous day from the compound, using a bundle of coconut leaf spines as a broom.

Everybody had to cleanse themselves by rubbing their body with soap, then wash it off using the water from the jar. Selene waited until the men had washed and breakfasted and, once they had left the hut, she, too, washed and dressed, then ate her breakfast and felt well enough to help Meme with some of the light chores.

Meme was happy to see her looking stronger. Selene's body was mending. Her legs had lost the temporary scarring produced by the leeches, the scratches and grazes that she had acquired during her escape from the cave had almost all disappeared, and the colour of her bruises was becoming fainter by the day. Selene planned to leave the following day, so she decided to take a look outside the hut, but she could not see any other hut or building nearby.

After having completed most of the chores, Selene seized the moment when Meme was working at the loom. The red-haired girl pointed her index finger towards the interior of the island, and then asked Meme, 'Lombok?' Meme shook her head and pointed towards the sea, to the southwest.

Selene's enquiries came to an abrupt end as, at that moment, the door was pushed open and the older man walked in. When he saw Selene standing next to Meme in a companionable attitude, he seized her arm and when Meme tried to help her, the man pushed her away, shouting what sounded like abusive words in Sasak. He then proceeded to manhandle Selene. His hand was like a vice round Selene's wrist. She tried to wriggle away from his powerful hold and to kick him in the shins, but he threw her onto the floor, gagged her and bound her wrists and ankles. He then picked her up and carried her in a kind of fireman's hold to a boat that was waiting on the shore.

Selene's heart was pounding with fear and frustration. She had been right to mistrust this man. After the argument with his brother, he must have made plans on the sly. That was why he had come to the hut at such an unusual time. Selene wondered whether he had borrowed the catamaran he was carrying her to. Where was he going to take her now? The man pushed the boat into the sea and jumped onto it. He concentrated on piloting the boat out of the reef, and then turned westwards.

'He's taking me to Lombok.' thought Selene, hope filling her heart. 'If he takes me there, David will surely find me.' She relaxed and almost enjoyed her sea trip. As they headed for the open sea, Selene was able to notice how small was the island where Meme lived. No tourists visited it for sure. The island was probably inhabited by a scanty community of fishermen. It was the ideal spot where to hide someone.

The crossing took longer than Selene had expected. They passed a group of islands, maybe the small archipelago near Sumbawa Island Beatrice had told her about. At some point during the day, the man directed the boat towards a deserted beach, where he ate and gave her some rice cakes and water. He did not loosen the rope around her wrists, though, but simply held the rice cakes close to her mouth, so that she could bite off some morsels.

After they had eaten, he tied a long rope round her waist and pointed his finger towards some mangroves, which would give her some privacy if she needed to relieve herself. Within a short time, they went back to the boat and set off once again.

It was a pleasant enough day. The sun was shining and the sea was calm. A light breeze caressed Selene's face. She was thankful, though, that she was sheltered under the light canvas roof that covered the middle part of the catamaran, as her skin was fair and burnt easily.

Although she was glad that they were travelling to Lombok, she could not help feeling the icy fingers of unease taking hold of her. Why was the man taking her to Chilli Pepper (Lombok's indigenous name)? And more worrying still, under whose orders was he acting?

Once again, the spectacle of the setting sun was so incredibly beautiful that, for a brief moment, Selene put aside all her cares and simply enjoyed this incomparable sight.

A few moments later, in the gathering dusk, Selene could make out the silhouette of Mount Rinjani, looming towards her. Memories of the days spent with Gabriel during their expedition on the slopes of the sleeping volcano assailed her and threw her into a depressive mood.

Looking back, she thought that they had been happy days, despite the pangs of jealousy that she had suffered on at least a couple of occasions.

It was dark now. The man lit an oil lamp and signalled to someone on the shore. Selene could see a light swinging from left to right, in reply. The catamaran turned, heading for the beach. They would soon go ashore, and Selene trembled inside at the thought of what expected her there.

It took another forty minutes before they reached the shore.

Two figures ran towards them. They helped to drag the catamaran onto the sand. Selene heard the three men talking animatedly. Finally, the man who had conducted her there grunted his assent. Selene recognised the sound of the voice of one of the other two men. She might have guessed it! They were the same men who had kidnapped her from *Inggris*. She had come back full circle.

It was pitch black and Selene was unable to make out their faces, nonetheless one of the men tied a scarf over her eyes. She was carried for a short while, until they stopped and she heard the sound of a metal door being opened. Soon after, she was unceremoniously thrown onto a pile of rough jute sacks. The door closed and the engine of the vehicle came to life. Selene realised that she was probably inside a *bemo.*

The road was bumpy and Selene sent a little prayer of thanks heavenwards that she had a pile of sacks under her to protect her body from more bruising. Her mouth was dry. She had not had a drop to drink since lunchtime, many hours ago. Her stomach was rumbling, clamouring for food and she felt dizzy with hunger and fatigue. Little by little, the monotonous movement of the *bemo* rocked her to sleep.

She was standing by the swimming pool at Inggris. She could see her image reflected in the water. Creeping up on either side of her, she saw the evil grin of two burly men, their faces concealed by Leyak masks. She tried to struggle, but the men held her tight. The three of them seemed frozen in time: immobile as if posing for a photograph. The silence surrounding this living tableau was suddenly shattered by a blood-curling laughter. Then, to her horror, a goggled-eyed face without a body sprang towards her. Selene looked on, mesmerised. Little by little, she saw maggots wriggling out of the empty sockets. Rangda's white fangs had turned black and from her mouth there exhaled a yellow cloud, a cloud stinking of rotten eggs. Then the cloud enveloped her and she started to fall into the pool. It was a fall in slow motion. Slowly the transparent waters of the swimming pool turned into a brownish babbling mess and she was falling right into it. Her eyes were stinging, her nose and mouth filled with the sulphurous gas. She began to choke. She tried to scream, her screaming bringing her back to wakefulness.

All shaken up by the hideous nightmare Selene was trembling from head to foot. Would these waking and sleeping nightmares ever end? She was at the end of her tether and was impatient to reach the destination of this endless journey, in order to know what fate awaited her. The movement of the vehicle, though, seemed to mock her wishes and Selene could only try to pull herself together and await her future with determination.

After a very long time the *bemo* stopped. The front doors of the vehicle were opened. The next thing that happened was the sound of someone talking in a soft voice, which barely reached her ears. This mumbling and whispering went on for some time, then, the side door of the *bemo* was slid back and rough, cruel hands grabbed her under her armpits, dragging her out. Someone else got into the act and took hold of her feet. Together the men smuggled her down some steps and through a door. She was carried across what she guessed was a wide room, and then she was dropped like a sack of potatoes onto a bed.

It was a western-style type of bed, with a mattress and soft pillows. This time, they tied her hands and legs to the metal frame of the bed, so that she was lying in a most uncomfortable and vulnerable position. She heard the men's walking noisily out of the room and the sound of a heavy door being pulled shut, and then locked.

'Well, here I am again. I am not in a cave this time, but I'm probably in a worse predicament than I was before. I certainly cannot escape now. Not without help. But who will help me?' No, there was nothing she could do except wait and hope.

Hours went by. Hours in which Selene felt her thirst and hunger increase. Were they going to starve her to death? No, of course not. She calmed herself down thinking of all the planning involved in bringing her to this place.

Eventually Selene heard a key turn into the lock. Someone came in, walked up to where she lay and sat on the bed.

A familiar voice said sardonically, 'Well, Well, Well ... My dear Selene, my bride to be. Here we are, together at last.'

CHAPTER TWENTY-EIGHT

So, it had been Michael Taun all along, just as she had suspected. 'Oh Gabriel, Gabriel. Please come and rescue me.'

'Well, what do you say, my sweet?' continued Michael Taun, in the same tone of voice, which made a mockery of his words of endearment, 'Shall we be married without you making a fuss, or do I need to use more persuasive methods? Will you make me a happy man and give back to my family the land of their ancestors, together with a bit of cash to cover all the expenses I have incurred so far?'

All Selene could do was making muffled sounds. 'Of course, dearest. You cannot answer me with that gag over your mouth. Wait a minute. As a matter of fact, you don't need to be gagged at all. Even if you shout at the top of your voice, nobody will hear you. Anyway, there are other methods to keep you quiet.'

Selene remembered the chloroform that had been used by Michael Taun's associates when she was kidnapped for the first time, and shivered. Meanwhile, Michael Taun was trying to remove the gag, but he was clumsy and the knots were tight, so that it took him longer than he had expected. This annoyed him, and he was rougher than the task required. After removing the gag, Michael Taun undid the scarf round her eyes and Selene was finally able to see the room where she was kept a prisoner.

The first thing she noticed was that there were no windows. By the soft light of the lampshades, shaped like two naked girls with enormous bosoms, she could see that it was a gaudy room, with red walls and a matching carpet. There was a huge mirror on the ceiling, just above the bed. On the walls, there hung explicit pictures from the Kamasutra. Next to the wall opposite the bed, there stood a dressing table completely strewn with body lotions, perfume bottles, false eyelashes, bottles of scarlet nail varnish and other telltale objects, which immediately made Selene realise that she was in a house of ill repute. The bed where she lay had silk red sheets, covered by a black brocade throw with the ugly face of a huge golden demon in the middle . She also noticed that the walls were soundproof. No wonder Michael Taun was not at all concerned whether she screamed or not.

'Well, Michael Taun,' Selene replied with a firmness she was far from feeling, 'I'm honoured to be chosen as your bride, but as I have already told you and your sister, I no longer have any claims on *Inggris*, therefore you have put me through all this for nothing.'

'Oh I know. You made that quite clear when we last met and I've had time to check that what you said is true. But...,' Michael Taun continued in a cunning voice she had never heard him use before, 'what is done can be undone. I know how persuasive Gabriel can be when something... or someone matters to him.'

'But what can he do? I signed the papers just before you had me abducted from *Inggris*. There is nothing Gabriel can do now. The terms I signed state as much. You won't gain anything by marrying me.' concluded Selene in a calm, even voice.

'You bitch! It'd better not be true, because if it is I'll kill you with my own hands. Or better still,' he added in a cold, cruel voice, 'I may have some uses for you in this establishment.' And with these parting words he left, slamming the door behind him.

Selene heard the key turn in the lock and let the tears that she had managed to hold back when Michael Taun was present, fall copiously down her cheeks. What was she to do? Michael Taun's words had scared her more than anything he could have said. She would never ever submit to the vile future that he had planned for her. She would rather die.

More time went by and Selene felt she really needed a drink of water. She was totally dehydrated. Her throat was beginning to hurt and her lips to crack. Her wait came finally to an end when the door opened and an ugly looking man entered bearing a tray.

There was a bottle of water, a glass and some rice cakes on the tray. He hesitantly walked up to the bed and laid the tray on a small table at the foot of it. He had some shifty, darting eyes with a lascivious look about him, which bore trouble for Selene. He was just about to put a hand on her knee when Dewi Rinjani appeared.

She looked at the man and started shrieking and shouting in Sasak. The man, who had had his back to the door jumped out of his skin. His face turned white, then green. Dewi Rinjani must have been telling him what she thought of him and was obviously shouting threats in a most impressive way, as he span around and hurried out of the room as fast as his short bandy legs would carry him. Selene, very much relieved, thought that for the first time in all her dealings with Dewi Rinjani, she was very glad to see her. A gladness she had never thought she would associate with the sight of the girl.

'Are you ready to become my sister-in-law?' Dewi Rinjani asked her, enjoying the disgust and contempt she could read on Selene's face at being thus addressed. 'It won't be long now. At last my mother's dearest wish will come true. She'll get that part of her heritage back, and I'll be free to become Gabriel's wife.' Dewi Rinjani concluded, with an evil grin.

Selene could not hide her distress, so much so that her rival was unable to contain her delight on seeing the depth of suffering her words were causing. Not satisfied with what she had just said, she added with gusto, 'You thought you had got your claws into him, didn't you? Well, think again. Once you are married to my brother, Gabriel will jump at the opportunity to make me his bride. Yes, it's about time you left the way open to me. I'll marry Gabriel. I've worked too hard and too long on him to see a slut like you snatch him from under my nose. You thought you were clever, didn't you? You should never underestimate people like Michael Taun, mother or me. My family has been dealing with people like you for centuries. We belong to the oldest aristocratic family on this island and you're nothing. Less than nothing.' Dewi Rinjani was raving now, pacing the length of the room and, occasionally, throwing glances charged with malevolence towards Selene. 'The only thing that stops me from clawing your eyes out and dispose of your carcass is the fact that you will be instrumental in gaining back for us what is my family's by right. I can't wait to see the fortune you don't deserve pass into my brother's hands.' With a final smug smile on her face and a parting look full of hatred Dewi Rinjani left the room, not forgetting to lock the door behind her.

Dear God, Selene prayed, what was she to do? Michael Taun would soon discover that what she had told him was true. What would he do then? Would he really use her in the ignoble way he had told her he would, to make money? Or would he kill her as he had threatened to do? Selene was beside herself with worry. Would David and Gabriel find her in time? These cogitations were only adding more discomfort to the physical pain caused by the way that she had been tied to the bed. Selene was so overwrought that she sobbed herself to sleep.

CHAPTER TWENTY-NINE

The sound of the door being opened awoke her. This time it was an old-looking Chinese woman in a sarong with birds of paradise printed on it and a light blue blouse. She was carrying a tray with food and water. On her tail there followed a dark, robust man. The man cut the ropes that tied Selene to the bed. Selene was just uttering a strangled sigh of relief, when the man pulled her up roughly from the bed and onto her feet. The woman accompanied her to a door leading to an ensuite and locked her in. Selene could not believe her eyes. She immediately hopped into the shower and let its powerful jets gently whip her body, ridding her of the dirt and stickiness that clung to it. After having carefully washed her hair, she patted it with a towel, and then wound another dry towel around it. She wrapped herself up in the fluffy white bathrobe she found hung on a hook on the door, after which she let her gaolers know that she was ready to come out, by rapping on the door.

The old woman opened the door and entered, carrying in her arms a beautiful white and golden Sasak dress. The sight of it reminded Selene of Michael Taun's words. This was a wedding dress, which meant that today he was going to make her his bride. What could she do? There was no way she could escape. The bathroom, like the bedroom had no window.

Selene was in utter despair. The woman was forcing her to put the dress on and she could see, through the door that had been left ajar, that the dark, robust man was waiting for them in the bedroom. Filled with hopelessness Selene submitted to her fate.

Once she was dressed, the old woman pushed her into the bedroom and sat her down at the dressing table, where she proceeded first to make her face up and then to do her hair. A basket had been brought to the room while she had been in the ensuite. The basket was full of fresh flowers and the woman was weaving these flowers into her hair. When she had finished, she motioned Selene near one of the full-length mirrors that hung on the walls. What Selene saw took her breath away. If she had been made ready to marry Gabriel, she would have been over the moon at the dazzling image the mirror reflected. She looked like a wood nymph. She had lost weight during the past weeks, which had added to her litheness and fragility.

Unfortunately her eyes betrayed how utterly miserable she felt at the thought that she would be forced to marry a man she despised with all the essence of her being.

Selene was contemplating what she could do to take her own life, if it came to that, rather than become the wife of such a despicable man, when there were three knocks on the door. The man went to answer it and Dewi Rinjani and Michael Taun himself entered the room. He was absolutely furious.

First of all he dismissed the man and the old woman, then, in a rage, he threw himself on Selene, his hands round her long slender neck. He wanted to choke her to death and was squeezing the life out of her, shouting abuse while doing so, when Dewi Rinjani came to her rescue once again.

'Wait, Michael Taun. Listen to me. All is not lost. Wait.' she made him release Selene, who fell onto the bed coughing.

'Listen, you fool. It's working out even better. You will get what you want and without having to marry her. You know now that she was telling the truth about signing *Inggris* over, but there may be ways of getting it back. We have her in our hands and Gabriel will have to pay a huge ransom if he wants to see her again.'

'But she knows it was us who had her kidnapped and, anyway, I thought you wanted to marry Gabriel.' said Michael Taun, beginning to calm down.

'Well, you see, once the ransom has been paid, we'll dispose of her. Gabriel will never know it was our doing. She was kidnapped by two masked men while we were moaning the loss of our father and of our uncle. Nobody will believe us capable of such a crime at such a sad time for us. All we need to do is take a picture of her holding today's edition of the Jakarta Post. Obviously, she will need to wear a different set of clothing and we'll need to take the picture with a neutral background. What do you say?'

'Brilliant. That's what you are, Sis. But when the time comes, I want the pleasure of killing her.'

After having uttered these words Michael Taun opened the door and barked a few orders in Sasak.

Meanwhile Dewi Rinjani walked up to the bed where Selene was recovering and hissed, 'Recite your prayers, because your days are numbered. I'm glad I don't need to have a disgusting creature like you for a sister-in-law. When we have back what is ours, Michael Taun will be able to pick himself a bride from the best society. Someone with distinction and breeding. Meanwhile I'll be consoling poor Gabriel until he won't feel his loss any more. And you, you miserable excuse for a human being, will follow your aunt. She was no fun either. My poor uncle was really distressed at the thought that he had to marry her. He, the descendent of one of the best families in Lombok! And she dared to refuse him. Well, of course she had to pay the penalty for her refusal.'

'What do you mean?' asked Selene, in a barely audible voice.

'Never you mind,' replied Dewi Rinjani, 'I may let you into the secret just before you die.' And she laughed a horrible laugh that chilled Selene to the core.

There were three taps on the door and Michael Taun let the old woman and the man in. After having explained something to them in Sasak, Michael Taun and Dewi Rinjani left.

Selene was pushed back into the ensuite where the old woman stripped her of the beautiful dress. She then gestured for Selene to wear a pair of jeans and a T-shirt she had brought. After Selene had complied, the woman led her back into the room, and, once Selene was sitting at the dressing table, she removed all traces of makeup and the flowers from her hair. When the woman had completed her task, the man tied Selene's hands and feet, then pushed her upon the bed. After that, they left the room, locking the door behind them.

Selene had plenty to mull over. She could not help but think of Dewi Rinjani's words. What did she mean by 'she had to pay the penalty?' Hadn't her aunt's death been an accident? Had Dewi Rinjani or Michael Taun or any other member of the family been responsible for her aunt's death? And what about herself? Was it her destiny to be murdered in this horrible room, in this degrading house, on this strange yet fascinating island? Where was Gabriel? Where was David? Where were all the friends she had made since arriving in Lombok? It was all too much for Selene who, once more, sought oblivion in sleep.

The noise of the door being unlocked awoke her from the usual nightmare. She could not tell whether it was day or night or how long she had slept. All she knew was that she was hungry and thirsty. Never in her life before had she felt the need to drink and eat so badly. The old Chinese woman who, earlier on, had helped her to dress, walked in with a jug of water and some boiled rice. She fed Selene then disappeared.

Selene was alone again. Alone with her wild thoughts of finding a way out, of regaining her freedom. But there was nothing she could do. The only way she could escape was through outside help.

Time moved on slowly, then the door was unlocked again and Dewi Rinjani walked in with a newspaper and a digital camera. Behind her came the dark, robust man, carrying a bamboo screen. The screen was positioned just outside the bathroom's door. A chair was placed against the screen. The dark, robust man pulled Selene up. He carried her to the chair and sat her down. Because Selene's hands were tied behind her back, Dewi Rinjani made her hold the newspaper up with her chin.

Once Dewi Rinjani was satisfied that the date on the Jakarta

Post was visible, she took a few pictures, then left without uttering a word. The man picked Selene up and dumped her back onto the bed. After that, he too left the room.

Now every time the door was opened, a cacophony of laughter, shouting, snatches of languorous music, and other unpleasant sounds invaded the room. Business was in full swing. The house must be brimming with people, but only a handful was aware of the recalcitrant guest in the soundproof room.

Selene lay there in the dark, thinking back to all that had happened to her since she had received the fateful letter that had brought her on the island. She was so lost in her musing that, at first, she did not notice the light click of the lock. It was dark in the room and Selene could not make out who was entering the room. Her heart started to pound. Who could it be? Was it that dreadful man with the bandy legs, who had given her such lascivious looks? Who was this person that was walking surreptitiously around the room and was coming near the bed? Then this mysterious visitor bumped into the screen that had been left there, and swore.

CHAPTER THIRTY

'Gabriel?' cried Selene, in an incredulous tone of voice.

'Selene? Thank goodness you're still alive. Where are you?'

'Over here, on the bed. I can't move. I'm bound hand and foot.'

'Wait till I've untangled myself from ... what...?' Gabriel replied.

'It's a screen Dewi Rinjani had it set up. I'll explain the whole story to you later. Haven't you got a torch? There are no windows in this room, so that light cannot be seen from outside.'

A narrow yet powerful beam of light broke the gloom. In a flash Gabriel was beside Selene, and was just bending over to untie her, when they heard the sound of a key being turned in the lock. Gabriel switched off the torch and managed to dive under the bed just in time.

The old Chinese woman walked in with the usual jug of water and rice cakes. She walked Selene to the bathroom, and then pushed her back onto the bed. As she was turning to go, the old woman dropped the plate that had held the rice cakes and Selene held her breath when she saw her bending down, so close to the bed, to retrieve it. Fortunately, the old woman did not see Gabriel hiding very near the spot where the plate had fallen. Selene thanked her lucky star that the throw was long enough to touch the carpeted floor.

After the old woman had switched the light off and left, Gabriel very quickly came out of his hiding place and, torchlight in one hand and Swiss knife in the other, cut the ropes that kept Selene captive. 'How are we going to get out of here?' Selene whispered, forgetting for a moment that the walls were soundproof.

'We'll need to walk upstairs. On the top floor there is a trapdoor that leads to the loft. From the loft, we'll gain access to the roof, which has a skylight. This was part of the original house and now permits the owner and some of the influent men on this island to escape if the police come to raid the place. The skylight we'll be our way out. I've brought some mountaineering equipment, which will help us reach the ground. We must be very careful, though, because there are some bouncers at the front door of this house and they may be attracted by the noise. They keep an eye to make sure that the girls don't run away. You must hide your hair. You'll be too easy to spot, because of its colour.'

'I know,' Selene replied, excitedly. 'I can use part of the throw as a headscarf. Can you cut a square off?'

Selene pushed her hair back into a bun, using the hairgrips from the dressing table. Then, she used the square of black brocade to hide it from sight. This was done very swiftly, as they both knew that they could not afford to be caught by Michael Taun, Dewi Rinjani or their accomplices. Gabriel leading, with Selene in close pursuit, walked very cautiously out of the room and looked down the corridor to make sure no one was coming. Selene followed him and she marvelled at how well he seemed to know his way around this place, but left all questions for a later date, when they would be out of danger.

On a couple of occasions, when they were climbing up the stairs leading to the loft, they had to hide from the girls who worked there, in their colourful costumes, walking into the upstairs rooms with a client in tow. Selene could feel her heart thumping with the excitement created by the flow of adrenalin in her blood, coupled with Gabriel's nearness.

They were now reaching the room where they would find the trapdoor to the loft. Gabriel looked around, making sure that no one was coming, then signalled to Selene to go on the other side of the door. He knocked, then listened, both of them holding their breath for fear that someone may be inside. After a few seconds, Gabriel rapped on the door again and when he was eventually satisfied that the room was empty, he turned the handle. He immediately realised that the door was locked and while Selene watched, incredulous, he pulled out a set of tools and after having selected a strange object she had never seen before in her life, he swiftly opened the door and waited for her. Selene followed him, closing the door behind her as Gabriel mimicked to her to do. He then gestured for her to come closer.

They were treading very softly, not to make their presence known to anyone in the room below. As soon as they were under the trapdoor, Gabriel explained to Selene where she would find the mechanism that opened it. He then lifted Selene up onto his powerful shoulders and she started feeling round the edges of the trapdoor. She quickly found the hinges and bolts of the trapdoor. Luckily, they were kept well oiled, for a fast retreat.

It would have been an easy task for Selene under normal circumstances to unfasten them. However, the limited diet she had been kept on had weakened her. Her arms felt like lead, and it took her ages to complete the simple task of sliding the bolts free and pull the trapdoor open. Apart from her weakness, the fear of being found out and the consequences to her and Gabriel made her hands shake. But Selene was a fighter. Forgetting about herself, she plucked up all her courage and strength and, as soon as she had opened the trapdoor, she heaved herself up through it. Gabriel very swiftly followed her. He then pulled the trapdoor up and hooked it into place with a special bar the present owner had had made to hamper the efforts of the police in hot pursuit of himself and his clients.

At the light of Gabriel's torch, Selene spotted the rope ladder that hung from the skylight. She grabbed the sides of the rope ladder and tried to lift up her left foot but a bout of dizziness prevented her from going any further. Gabriel, seeing her distress held her close to him and whispered, 'Don't worry, Selene. I'll climb up the rope ladder, then all you have to do is to hold on to the ladder and I'll pull you up. He kissed her gently on the lips, then he was up the ladder and out onto the roof in a flash. Selene held on tight to the rope ladder with the little strength that she had left and Gabriel pulled her up with ease, so light she had become during her captivity. She looked so fragile and lost that all Gabriel would have wanted to do was to fold her in his arms and kiss her. But there was no time for that. Instead, he cut the rope ladder with a knife, pushed down the skylight, and used the rope to secure it. This way he made it impossible for anyone to try to follow the two of them by that route.

Gabriel helped Selene walk the few steps to the edge of the roof that was in darkness. He fastened her into the harness he had brought, put on his own, passed the rope round her waist and secured it with some *locking krabs* (locking device used in mountain climbing). He did the same for himself, then, after having put into place the *descender*, (locking device used in mountain climbing) he fastened the other end of the rope to the metal pole that held into position a huge satellite dish. He slowly lowered Selene to the ground, and then deftly and silently followed her.

Once they had both reached the bottom, they noticed the lights of a car that was approaching the house. Afraid of being discovered, they quickly dived down to the ground, hiding in the darkness.

In the light streaming from the front door of the house, which had been opened by the bouncers, Selene, to her dismay and horror, saw Michael Taun walking into the house.

'Quickly, we must run for it.' urged Gabriel and, taking her up into his arms, he raced ahead into the darkness. He had run but a few yards into the jungle, when they heard shouting and the sound of several men running in hot pursuit of them. Gabriel put Selene down and led her frantically through a maze of narrow paths until they found their way barred by a fallen tree. All of a sudden, the sound of shots being fired reached them. Selene heard a noise resembling the buzzing of a bee, very close to her left ear and Gabriel, realising a bullet had just missed her, pulled her down with him into some prickly bushes, his hand over her mouth. Soon after, six men appeared and started looking everywhere, seeking them out. Michael Taun was among them, holding a gun in his left hand. They were looking in all directions, probing the thick vegetation of the jungle, trying to find them.

Selene held her breath, but her hands were trembling with fright at the thought of what awaited her if they were discovered. She knew she could not bear to be taken captive again. Her face was full of small scratches and even the limited amount of blood they produced attracted all kinds of insects, which fed on it. The ensuing irritation was torture, but she had to hold still, keeping her head down, only hoping that her enemies would head their chase to another part of the jungle. Gabriel, too, was lying with one ear to the ground, listening to any telltale sound that would indicate the direction their pursuers had taken.

The men were thrashing about the ground nearby. Now and again, they heard Michael Taun's 'voice, coming from somewhere very close to them. He was giving orders in short, clipped sentences. Night was on Selene and Gabriel's side, but soon the first light of dawn would appear and they would certainly be discovered.

Selene was giving up hope when she heard shots fired, but this time at Michael Taun and his men. She heard their footsteps retreating towards the house, while their weapons started a tattoo of their own, in answer to the gunfire that was deployed against them.

There was a real barrage of gunshots now, and Selene thought with apprehension that she and Gabriel appeared to be in the middle of it all. Gabriel was shielding her with his body, whilst he was considering whether it would be safer to leave their hiding place. Their rescuers were moving forward and soon passed the spot where the two lovers were hiding. Gabriel decided to come out of the prickly bush, which had sheltered them so well from Michael Taun and his men, but signalled to Selene to remain there.

Other shots were fired and then, after a short pause, everything went quiet. Selene heard a scurrying of feet, then someone running towards the spot where she was hiding. Gabriel had come back to her.

He looked exhausted. He had bruises on his face and neck. Blood was trickling down his face from a cut on his forehead. His shirt was in tatters and there was a gash in his right arm. He helped her out of the bush, kissed her and hugged her with an intensity of passion that surpassed any he had displayed before. This showed to Selene how real the danger had been and how relieved Gabriel was that nothing had happened to her. They stood there locked into an endless embrace, just happy to be alive.

Soon after, they were joined by David and four other Englishmen, who introduced themselves to her. They were all David's friends. They were ex-Army men, who had fought bravely in Iraq and Afghanistan, and who were now part of David's team.

'Michael Taun is dead,' Gabriel informed her. Two of his men are badly wounded, while the others have surrendered. The owner of the brothel said he had been forced to keep you segregated there by Michael Taun, as he owed him a lot of money. He has handed over the old Chinese woman and the dark, robust man who guarded you. They are tied up at the back of one of the jeeps. If we hurry up, we'll be out of this jungle and in Singiggi in forty minutes or so. From there we'll take the road to Mataram and stop over at Beatrice's home.'

There were a thousand questions Selene needed to ask him, but she felt she could leave them unanswered for a few more hours. She had to save what little energy she had left to cover the ground that separated them from the place where the jeeps awaited them.

They trudged through the jungle accompanied by its incredibly disturbing night sounds. When they reached the three jeeps, they found one of the detectives from Mataram that Gabriel had engaged, guarding Selene's former jailers. The old woman looked at her with a mixture of spite and fear, while the man seemed to be resigned to his fate.

Selene, now that the adrenalin that had sustained her in her flight had subsided, was very near to collapse. She looked with relief as Gabriel pulled open the back door of one of the jeeps, lifted her up and deposited her gently on the back seat, as if she were a very precious and fragile life-size porcelain figurine. He then took a First Aid box from under one of the seats and, with trembling hands, administered an ointment on Selene's scratches. Then, helped by Selene, he took care of his own wounds. When that was done, he replaced the First Aid box, sat down, and put his arms around her as if to shield her against all the evils of the world.

David, after having discussed the best route to take with all of his men, hopped into the front seat of the jeep where Selene and Gabriel were. Two of his men joined him at the front, and, once he saw that they were all settled and ready, drove off at the speed allowed by the uneven, muddy terrain.

The first part of their journey, in fact, was on dirt tracks, and was full of potholes. It was a very bumpy road of twelve kilometres, which jolted both driver and passengers nearly out of their seats. The last stretch was covered in brown dust, which settled over their clothes, hair, and faces. Once they reached Singiggi, though, the rest of the journey was smooth and uneventful.

Throughout the journey to Mataram, Gabriel cradled Selene in his arms, as a father would a child, a loving, protective father. It was like a joyous homecoming to Selene who, feeling warm and safe, and, lulled by the motion of the jeep, left all her cares to Gabriel and David and fell asleep.

She awoke when they reached the town, but absolutely refused to be taken to a hospital as Gabriel suggested. He had lifted her in his arms and was about to alight from the car in front of one of Mataram's most renowned clinics, when Selene voiced her objections in no uncertain terms.

‘Put me down,’ ordered Selene who, though filled with joy, was becoming a little impatient at all that fussing. ‘I’m not a cripple. I don’t want to go to the hospital. I want to go home. I tell you what I really want. First, I want to have a long soak in a spa bath. Then I want to put on clean clothes, see my friends and, finally, I want answers to my many questions,’ While uttering those words, she pushed against his chest and wriggled so much that he had to put her down, lest she slipped out of his arms.

Gabriel laughed, ‘I can see what our daughter will be like. Full of character and determination, just like her mum.’ That was music to Selene’s ears. He too, like herself wanted children. However, that was beside the point. She needed to keep a grip on herself and start getting some answers out of him.

David, meanwhile, had restarted the car and within a few minutes parked outside the building where Beatrice and Vincent lived.

‘Beatrice would not hear of your going anywhere else. I was under strict orders to take you here as soon as you had been freed’ Gabriel answered her unspoken question.

As soon as David left, Gabriel put his arm round Selene’s waist and held her close to him as if he were afraid that, if he let her go, she would disappear again. Gabriel spoke on the intercom, and then they entered the building and called the lift. There were other people in the lift and Selene was too shy to kiss Gabriel in front of an audience, but she was happy that he held her close to him.

When the door of the lift opened, they found Beatrice standing there, waiting for them.

Beatrice and Selene fell on each other’s neck, and hugged and kissed, tears streaming down their faces. Beatrice frowned to see how much weight Selene had lost, but said nothing. She simply took hold of Selene’s arm and led her into the apartment. Vincent came forward, followed closely by Jessica and Patrick and then, Selene had the indescribable pleasure of seeing her friend Vanessa.

Vanessa hugged and kissed her then introduced her to a tall, fair-haired young man, who turned out to be Darren, her husband. It was such a surprise to see all her friends together, greeting her and making her feel welcome that Selene was pervaded by the kind of warmth that told of friendship and love and belonging. Something that she had never experienced before in her whole life.

All the excitement of her escape and the strain of the journey to Mataram had taken their toll. Selene needed a rest to recuperate her strength, therefore Beatrice accompanied her to the beautifully furnished guestroom Selene remembered from her previous visit, drew the curtains, and said kindly, 'There'll be plenty of time to talk later on. Now, have a long soak in the bath, then lie down and have a rest my dear.' She closed the door behind her quietly and went back to entertain her other guests.

Selene luxuriated in a jasmine-scented spa bath. She washed and rinsed her hair four times, before she felt that the dirt of the past few weeks had all disappeared. She brushed her teeth again and again, trying to make up for the time when she had been unable to carry out even this simple task. After she had patted herself dry, she sat in front of the mirror and examined her face. Her scratches were not stinging quite as much, a sign that the ointment worked. There was still a shadow under her eyes and she looked thinner. The golden tan had faded, leaving her looking pale, but interesting.

She found one of her nightdresses on the four-poster bed and she put it on, her body craving a trouble-free sleep.

CHAPTER THIRTY-ONE

She was standing near the steps of the pool, arguing with someone. She was pushed violently into the water. She tried to come back up to the surface, but someone kept pushing her head down. She was out of breath. Her lungs were on fire. Someone was laughing a high-pitched maniacal laugh and she was falling down, down to the bottom of the pool. She struggled against the black vortex that was swallowing her up. She screamed and screamed and woke herself up.

'Wake up. Wake up. What is it darling?'

'Oh Gabriel, it's the nightmare again. It gets worse all the time. If I carry on having this horrid dream I think I'll go insane.' cried Selene.

'No, my love, it's the trauma you've suffered since they've kidnapped you. You've experienced such an emotional upheaval in the past few months that it's surprising you haven't had a nervous breakdown. From now on, I'll take care of you. Don't forget you and I were supposed to be already married. We couldn't make it on the day for obvious reasons, but I've already fixed another date. We'll be married in three days' time. But we'll talk about this later. If you feel up to it, you should get dressed now and we'll both go and join our friends.'

'I'd like to make up and change before meeting them again.'

'Of course my darling. Look. Here is a suitcase with some of your clothes. Mei-Lin packed it before I came to find you. You make yourself beautiful, meanwhile I'll go and ask our friends to be patient for a little while longer.'

Spurred into action by Gabriel's words, Selene dressed herself in a silver and emerald green dress that covered her shoulders, but left exposed a little of her cleavage. She brushed her hair until it shone like the flames of a blazing fire, and then let it down to her shoulders. She put some foundation powder on her face and arms, to hide away the scratches. She added a small amount of blusher on her cheeks to give her face a little colour. A touch of lipstick, eye shadow, and mascara made her feel human again. Finally, she clipped the emerald necklace round her long, fragile neck, fastened the clasp of the matching bracelet round her wrist, and wore the emerald earrings that she had bought in Singapore. On the dressing table, in a small box containing the rest of her jewels, she found her engagement ring, a reminder of Gabriel's love. She picked it up and slid it on her finger, thinking how fortunate it had been that she had taken it off and put it in the dressing table drawer before her kidnapping, or it would have been lost forever. One last look in the full-length mirror, a spray of her favourite perfume and she was ready to meet her friends.

'My dear, you look fabulous,' Beatrice greeted her. Selene sent a 'thank you' to the manufacturers of the cosmetic cream and powder that had helped her cover all the ravages that her capture and escape had left on her face. 'Now sit down,' continued her hostess, 'We'll have dinner, then you'll tell us all that has happened to you and we, in turn, will fill you in on what we did when you went missing.'

Dinner was delicious. The wine was ambrosia and went down well. Her friends kept on telling her how wonderful it was to have her back amongst their midst and Gabriel was looking at her with eyes filled with love. She felt protected by her circle of friends, enveloped in a cocoon of love and savoured every moment of a perfect evening.

When coffee was served, Selene decided that the time had come to tell her tale. Everyone listened to her without interruption, exception made for the occasional gasp of horror when she described some particularly unsavoury moments, like when she had been given chloroform to keep her sedated. Or about the evil intentions of the lascivious man with the bandy legs in the house of ill repute. Her narrative was so vivid that she managed to convey to them how ill she had been as well as the fears which had seized her on a couple of occasions when she thought she would be killed.

After she had narrated to them all that there was to tell about her kidnapping, her astonishing flight from the cave, her forced confinement in the dreadful house, where she had been at the mercy of Michael Taun and Dewi Rinjani, it was her turn to hear what the others had felt and done. 'When did you discover that I was missing?' she asked encouragingly.

'We realised something awful must have happened to you as soon as we returned from the festival on the beach,' replied Jessica,

'I came back from the festival early for I had developed a headache and asked Patrick to accompany me, because I didn't fancy the long walk from the beach to the back of the house on my own. We let ourselves in through the patio doors, and then I stopped in the kitchen to drink a glass of water. I knew that there were some tablets in my ensuite and Patrick and I headed for the hall. As soon as we walked out of the kitchen, we could see that the lights were on in the entrance hall. At first, we thought that you had left them on, so that people coming to the front door would not be in the dark, but when we reached the hall, we noticed that the door was wide open. Puzzled, we looked outside, thinking you might be out there somewhere….'

'But when we didn't see you,' continued Patrick, 'we ran up to your room, and saw the half-packed suitcase on your bed. We called out, thinking that you were in the ensuite, but when you did not answer, we looked everywhere in the house, but there was no sign of you. Then we resumed our search outside. We walked a little down the driveway, but you were not there. Bothered and a little uneasy, not sure about what to do, we waited for the others to return.'

'We should have realised that something was afoot,' Beatrice said, picking up the thread from Patrick, 'because Dewi Mas looked peculiar, somewhat feverish, but also distracted and on tenterhooks. We didn't think much of it then, of course, because we assumed the news of the death of her husband and brother had affected her to the extent that she was unable to concentrate on anything that was happening around her. Dewi Rinjani and Michael Taun, too, appeared altered, but in a manic sort of way.'

'Having seen the state they were in, we were all for leaving them to their grief, but every time we mentioned that it was time we left, they were adamant we should stay a little longer and how they didn't want to be left alone.' Vincent added.

'I should have known that they were up to no good.' joined in Gabriel, 'Michael Taun kept on looking at his watch and pacing up and down the room, while Dewi Rinjani tried to catch his eye every so often. Dewi Mas kept the conversation going, only stopping to sigh or reach for her handkerchief. She kept on talking about her marriage; how she and her husband had met, and what a wonderful husband and father Sir Edward had been. Whenever she mentioned her brother she let out some little sobs, but she tried to maintain a dignified air. She really played the inconsolable widow and sister well, except, as Beatrice has already remarked, for the heightened colour on her cheeks and the quick look she darted at Michael Taun every now and then. Anyway, by the time we managed to disengage ourselves it was already around two in the morning.' concluded Gabriel.

'We'd been waiting impatiently for them to return and even hoped that you had decided to join them at the Fairchilds,' said Patrick, 'but all our assumptions came to an end when they came back and you were not with them. We panicked then and explained to them that you were missing.'

'Gabriel swore.' added Jessica, brightening up, 'I'd never have thought he could or would swear quite like that.'

'Well .... Ahem,' Gabriel butted in, 'I was raked with guilt at having left you on your own after we had been discussing Michael Taun's behaviour only a few hours earlier. I felt a real fool not to have read the signs and to have dismissed the possibility of his being such a cad. Besides, I was worried sick about you,' he pulled her closer to him, 'I thought I'd never see you again.' Selene could feel his body quiver at the mere thought.

'The problem was that we couldn't contact the local police,' Vincent went on, 'because we knew, from what you had overheard, that they were on Dewi Mas's side. We couldn't confront Michael Taun or Dewi Rinjani, because they might decide to do something drastic. Our only option was David.'

'It was agreed that I should return to the hotel and contact David immediately, in total secrecy, so as not to alert the Fairchilds or their associates.' Gabriel disclosed. 'I made sure that there was no one in sight, and then tapped on his door. There was no answer at first, so I tapped a little louder. This time David opened the door. I took another surreptitious look, and then slipped in. David had been asleep, so his mind was a little fuzzy at first. However, as the story of your disappearance unfolded, he listened attentively until I'd finished. He told me that the man he had engaged had been shadowing Michael Taun and Dewi Rinjani all day long, but that they had not been approached by anyone in particular. Then David had a quick shower, got dressed and we drove back to *Inggris*. David had a good look around and, in the light of day, he noticed the deep marks left by the tyres of a vehicle, probably a van, which had left at speed. He also found a fingerprint on the doorbell, which Vincent and I immediately took to the forensic lab in Mataram.'

'David, meanwhile, asked Patrick, Jessica and myself to talk to Mei-Lin and her family to see whether they had noticed or heard something related to your abduction.' added Beatrice, 'Mei-Lin was in tears when she heard. She couldn't believe that anybody would be so wicked as to do something so horrible to such a kind and beautiful lady like you. Once the initial shock was over she thought hard, but all that she had seen was Michael Taun flirting with a couple of local girls on the beach the night before.'

'Wayan, instead, had something interesting to relate.' carried on

Patrick, 'He had been talking to one of his friends when he spotted one of Michael Taun's servants whispering something in Michael Taun's ear. Whatever he told him seemed to please him and he immediately informed his sister. Then the fellow was dismissed, after some more whispering. Wayan thought that kind of behaviour rather unusual as Michael Taun doesn't treat servants very well and would never be seen talking to one of them in such a familiar way.'

'We decided to wait until Gabriel got back, to convey this piece of information to David, as we didn't know how to approach him without being noticed.' continued Jessica. 'Gabriel and Vincent came back in the early afternoon with the news that two plain clothed detectives would come down from Mataram in the next day or so and stay at the same hotel as Gabriel and David.'

'Meanwhile Wayan offered to try and find out what the servant had said to Michael Taun. Wayan has lived in the village all his life and knows all of the Fairchilds' servants.' Patrick explained. 'His plan was to "accidentally" bump into the servant and get him to talk.'

'Where do the two of you fit in all this?' asked Selene, turning to Vanessa and her husband, who sat there quietly listening to what the others had to say.

'Honestly, Selene. Don't you remember? You invited us to your wedding. I emailed you for two days without receiving any answers, so I decided to phone you. Gabriel took the call and informed us about what had happened. Well, after that, no team of wild horses could keep Darren or me from flying over.' Vanessa sat next to Selene and hugged her. 'I couldn't let my best friend be kidnapped and sit there doing nothing.' she concluded, Darren assenting during his wife's speech.

'I figured two extra helpers wouldn't go amiss.' he chipped in.

'Anyway,' Vincent said, resuming the tale, 'Wayan was unable to approach the servant in a casual way, therefore the detectives Gabriel had hired from Mataram shadowed him twenty four hours on the trot, swapping shifts with each other.'

'On day two of your absence, there was still no ransom note and you were still missing from *Inggris.* We couldn't understand why you had been kidnapped. If the Fairchilds didn't want money, why would they abduct you? We were beginning to think that, maybe, someone else was responsible for your disappearance.' Gabriel explained, 'We were frantic with worry by then. The Fairchilds were staying at home making arrangements for the double funeral, the servant seemed to follow a home-work-home routine, and all traces had been lost of the rough man.'

'By then, we were bashing our heads against the wall, metaphorically speaking,' put in Patrick, 'when a ...' 'Wait a minute. It's my story. Let me explain.' Patrick proceeded, checking his sister and taking on his lecturing voice, making everybody chuckle. 'Well, Wayan was at the local market helping his cousin sell his wears, when he saw Michael Taun's servant gambling. Wayan observed him for quite some time, and noticed that he was losing heavily, but did not seem too worried about it. Still, despite this unusual behaviour, nothing else emerged for a few days. Wayan, though, would not let himself be deterred by this apparent inaction and a few more days brought an incredible change.'

'Yes,' Jessica exclaimed, picking up the thread from Patrick, 'All of a sudden there was great activity around the place. For one thing, Wayan saw the rough man moving about the market in a furtive fashion, then, when he thought no one was looking, he sent a little boy to the place where Michael Taun's servant was playing. The little boy whispered something into the servant's ear and soon after the servant interrupted his gambling and roamed about the stalls until, 'accidentally', he found himself within earshot of the rough man.

There was a frantic whispering, after which the servant ran back to the Fairchilds' home. David had the place under surveillance, the detectives from Mataram using powerful binoculars. They saw the servant run up to Michael Taun, who was relaxing by the swimming pool. As soon as the servant had imparted his news Michael Taun sprang up, angry and red-faced, gesticulating furiously.'

'Two weeks or so went by and still nothing happened,' interjected Vanessa, 'apart from a couple more encounters between the rough man and Michael Taun's servant, which Darren and I observed while playing as tourists looking around the market for souvenirs to take home.'

'We were very concerned that we had no news of you and were considering changing our tactics, when, as fast as he had appeared, the rough man was gone again, but one of the detectives 'contacts in this part of the island followed him.' Gabriel said, picking up the tale once more. 'Meanwhile Dewi Rinjani kept on coming over, asking after you and we made up stories that you had had to fly back to England. We did that because we didn't want her to realise that we suspected that she and her brother were behind it all.'

'She was constantly followed, but we employed different people.' continued Vincent. 'And, fortunately, this constant shadowing of the brother and sister yielded very good results, particularly when you were taken to that awful place in the middle of the jungle.'

Selene shivered. 'It was horrible. Michael Taun first wanted to marry me, then Dewi Rinjani told him that he could ask for a huge ransom and that would help them gain back what they called 'their land'. She took a picture of me holding the Jakarta Post herself and she told me outright that once they had obtained what they wanted, they would dispose of me.' Selene's voice was in danger of betraying her emotions, while she was speaking about the distressing period of her captivity. Gabriel tightened his hold on her, pulling her so close to him that she found it almost difficult to breathe.

Vanessa came up to her and Gabriel momentarily released his hold on Selene, so that Vanessa, then Jessica and Beatrice, in turn, could give Selene a hug of understanding and support.

Reassured by her friends' display of affection, Selene urged them to carry on relating the events of which she had been the protagonist. 'How come that a building made of stone and mortar was built in the middle of the jungle?' she prompted.

'Well, you see,' Vincent answered, 'the building had been commissioned by an extremely wealthy Dutch merchant in the middle of the 19th century. This merchant had eight daughters and three sons, so he had this mansion built to accommodate all his children. He engaged a Dutch architect because he felt nostalgic towards his native country and had a big skylight added to the roof, in order to indulge in his hobby of stargazing, in comfort. The mansion was built far enough from Singiggi to assure him and his family all the privacy they wanted, but at the same time, it was close enough for him to require only half a day on horseback to reach his warehouses. When he died, most of his children had already returned to Holland or had moved to Australia. Only one of his sons stayed on, then his son's heirs and so on until, eventually, the house was sold to a local man, who turned it into what it is today.

Wealthy tourists are lured there by the gambling tables and other illicit activities of a sexual nature that go on there. You were very lucky to escape unscathed, my girl.' he concluded, patting Selene's hands.

'How come that you, Gabriel, could find your way around the house so easily?' Selene could not help asking.

'Because the two detectives from Mataram managed to find the layout of the house at the Planning Office in the capital. The plans for the changes made to the original building had to be submitted and approved by that office. After they had photocopied them, David and I went over them several times, until I knew it by heart.' Gabriel answered her, smugly.

'How was Michael Taun killed?' Selene went on, relieved at the explanation Gabriel had given to her previous question.

'While his men were fighting against David and his companions, Michael Taun was trying to run off. I followed him and we started punching and kicking each other. Then he took a flick knife out of his pocket and started waving it about. He managed to strike my arm with it, but I managed to wrench it from him. He lunged for the passenger seat of the jeep and when I jumped on him, he produced a revolver. We struggled when suddenly a shot was fired and he fell down dead.'

It was Selene's turn to hold on to Gabriel, trembling at the thought of what might have happened. 'What will happen to Dewi Rinjani, now? And what about my aunt's death? I don't believe she died accidentally. I think someone murdered her.'

Selene had barely formulated the question, when the phone rang. A few seconds later, Beatrice's maid walked into the sitting room and, looking at Gabriel, said, 'Mr Wayan on phone. Urgent matter.'

Gabriel left the room, while the others looked at each other wondering what was happening.

When Gabriel returned, his face betrayed the shock and concern he felt. Selene got up and took some tentative steps towards him, but he motioned to her to sit back in her chair. 'You must be brave darling,' he almost whispered, 'Something awful has happened. Someone has been to *Inggris* and...'

Selene, deathly pale, shot up from her chair and exclaimed, 'What has happened? Mei-Lin. Where is she?'

Gabriel seized her gently by the arms and led Selene to one of the sofas. He sat her down, then, still holding her, he related to her that Mei-Lin and Komang had been murdered and that the house was in shambles.

On hearing this ghastly news, a heart-wrenching sob escaped from Selene's lips. No. Not Mei-Lin. Her sweet, gentle Mei-Lin. Her first friend on Lombok. 'How... How was she killed?' murmured Selene.

'She was drowned in the swimming pool.' replied Gabriel,

imparting only a fraction of what he had been told. 'Komang, instead, must have fought like a lion. Wayan said he was stabbed several times. His blood is everywhere. The house has been ransacked. Wayan said it looks as if a tornado has hit it.'

'Has he called the police?' asked Vincent, his voice not quite steady.

'No. He doesn't trust the local police and, after what Selene told us, neither do I'. I'll call the detectives we have engaged, then David and myself will go to *Inggris*.

'Not without me!'Selene cried out.

'Or me!' shouted all the others.

'Now then. Let's all be sensible.' Gabriel interjected, as everybody started to speak at once. 'We need to leave the scene of the crime undisturbed. I believe we'll need our detectives to call the police in Jakarta, so that a proper investigation can be carried out. Meanwhile, David and I shall go to *Inggris* and will give all the support we can to Wayan.

Selene strenuously opposed that plan of action, but Gabriel was firm and nothing she could say moved him into taking her with him.

CHAPTER THIRTY-TWO

While Gabriel contacted David, the rest of the party commented on the event, wondering who could have perpetrated such a hideous crime.

'There must be Dewi Rinjani or her mother, or both behind it.' Selene blurted out, 'It must be their way of avenging Michael Taun's death. Both of them hate me. Dewi Rinjani wanted me killed, but I never expected she would be so despicable, so mad as to take it out on Mei-Lin.' And here a tear trickled down Selene's cheek.

Beatrice and Vanessa sat next to Selene and tried to comfort her as best they could, but Selene's heart ached too much and after uttering her excuses, she sought the haven of her room, where she let open the floodgates, until she had no more tears left and fell asleep.

Selene was being chased by something evil. She arrived at the edge of the swimming pool. She heard someone laughing a demoniacal laugh, and then strong hands pushed her down under the surface of the water. The laughter echoed in her head while she was slowly drowning. She was unable to resist and let herself drift to the bottom of the pool, her lungs filling up with water. She was about to hit the bottom when...

'Wake up Selene,' Vanessa's voice reached her through the shreds of her dream, 'It's ten o'clock in the morning. Gabriel and David left ages ago, and Darren, Patrick, Jessica and I have something to propose to you.'

Selene stirred and stretched, muttering something incomprehensible, but then, under Vanessa's gentle probing, she shook herself awake.

'What was that?' she mumbled.

'Look Selene, why don't you freshen up and join us in the sitting room?' suggested Vanessa.

Selene did as she was bidden, and by the time she walked into the sitting room she was perfectly alert.

'Where is Beatrice?' Selene enquired.

'Vincent and Beatrice left for Jakarta half an hour ago. Vincent knows the Commissioner of Police there, and thought it would be best if he paid him a visit to obtain his help. Beatrice, being satisfied that we would look after you, decided to go with him.'

'And how are you all going to look after me?' asked Selene, the beginning of a smile playing on her lips.

'Well, as you well know, I can read you like a book.' Vanessa began, 'I figured you wouldn't be satisfied with sitting here quietly waiting for news from Gabriel. Therefore, we put our heads together while you were sleeping and decided we'll hire a *bemo* and go to *Inggris*, where you'll be able to see with your own eyes what exactly happened there. Obviously, you won't be able to stay there, hence Darren has booked two rooms at the Kunta Indah Hotel. One room for us girls and another for Darren and Patrick.'

'Wonderful.' cried Selene, looking at her friends gratefully. 'I like your plan.'

While everybody retired to their room to pack a few things, Patrick was busy hiring a *bemo.*

There was hardly any conversation at all during the journey from Mataram to Kuta Beach. Each friend lost in thought of what they would find once they arrived at *Inggris.*

It had been agreed that they would go to the hotel first and then, after lunch, they would walk all the way to *Inggris*, but first Patrick was to call David on his mobile, to alert him of their coming. Selene dared not contact Gabriel, well aware of what his reaction would be.

David was not amused when he received Patrick's call. He told him in no uncertain terms, how foolish he thought they had all been, and how dangerous their coming there was for Selene. 'Besides,' he added, 'I thought Gabriel had made it quite clear that you must not go on the scene of the crime until the forensic team from Jakarta have been. If you're really keen on seeing the devastation that has struck *Inggris*, you'll have to wait at least another two or three days. I'll let you know. Meanwhile try not to expose Selene to any harm.'

'Please, David, before you ring off...is it really that bad?'

'Yes Patrick. It's the worst scenario you can imagine. Every single item of furniture has been smashed. All the pictures, including photographs of Selene's aunt have been slashed or burnt. The bedrooms have been set on fire and the hall is full of blood. Komang's body has been cut in a most macabre way, and peculiar symbols have been drawn on the walls, using his blood. I can't tell you what they've done to Mei-Lin. I feel sick only to think of it. Sorry Patrick, I have to go now.' And with that David rang off.

CHAPTER THIRTY-THREE

Patrick put down the receiver, and tried to compose himself before joining his friends. One look at him, and they realised that David had not been happy that they were in Kuta Beach.

Selene was the only one who questioned him, and Patrick explained to her what David had said about forensics, but kept the rest of what he had learnt to himself.

Thwarted in her purpose of seeing for herself what had happened to *Inggris*, and annoyed with David and Gabriel, Selene invited her friends to have a look at Kuta Beach as she wanted to know if anyone was yet aware of the crime that had been committed at *Inggris*.

The exercise proved tiring yet futile, therefore, after consuming a cheerless dinner at the hotel, they all retired early to their rooms and within minutes were fast asleep.

Danger! There was danger in the air. Selene was in a small dark place and found it hard to breathe. She was on her hands and knees, but the dark walls were closing in on her at a terrific speed. Then, as she was on the verge of suffocating, she was out into the open, by the swimming pool at Inggris. She could feel the warmth of the sun on her back, the water beckoning to her. She was stepping down, eagerly savouring the moment when her body would make contact with the lovely cool water of the pool when a shadow appeared on the surface of the still water. She tried to turn, but a maniacal force pushed her down into the swimming pool. The hand that kept her head ducked into the water was pressing harder and harder. Her eyes were popping out of her head, her lungs were on fire, and she found it increasingly difficult to struggle. She was going to die. She knew that for a fact, and while she was labouring for breath, a chilling, crazy laughter reached her ears. The laughter went on and on and, the louder it was, the closer to drowning she came.

Selene woke up in a pool of sweat. Her breath was laboured, her pulse racing and her head was throbbing. It was the nightmare again. Will she ever be rid of it? She pushed the light button on her watch: three thirty in the morning. It was raining. Both Jessica and Vanessa, who shared the room with her, were sleeping peacefully, one snoring lightly, the other with mouth open. Selene observed them for a few minutes, enviously.

Dawn caught her thinking about Gabriel. Was he all right? What would she do if something happened to him? She bit her fingernails, something she had stopped doing when she had started secondary school.

Selene heard people stirring. Some were getting ready for their daily tasks. Others were there for the holiday of a lifetime. She, instead, seemed to be suspended on the edge of a dark, unfathomable abyss. She would be there, dangling in the void, until she received some news, any kind of news. This waiting around was just killing her. It was what she had tried to avoid all along.

Eventually, tired of waiting, she picked up her towel and headed for the shower. She was about to press down the door handle to the ensuite, when she heard someone tampering with the lock of the bedroom door. She turned around quickly, trying to wake Vanessa and Jessica, when a figure wrapped up in a long bathrobe suddenly catapulted into the room.

Scared out of her wits, she was about to scream when a hand sneaked up to prevent her from doing so and a voice she knew whispered, 'Don't panic, Selene. It's me, David.'

Jessica stirred and opened her eyes. 'What .... What's going on?' she mumbled, still half asleep.

'Who's there?' shouted Vanessa.

'Don't worry, girls. It's only David.' Selene reassured them.

These words brought both girls into a sitting position, mouth gaping. Selene was about to say something more, when there was a rap on the door.

'It's Patrick and Darren.' Selene informed David.

'Good. Let them in.' was David's curt reply.

'My, we're crowded in here. Have you organised a party Selene?' Patrick remarked cheerfully, sitting down on his sister's bed, while Darren joined Vanessa.

David, meanwhile, had taken off his bathrobe to disclose the fact that he was fully clothed. He then sat down on the edge of Selene's bed and filled them in with the news he had brought.

'When Patrick contacted me yesterday, I was really annoyed. Gabriel is bad enough, but at least he is capable of looking after himself, or so I thought. But you lot are real amateurs and what I need are professionals.'

'What do you mean by "or so I thought"?' asked Selene, panic-stricken.

'Well...Gabriel and I met Wayan early yesterday morning. Wayan was distraught as you may well imagine. While I was carrying out a preliminary survey of *Inggris*, I told Wayan to go and find out if Dewi Mas and Dewi Rinjani were still at Dewi Kunta. Gabriel, instead, had to go back to the hotel and wait for Vincent's call about the police in Jakarta.

It was about lunchtime when Wayan came back. The three of us had lunch at the hotel, and it was then that Wayan told us that both women had vanished. Some people that Wayan knows, told him that they thought Dewi Mas and Dewi Rinjani had absconded in a village near Aibuka, on the slopes of Mount Rinjani.

The inhabitants of this hamlet are extremely superstitious and think that Dewi Mas is a sorceress with magic powers. They have been strict followers of an animistic religion based on witchcraft. Nowadays, practising the beliefs they hold is against the law, therefore most of the followers have had to hide, and what a better hiding place than on one of the slopes of the holy mountain of Lombok?

Anyway, soon after Wayan had imparted his findings to us

Gabriel left, saying that he was going for a walk along the beach to think matters over. I went back to *Inggris* to look at the grounds and came back at dinnertime.

As we were due to have dinner together, I tried to contact Gabriel in his room, then on his mobile, but there was no answer and his mobile was switched off. I asked at reception, and I was told that his keys were not there and that he had left no message.

It was at that point that I had the first inkling that he might have decided to go and try to find mother and daughter himself.

CHAPTER THIRTY-FOUR

There was a gasp from Selene, who turned as white as a sheet and would have fainted if Vanessa had not helped her to sit on the bed and Jessica had not brought her a glass of water to drink.

'How do you suggest we proceed now?' enquired Selene after she had somewhat recovered.

'Apart from going to Aibuka with my team and try to locate him there, I haven't come up with any other plan.'

'Can you tell us a little bit more about Aibuka, the village in the area where Dewi Rinjani is?' asked Darren.

The friends sat there, listening while David explained to them that in the village of Dagnar, near Aibuka, there existed some kind of sect that worshipped Rangda, the Queen of Leyak.

When she heard the name of Rangda, Selene cried out, 'It can't be. Oh please, not Rangda. I've had forebodings as soon as I read about her in London. I've had nightmares where there has been an obscure force trying to drown me and now I realise I was dreaming of Rangda all along. If Gabriel is in her hands, he's doomed.'

'Please Selene, don't upset yourself in this way. Rangda is only a myth. It can do you no harm. Remember, it's what you believe that can harm you, not the belief in itself.' Patrick patted Selene's hand, trying to reassure her. But Selene felt a chill run down her spine and shivered. She had to find Gabriel before it was too late.

In the meantime, David had been saying that a new trail had just been opened to go from Aibuka to Gurung Baru, from inside the caldera up to the summit of the ridge. This was part of a new adventure tour for people who liked danger.

'But then we could ask one of the guides to take us there!' exclaimed Patrick.

'Well. It's not so easy. People have to book in advance and not all the guides offer this service, as it is quite dangerous.' replied David.

'Come on, David,' continued Patrick, 'don't tell me that, if the price is right, we won't find someone willing to help us.'

David considered Patrick's words, and answered him that it was far too dangerous for amateurs to embark on this type of mission. 'Let me and my men take care of it. If I were you I would go back to Mataram, to Beatrice's apartment and wait for news there.'

At these words, Selene exclaimed, 'No David. That's enough. You know how much I have grown to respect you and your team, but this is my show. I'll pay a guide to take me up to Dagnar . Dewi Rinjani won't be able to resist trying to grab hold of me. She hates me. She'd like to see me dead and if she learns that I'm in the area, she'll do all she can to entrap me. She's not a fool. If she knows that I've come with a party of devoted friends, she'll stay away, but if she believes me to be alone, she'll make a move, and then you, David, can intervene with your men and catch her.'

They all argued with her. Nobody wanted Selene to offer herself as bait for Dewi Rinjani, but she stood her ground and eventually they had to submit to her wishes. David, though, made her promise that she would wear all kinds of electronic gadgetry, including a GPS tracker with panic button incorporated fitted under the skin inside her left armpit.

After Selene had agreed, David performed the small, painless operation on her armpit, to fit the device. The six of them then spent the remainder of the day travelling to Mount Rinjani, and trying to find a guide who would accompany Selene on a solo trip from Aibuka to Gurung Baru on the following day. Selene was paying a high sum for the privilege and eventually she found someone ready to take her inside the caldera, despite some talks that there seemed to be some geological activity around Gurung Baru.

Selene felt a new excitement growing within her. Never in her life before had she been so close to accomplishing something so daring.

The danger, she thought, did not lie so much on the trekking, but on her encounter with Dewi Rinjani. She knew the girl was desperate, and possibly unbalanced. As David had reminded her, Dewi Rinjani had always wanted to marry Gabriel, in spite of everything. The only person who stood in her way was Selene herself. She was conscious of how much Dewi Rinjani loathed her. She had felt the girl's hatred grow from the first time that she had met her. She recalled her last encounter with Dewi Rinjani and shivered. Yet she had to face her once more, hopefully for the last time. If Gabriel was in her and in Dewi Mas's clutches, it would be a mammoth struggle to free him and save herself.

CHAPTER THIRTY-FIVE

Selene did not sleep a wink. The night was long and restless. Selene kept on tossing and turning, thinking of Gabriel. The adrenalin was carousing through her veins, ready for the challenge that faced her. Tomorrow was going to be May 1, the month the Romans devoted to the dead.

Selene was up at dawn. She washed herself meticulously, and then dressed in jeans and T-shirt, with a light woollen jumper and a windbreaker on top. She put on heavy socks and a pair of strong hiking boots. She forced herself to eat breakfast and, after having parted from her friends, she joined the guide that she had engaged.

The guide was a short, slim, wiry man, in a woollen hat, check shirt, and black jeans. He was well equipped with ropes and mountain gear and, after shaking her hand, they set off right away.

First, he led her through the thick rainforest, along the trail Selene remembered so well. The air was still full of rain droplets and early morning dew and Selene was glad that she had on her light jumper and windbreaker. The trail along the emerald green savannah was reinvigorating and exciting, accompanied, as they were, by the sound of birds and monkeys. Soon, though, the terrain became more rugged and the steep ascent began.

Up and up they climbed, straight up the side of the steep active volcanic cone. All of a sudden, Selene saw a plume of ash issue from Gurung Baru, shooting up high into the sky. She called to her guide who turned round with an enquiring gaze and she pointed at the cloud. 'What is it?' she asked in what she hoped sounded a calm tone of voice.

'Nothing. Lady. No worry. Sometimes spirit of Gurung Baru angry.'

The climb was becoming more arduous by the minute and Selene found that she was feeling hotter and hotter and had to stop to remove the windbreaker and the jumper, which she tied round her waist. She needed a rest and said as much to her guide. Selene sat on a flat rock. Her throat was parched and she drank some of the supply of bottled water that she had brought with her. Her skin felt uncomfortable, like when one works in a dust-filled environment. Selene looked at her arms and noticed that they were covered in a greyish layer of ash. Her face, too, felt caked with it. After a thirty-minute stop, they returned to the trail, descending towards the crater. They walked along the edge of the crater, leading to the lake, with its new volcano, which made its smoky presence felt in the middle of it.

Just as they were reaching the lake, the earth shook. Selene, alarmed, was about to turn towards her guide to ask for an explanation for this phenomenon, when something hit her hard on the back of her head and she fell into a world of nothingness.

Someone was slapping her remorselessly and relentlessly on both cheeks, until water was thrown on her with savage glee.

'How kind of you, Miss Heiress, to come all the way to my humble abode.' Dewi Rinjani's voice and maniacal laughter greeted Selene's return to consciousness. 'Oh but we're looking more like a boy than a woman with all the weight you've lost. Look at her Gabriel. Look at her! Is this the woman of your dreams? The one you refused me for?'

Selene opened her eyes and saw Dewi Rinjani holding Gabriel by the hair to pull his head up, so that he could look in her direction.

Her poor, darling Gabriel! He had his arms stretched out wide apart, his wrists chained to the rocky walls of this peculiar dwelling, carved out of the slope of one of the sides of Gurung Baru. His feet too, were chained to the floor. His body was slumped forward. He was half-naked and bore the marks of recent beating. His eyes were swollen and his lips were bruised and cracked.

What was the usual quotation in this kind of situation? 'Hell hath no fury like a woman scorned.'

‘Well, my dear.’ Dewi Rinjani went on, ‘How do you like your betrothed? Handsome, isn’t he?’ she mocked. ‘Don’t worry. Although it would be one of my dearest wishes to match the bruises and cuts of his body with yours, my mother has other plans for you. Did you really think I would fall for your pathetic attempt to draw me out of this comfortable hiding place in order to be captured by that English detective and his murderous men? The men who killed my dear brother? You’re a real fool, you, awful creature,’ Dewi Rinjani said, addressing Selene, ‘You are simply laughable. Did you believe, even for one moment, that those electronic devices you had in your belt would escape me? You’ll pay. Yes. You’ll both pay for my brother’s death and for cheating my family’s hopes of regaining what was their rightful inheritance.

Neither of you knows that tomorrow will mark my initiation, not as a mere sorceress, but as the assistant of Rangda, Queen of the *Leyak*. I shall be at the side of the head of one of the most ancient animistic sects. A sect that has escaped the vigil eye of the police for generations. A sect that my mother has led ever since she was a girl, and that I shall lead after her.

The first deed I shall perform will be to help my mother carry out a human sacrifice to placate the ire of Mount Rinjani.

It will be an amazing ceremony and you, Selene, are going to have the privilege of being killed for the good of my people.’ Dewi Rinjani then laughed and laughed and her laughter echoed and bounced off from one rocky wall to the other.

Dewi Rinjani was still laughing when a slight tremor made the whole room vibrate. ‘You see? Mount Rinjani, or rather his son Gurung Baru is clamouring for human blood. Rangda shall regale the spirit of the young mountain with your blood slowly dripping from the incisions she shall make on your body, and afterwards, I shall distribute pieces of your heart to my mother’s followers.’

At these words, Gabriel raised his head and tried to shout something, but the only sound that issued from his mouth was a muffled growl.

'Don't fret, dear Gabriel. You shall be there to watch it all. Afterwards it will be your turn.' Again, a ghastly laughter burst out of Dewi Rinjani's cruel lips.

She was certainly a sight, thought Selene. Dewi Rinjani was wearing a beautiful brocade sarong, its red and gold wavy pattern complementing her curvaceous body. Her fingers were all adorned with precious gold rings; her ears were studded with diamonds. She was heavily made up, the red coral lipstick accentuating the hardness of her mouth. Dewi Rinjani looked both beautiful and terrifying, like the demons painted on her dress.

After a final malevolent look in their direction, Dewi Rinjani left the room, the scent of her favourite perfume lingering in the air.

The girl had barely left that Dewi Mas made her entrance. She wore a black sarong with mock flames leaping from the hem up to her breast. Her hair was loose and reached down to her waist. She wore rings on every finger and toes, with a black pearl on each band.

When she approached Selene, she could not disguise her glee. 'Here you are, you nobody. It was a pleasure to drown that spineless maid of yours, and then eat her pulsating heart.'

Selene opened her eyes wide and looked at this monster, speechless with horror.

Selene's look seemed to gratify Dewi Mas who continued, 'Yes. The end of your time on Earth has finally arrived. With your death, it will be easy to claim the land back. The land that was left to my father by my ancestors and that he gambled away. And the rest of the land. The land where Dewi Kunta is built. I had to save it at all costs, including having my followers kill my husband and my brother...Yes, you may look at me that way, but my husband was going to sell Dewi Kunta to pay off my brother's debts. I've had to do all this because your aunt refused to marry my brother. Oh yes. She dared to refuse him. Yes, she dared to snub him. He, a descendent of one of the noblest and most aristocratic families on this island. Just like you, a nobody, who turned down my son. My son! Whose father was knighted by the Queen of England. But you'll pay for it, like your aunt did.'

Sick at heart, Selene still found the strength to ask, 'How did my aunt die?'

'Oh I went to her house with Tut, one of my servants. She laughed at me when I asked her if she was going to marry my brother. But I had the last laugh. I can see her now. She was standing on the steps of the swimming pool. I grabbed her by the neck, but she fought me off. I pushed her then and Tut came and held her head under the water. She struggled, but Tut is tall and strong and one of my most obedient servants. He held her down until the water found its way into her lungs. She hit the bottom of the pool, and when she came back to the surface, she was dead.'

Selene was horrified. Now she could explain all those nightmares that had marred her nights. Ill as she was feeling, she still tried to speak up for the man she loved. 'Why don't you let Gabriel go. After all, it's me you want to punish.'

'Him? Let him go?' Dewi Mas continued, looking at Gabriel with hatred, 'let free this murderer, who killed my precious, my only son. Who rejected my daughter for you! You must be insane.' cried Dewi Mas, her voice rising. Tomorrow, after I have killed you both, will see me rising from the ashes to take back what should have always been mine!'

After she had finished uttering these words, Dewi Mas turned her back majestically on Selene and Gabriel and exited the room, followed by a tall, strong man, who had been in waiting, and who now pulled the door to and locked it.

As soon as she was alone with Gabriel, Selene looked at the state she was in. She was kneeling on the rocky floor, her legs and feet chained to it, her hands above her head, both wrists chained to the wall. This time, too, escape was impossible, unless David and his team came to the rescue. Before leaving her, David had assured her that he would move when the signal from the GPS device showed that she was stationary in a place for longer than one hour. How long had she been here? She wondered.

Selene looked at Gabriel. He had passed out again. She could only imagine the corporal and mental punishment Dewi Rinjani had put him through. How could she be so evil? Or was it madness? A madness that ran in the family? That was the more probable explanation, but it was no consolation to Selene. To make matters worse the pain at the base of her head, where she had been hit, intensified. She closed her eyes and, after what seemed a very long time, she lost consciousness.

Selene was in the throes of the worst nightmare that she had ever had when a rough hand jerked her out of her dream. Two natives, dressed in ceremonial robes, unlocked the chains and, holding her by the arms, led her out of the room and along a steep corridor. She heard other natives taking hold of Gabriel and dragging him up the slope leading to the caldera. The heat was so intense that Selene started to perspire. After a few minutes, the party stopped by the entrance to a small cave. The jailers pushed her into the cave, where four women, also in ceremonial dress, took her up to a huge tub filled with sulphurous water. She was forced into the tub and given a vigorous scrub. She was then dressed in a white linen sarong that covered her from her shoulders down to her feet, leaving her arms and neck exposed. A crown of fragrant white flowers was placed on her head.

The heat kept on increasing and Selene noticed that even the women who had washed and dressed her were feeling uncomfortable. The jailers entered the cave and seizing her by the arms, escorted her to another cave, a larger, more beautiful cave with a high ceiling, all adorned with effigies of demons, and lit by a myriad of candles.

CHAPTER THIRTY-SIX

As if in a dream, Selene saw Gabriel being strapped to the pillar of a wall next to a sacrificial altar, made of black volcanic stone. At the four corners of the altar there stood four tall statues of the *Leyak*, the human servants of Rangda, the demon queen of black magic. Each statue had the heart, lungs, and all other organs attached to the head. From each grotesque mouth, complete with long fangs, an unusually long tongue reached down as far as the floor.

Above the altar, there hung the huge, hideous effigy of a demon with round bulging eyes. Skilfully carved flames seemed to be leaping out of the monstrous head and issuing from the enormous mouth, sporting very long fangs. Selene, in her somnambulistic state, thought it a well-portrayed representation of the spirit of Mount Rinjani.

A crowd of natives in beautifully woven *songet ikat*, made an impressive audience. They were all chanting 'Rangda, Rangda,' following a ceremonial ritual as old as was the animistic belief on Chilli Pepper Island.

As the chanting reached a crescendo, an astonishingly striking figure made her entrance. It was terrifying yet it held its audience as if bewitched. All eyes were glued to her and followed her every move. A beautiful, priceless, solid gold flame-like headdress was firmly placed on the head of an incredibly sharp-fanged and goggle-eyed mask, with a long, red, protruding tongue. Red and white strands of hair flowed down to her ankles. Calf-long, silk red trousers, striped with gold and silver thread emphasized the bare bejewelled feet with blood-red varnished toenails. In between the strands of hair, Selene was able to see a gold bodice and a long white cloth wrapped round the waist of Rangda, the Queen of the Leyak.

The witch proceeded up the aisle, her fingers encased in

extremely long fingernails, made of pure gold. As she reached the altar, the mask could not hide the glint of triumph and hatred in Dewi Mas's eyes.

Strong male arms forced Selene to lie down onto the altar. Then, they tied her ankles and wrists, using thick leather straps. Above her, there loomed the massive wide mouth of the demon representing Mount Rinjani.

The ceremony was about to begin.

A hush descended on the crowd and Dewi Mas started her mantra. Now and again, during Dewi Mas's chant, the earth vibrated. The heat in the cave was becoming more and more intense. From the other end of the cave, a most amazingly beautiful woman advanced solemnly, carrying a red cushion where a *keri* (dagger) lay. Her sarong was gold with silver threads. She wore a solid gold headdress with a beaked front design extending up in golden leaf shapes, mounted by a fretwork arching design. Her face was heavily made up, with gold eyelids and purple cheeks. Behind her, two very young girls, nine or ten years of age, carried two round gold bowls.

The woman in the gold sarong advanced slowly, each step bringing her closer to the altar. When she reached the place where Dewi Mas stood, Selene realised that it was Dewi Rinjani.

Dewi Rinjani knelt down, lifting up her arms, offering Rangda the cushion with the *keri* resting on it.

Slowly, majestically, Dewi Mas took hold of the priceless dagger. It was made of solid gold, adorned with black pearls in the effigy of the demon presiding over Mount Rinjani. Dewi Mas lifted up the *keri* with both hands and paused. The girls with the gold bowls took up their place: one on each side of the altar. They positioned the bowls just under Selene's outstretched arms. Slowly, savouring the moment, Dewi Mas lifted the precious *keri* even higher, holding it poised over Selene's right wrist.

The audience recommenced their chanting.

'My time has come.' thought Selene, 'Goodbye Gabriel. Goodbye my love. Ours was a wonderful dream. How I would have loved to bear your children...'

Suddenly the entire cave shook, unbalancing Dewi Mas, who spun and fell onto Dewi Rinjani, involuntarily stabbing her through the heart with the *keri*. Incredulous and horror-stricken, Dewi Mas tried to straighten up, but a new tremor unbalanced her again, making her fall sideways, so that she struck her head against one of the pointed corners of the altar. This event was followed by a terrific crash.

A party of men in gas masks and in army uniforms stormed the cave. They threw something on the ground in several directions. Choking fumes invaded the cave. Selene's eyes were filled with tears. She could not breath and started to cough and splutter.

Strong hands released her from her bonds. Burly arms carried her for what seemed ages, out of the cave, along the long sloping corridor, then out into the open air. She was strapped onto a stretcher and lowered down the face of a steep cliff, and then she was thrusted into the back of an army vehicle.

Selene heard a voice shout out sharp clear orders, then the vehicle doors were closed and there started the craziest, fastest, neck-breaking race she had ever been involved in. At times, the truck was travelling so fast that it threatened to overturn, but at no time the speed was reduced. After what seemed hours, the truck stopped.

Someone jumped out and opened the doors at the back of the truck, letting the first lights of dawn through. David lifted her into a sitting position and pointed to the spectacle that met their eyes.

The cloud of ash that had been issuing from the crater of Gurung Baru was spreading in all directions, and then a fierce jet of molten lava spewed out into the air. More powerful and beautiful than any fireworks display, the lava kept on spouting out of the bowels of the volcano, covering its slopes, killing everything living.

Selene watched, though her eyes were stinging, unconsciously holding her breath. If David and his men had delayed only a few more moments, she would not be here to admire the incredible show that nature was staging. She would have died either at Dewi Mas's hand or burnt to a crisp by Gurung Baru's steaming hot lava.

Gabriel. Where was Gabriel? As if sensing her anguish, David whispered, 'He's safe, Selene. He is in the other truck. Now we're taking you both to the best hospital in Mataram where they can treat you for the side effects of the gas bombs we had to use and for any other problems.

Reassured, Selene, despite her throat being on fire, could not help but ask, 'What time is it David?'

'A few minutes past 5:00 am, on Sunday, 3rd May 2009.'

She bowed her head to thank him. She knew she would remember this day and this moment for the rest of her life.

CHAPTER THIRTY-SEVEN

A few hours later Selene and Gabriel were taken into Mataram's most renowned private hospital. The prognosis for Gabriel was better than she had expected as, apart from the side effects of the gas bomb, he was diagnosed as suffering from concussion, a few cuts and some broken ribs. The doctor decided that Gabriel would have to spend two days in hospital, provided that he followed that up with a period of rest for a full recovery.

As a precaution, Selene was to be kept under observation overnight and would be released around eleven o'clock the following morning.

Selene was still unable to see properly because of the effect of the gas bombs, but as she had some instructions for David, she scribbled a message then gave it to him. In her message, she thanked him and his team for all they had done and to show her appreciation, she gave them a hefty bonus. She also asked him to contact Vincent and Beatrice, to inform them of what had happened and of where they were now.

In the afternoon, the stinging sensation in her eyes began to wear off, so Selene went to visit Gabriel in his room. When he saw her, he regaled her with one of his incredible smiles and she, relieved, bent down and gently kissed him on the lips. Then she sat by him, took his hand into hers, and stayed there until nightfall.

The next morning Selene went back to see Gabriel, but the doctor was there and she was asked to return to her room, as the doctor would see her next. After having declared her well enough to leave, one of the nurses informed her that a friend of hers had brought her some clothes and was taking her home.

Beatrice was ushered into the room and Selene hugged her and smiled at her, so happy was she to see her again. She dressed quickly, and then she and Beatrice went to see Gabriel. Beatrice was horrified to see the bruises on his face and arms and his swollen lips, but she did not show it. Instead, she congratulated them both for their near escape and after assuring him that she would take good care of Selene and that they would go back and visit him again, she left them a moment of intimacy.

Selene very gently stroked Gabriel's forehead and kissed him, then left him and joined Beatrice.

Back again in Beatrice and Vincent's apartment, Selene and her friends had plenty to relate to one another. The few days that had passed had been full of momentous happenings. Although Selene had lived more dramatic events than her friends, Patrick, Jessica, Darren and Vanessa had had a close encounter with the erupting volcano, too.

Annoyed at being left behind by Selene first, then by David and his men, Selene's friends had decided to follow them anyway. They had nearly reached the bottom of the cliff when they had seen Selene being lowered down in a stretcher. When they saw the urgency with which David and his team were leaving and noticed the cloud of ash getting higher, they realised the danger and lost no time in getting into the jeep they had hired and drive off. It was very difficult to follow David's trucks, as his drivers were experienced and were able to push their vehicles at a terrific pace over the uneven terrain. Selene's friends soon lost sight of them, but covered enough ground to flee before the eruption took place. They, too, had stopped once they had reached a safe distance, to observe the eruption in all its deadly beauty.

'I wouldn't have missed this incredible adventure for anything in the world. Think what marvellous story we'll be able to tell our children.' exclaimed Vanessa.

'Yes,' reiterated Darren, 'thanks to you, Selene, our life together has spiced up considerably.'

'Hear, hear!' interjected Patrick and Jessica.

The following day Selene went to the hospital alone to see

Gabriel. He looked much better, despite the black-yellowish colour of his bruises. She brushed his lips with hers, trying not to cause him pain in the process. She had brought him some nice new clothes, to replace the scanty tattered garments that he had worn the day before. He had showered but not shaved, so that he had a day's growth on his cheeks and chin, making him look wild and macho.

'What have you got in store for me today, Selene?' he enquired in a humorous tone of voice, 'Will it be a tumble with a grizzly bear, or a tag-of-war with a jaguar?'

'As neither animal lives on this island, I think not. I thought we'll give ourselves and everybody else's a rest and enjoy life for a change.' she replied, giving him a peck on the nose, 'What do you say to a trip to Sengiggi and a relaxing time sunbathing, while a hoard of waiters brings us anything we desire?'

'I favour the motion, Ma'am. When do we start?'

'Right now. Please follow me.'

They had a perfect day for it. The trip to Sengiggi was just as Selene had promised and Gabriel felt like a new man at the end of the day.

Three weeks passed quickly by. Gabriel's bruises had disappeared, but he still felt some discomfort around his ribs. He knew that soon, too soon for his liking, he would have to take Selene to see what was left of *Inngris*.

It was the day before they were due to travel to *Inngris*. Selene and Gabriel had just come back at Beatrice's apartment from a shopping spree, when a loud peal of laughter announced the return of Patrick and Jessica.

They burst through the sitting room door, brimming with gaiety like children returning from an adventure park. Patrick, clowning as usual, was wearing a cooking pot on his head, as if it were a hat.

'What on earth have you got there?' laughed Selene who, despite all her cares, could not help but be amused by him.

'It's one of the many presents I bought for mother for when we go home, after your wedding.' replied Patrick in a half-serious, half-joyous tone of voice.

'Come on, you clown,' laughed his sister, 'it's a cooking pot, not a hat.'

'Mother's not to know. Besides, she certainly doesn't excel in the cooking department. Instead I can see her sunbathing, her head and face well protected by my wonderfully practical 'hat', even if it's only a cooking implement.'

'Now, now, children,' Beatrice reprimanded them with merriment, 'stop squabbling. Come now, put all your parcels in your rooms, wash your hands, and then join us for tea.'

'Yes, Ma'am,' replied Patrick, giving Beatrice a salute, 'I think I shan't bother to go home. You make me feel right at home here. You sound just like our mother.' Then the pair of them scuttled off to their respective rooms.

Selene felt happy and at peace, too. From now on, no more dreams of Rangda would haunt her nights.

She also knew that she didn't want to get married in Jakarta. She wanted to get married by the shrine near Elizabeth's resting place and, at her wedding, she wanted her friends, Gabriel's family, Wayan and his wife, David and his men, Vikram and his family, and Mr and Mrs Berry...and ... the list kept getting longer and longer...

'We'll have anyone you want at our wedding and we'll get married wherever you want, darling, so long as it is soon.' Gabriel whispered, his voice filled with love, when Selene told him about her plans.

CHAPTER THIRTY-EIGHT

The following day, which marked almost a month from the tragedy, Selene finally went back to *Inggris*. And what a sight met her eyes.

The main part of the house had been destroyed by the fire that had been started in the bedrooms. All that was left of her Aunt Elizabeth's study was the telescope. Komang's blood had been scrubbed from the hall, and most of the mess had been cleared away.

Selene, her heart full, tears in her eyes, but a resolve within herself, told Gabriel that she wanted to start anew. What was still standing would be knocked down and little honeymoon bungalows would be built instead. Wayan and his wife would take over what was to have been his parents' position, and the *Inggris Co-operative* had to go ahead as planned.

The Japanese garden was in need of restoration and the stables were to be built back. Selene wanted Vikram, Vincent and Wayan to get together and make some new plans.

Unbeknown to her, Gabriel had had a new headstone made for Elizabeth's grave, to match the one that had been destroyed by the fury of Dewi Mas. A headstone with the simple words Beatrice had had carved on the original one.

The Hindu temple had been rebuilt, too, so that Selene could have her wish to be married there, by her aunt's grave.

The night before the ceremony that would bind her forever to Gabriel, caught Selene sitting in the wicker chair that had been on the balcony outside her room at *Inggris* and that she had brought with her to the hotel. She had told Gabriel that she wanted to spend this night alone and he had respected her wishes.

Gazing up at the star-filled sky above her, Selene thought about how much she had changed since coming to Chilly Pepper Island.

She had spent her childhood and early womanhood as an introvert, unconsciously dominated by her grandmother's fears. She had learnt to distrust men from an early age and yet, since she had reached this fabulous place, away from everything that was familiar to her, she had made many true male as well as female friends. She had become stronger and had learnt to trust men like Patrick, Vincent, Darren and David.

Above all, she had fallen in love. Selene understood now that what she had felt for Simon had been only a young girl's infatuation. What she felt for Gabriel, instead, was the real thing. A feeling so strong, so compelling that it had helped her overcome all the obstacles in her way. Because of it she had become a better person, open to the needs of others. She had learnt to trust and to put her life and happiness into the hands of one man.

Her last thoughts, before she retired to her bed, were for Gabriel who had opened the cocoon where her true self had been hiding, and had let her free to fly.

It was a glorious sunny day when the British Ambassador first, and the Anglican priest after, joined Selene and Gabriel together as man and wife. It was a beautifully moving ceremony under the clear Lombok sky.

Afterwards, while their friends and relatives were toasting their happiness, they went off on their honeymoon, for a last exploration of this paradise island, before flying home to England to begin a new wonderful life together.

Lightning Source UK Ltd.
Milton Keynes UK
22 May 2010

154509UK00001B/7/P

9 781899 820986